SLEEPAWAY
GIRLS

by Jen Calonita

poppy

LITTLE, BROWN AND COMPANY
New York   Boston

Teen
Calonita

Poppy

Hachette Book Group
237 Park Avenue, New York, NY 10017
For more of your favorite books, visit our website at www.pickapoppy.com

Poppy is an imprint of Little, Brown and Company.
The Poppy name and logo are trademarks of Hachette Book Group, Inc.

First Paperback Edition: May 2010
Originally published in hardcover in May 2009 by Little, Brown and Company

The characters and events portrayed in this book are fictitious. Any similarity to real persons, living or dead, is coincidental and not intended by the author.

Library of Congress Catalog-in-Publication Data
Calonita, Jen.
  Sleepaway girls / by Jen Calonita. —1st ed.
    p. cm.
  Summary: When the exceptionally people-pleasing Sam spends a summer as a counselor-in-training, she learns how to say no, how to stand up for herself, and what it feels like to have a crush on a great guy.
  ISBN 978-0-316-01718-3 (PB) / ISBN 978-0-316-01717-6 (HC)
  [1. Camps—Fiction. 2. Camp counselors—Fiction. 3. Assertiveness (Psychology)
—Fiction. 4. Interpersonal relations—Fiction.] I. Title.
  PZ7.C1346Sl 2009
  [Fic] —dc22

                                               2008029896

10 9 8 7 6 5 4 3 2

RRD-C

Book design by Tracy Shaw

Printed in the United States of America

Praise for Jen Calonita:

"As always, Jen Calonita keeps it fresh and funny! Sleepaway Girls is this summer's must-read."

—Meg Cabot, author of the #1 New York Times bestselling The Princess Diaries

"Opening Jen Calonita's debut novel is like entering a glamorous party where fame, friendship, betrayal, and love are all on spectacular display."

—Zoey Dean, author of the New York Times bestselling A-List series

"Kaitlin Burke is the perfect teen starlet—cute, funny, and totally nice to interviewers. We'd feature her in our pages any day!"

—Lori Majewski, Executive Editor, Teen People

"At last! A witty, entertaining, and refreshingly honest take on what it's like to be a celebrity 'It' girl."

—Mara Reinstein, Senior Writer, Us Weekly

"Sleepaway Girls has it all. Throw in Color War, camp pranks, food fights, and some valuable lessons about friendship, heartthrobs, and standing up for yourself and what do you get? A perfect summer read."

— Sara Shepard, author of the New York Times bestselling Pretty Little Liars series

"Filled with lifestyles of the rich and famous, designer clothes, and teenage angst."

—School Library Journal

"Wide appeal, smart writing, and an entertaining cast of characters . . . A quick, stylish read."

—VOYA

"Who knew summer camp could be so fun?!"

—Alyson Noël, author of the #1 New York Times bestselling Evermore

SECRETS OF MY HOLLYWOOD LIFE novels by Jen Calonita:

SECRETS OF MY HOLLYWOOD LIFE

ON LOCATION

FAMILY AFFAIRS

PAPARAZZI PRINCESS

BROADWAY LIGHTS

Also by Jen Calonita:

RealityCheck

SLEEPAWAY GIRLS

To Briel Gradinger, Ashley McGetrick, Grace Barrett-Synder,
my MySpace buddy Emily Kate, and to sleepaway girls everywhere
who shared their stories

The Newbie

It was 8:45 AM and I was doing what I did best — talking to myself.

"I'm going to start recording now," I announced to my mom as we zipped along the I-95 expressway on the way to camp. I cleared my throat and pressed record on my brand-spanking-new palmcorder. "Hi, Mal!" I greeted my best friend excitedly. "I know it's only been an hour . . ."

"Forty-five minutes," my mom interrupted, side-eying me.

"I know it's only been *forty-five minutes* since we said goodbye," I corrected myself, "but I wanted to send you your first of many messages. I know you're bummed about my decision, but I swear I'm going to send you as many videos as I can to keep you company, and you're going to be so busy with Mark you'll barely notice I'm gone."

"The allure of Malomark," Mom said with a smirk.

My jaw dropped. Mom had interrupted my first message by

uttering the secret moniker I'd given Mal and Mark's relationship out loud. I fumbled for the pause button on the recorder, panicked. "Mom!" I complained. "Now I have to start over." I pressed the rewind button. "What if Mal heard you say that?"

"I can't help it." My mother laughed, gripping the steering wheel of our car tightly for support. "It's funny, Sam."

In past years, the day after school ended for the summer, I would sit on a faded pink plastic beach chair in Mal's backyard, slathered in SPF 30 while we read aloud the latest Britney Spears incident in US Weekly. But that was before Mal became Mal and Mark, Mark and Mal, or as I now secretly referred to them: Malomark. I got the idea because their names fit the description and definition of a Mallomar cookie: super sticky sweet, and if you eat too many you get sick to your stomach.

That's why I was worried about that upcoming summer. I knew how it would play out: Mal would beg me to hang out and I'd be Malomark's third wheel 24/7. The thought of being with them (I can imagine it now: "You're cuter, babe!" "No you are, baby!" Gross.) was more torturous than getting a wisdom tooth pulled. I made up my mind to make the first bold move I've ever made in my life: I signed up to be a camp counselor-in-training (CIT) at a sleepaway camp two hours away from home, Malomark, and any "baby" references. But now that the first day of camp was finally here and we were an hour away from Whispering Pines, part of me was so nervous that I wanted to jump from the moving car. The other half of me couldn't wait to get there. I looked over my outfit again. It took me weeks to settle on one I was happy with. I finally went with a red (my favorite color) cotton halter top, lightweight denim shorts that were fringed mid-thigh, and black flip-flops.

"I hope you'll consider going into advertising someday, Sam. 'Malomark' is such a clever name." Mom was still talking and had tucked a strand of her shoulder-length brown hair behind her ear. I'd always been jealous of how Mom's hair hung perfectly straight while mine frizzed up five minutes after I flat-ironed it. "It shows real creative thinking. I think you were born to be in the business, just like me," she added, and then a devilish smile spread across her full lips. "You'll have no trouble getting a job. You're already a media sensation in the field."

I practically felt the light tan I'd been working on slide right off my face. "You promised to stop bringing that up," I begged weakly.

"I will," Mom protested. "But you should be proud of your accomplishment. Not everyone gets to star in a —"

"Mom," I warned, interrupting.

"Fine." She sighed and then the two of us lapsed into silence. I hated when Mom brought up my Dial and Dash moment, as we called it. I just prayed no one at camp figured it out and drove me crazy about it the way the kids at Carle Place High had been for months. I stared out the car window at the pine trees as they whizzed by.

"I think you're really going to enjoy yourself this summer," Mom said. "Alan was telling me all about Whispering Pines the other night and your camp sounds wonderful."

"Who's Alan?" I asked, confused.

My mother's face colored slightly. "Alan Hitchens is your camp director."

"I thought his name was Hitch." I stared at my mom curiously, but she was looking straight ahead with her long, manicured fingers placed firmly on the wheel.

"It is. I mean, you are supposed to call him that," Mom muttered. "He asked me to call him Alan since I'm a parent." She cleared her throat and made that weird gurgling sound she always made when she was nervous. Thank God I didn't inherit that habit.

"Anyway, he seems very nice," Mom said quickly. "I've talked to him a few times — just about signing paperwork — and he told me he's been running this camp since his thirties. His wife ran it with him until she passed away from cancer a few years back. Now it's just him and his daughters Alexis and Ashley. Ashley is the same age as you."

"Uh-huh," I said blandly, but inside I was sort of shocked. My mom had a thing for my camp director! Too bad camp was so far from our home on Long Island; otherwise I would have rooted for Mom to snag a boyfriend. She hadn't met anyone she liked since my dad left a few years ago. I hoped this camp director crush worked out for her, but if it did there was no way I was moving to the boonies. I'd been a suburbanite New Yorker since I was born and that was not about to change now.

"So you like your present?" Mom changed the subject quickly. "Al — Hitch — said you can't have electronics, but I'm sure he means cell phones." Mom winked at me. "Besides, if you hide this at the bottom of your trunk, no one will find it."

I was not going to let this camera out of my sight. It was much better than the clunky five-pounder I had been using to record my video diary. (I had been taping my woes since the seventh grade. I wanted my future children to understand the hardships faced by teens in the new millennium. Sure, we had iPods and things like *The Hills*. But we also had to deal with global warming and killer hurricanes.) "I love it," I gushed.

"I expect you to send me a few video postcards — that is, if you have time after doing all the ones you promised your friends," Mom said wryly.

"I didn't promise *that* many," I said.

Mom looked at me skeptically. "You promised at least four people I know of, plus Mal, video postcards. How you're going to have time to sleep or shower I have no idea."

"I'll have plenty of time," I insisted stubbornly.

"I keep telling you, Sam, until you learn how to say no to people, you're never going to get the things you truly want out of life and — oh no."

Thankfully our car came to a screeching halt, distracting Mom from her well-worn Sam lecture. I looked out the front window. There were red brake lights as far as the eye could see. Mom frowned. "Must be an accident." She turned on the radio and scanned the dial for traffic news.

I looked nervously at the clock on the dashboard. It was 8:58 AM. I was supposed to be at orientation at ten. Being the new girl was nerve-racking enough. Being the new girl who was late was ten times worse.

Mom read my thoughts. "I'm sure we'll be past this jam in

a few minutes." She didn't look sure about that and neither was I as I heard a siren wail in the distance.

I pressed record on the palmcorder again as my stomach started to do flip-flops. "Mal, I think my first message will have to wait."

❧ ❧ ❧

Two hours later, Mom and I were practically running to the mess hall, which according to the map was right down this super-green, grassy hill. My heart was in my throat as I raced up the wood building's well-worn wood steps and pulled open the double doors. The large, open room had high ceilings with wood beams that held up rows and rows of camp banners. THE GREEN MACHINE — 2003 COLOR WAR VICTORS! announced one. WELCOME (BACK) TO THE PINES! declared a large red one. And across the back wall was a glass cabinet full of trophies. The only thing missing were the people. Mom and I were standing in front of rows of empty picnic tables covered with folders and papers and discarded jackets. "They're not here." I freaked out. I was actually yelling. One of my biggest pet peeves was being late.

"Samantha Montgomery?" I heard someone bellow, and I turned around.

"Yes?" I said uncertainly.

A tall man wearing camouflage fatigues and holding a megaphone was walking toward us. He had white hair, was tan like it was the middle of August instead of late June, and his teeth were an eerie shade of white. The man bounded up the steps and shook my hand vigorously. "Alan Hitchens, but you can call me Hitch."

"Hi, Hitch," I shook his hand lightly and smiled nervously. "I'm really sorry we're late. There was an accident on the expressway and . . ." I stopped talking.

Hitch had dropped my hand and was looking at my mother. "Pamela, it's so nice to finally meet you," he said with a large smile.

My mom made that weird gurgling sound again. "It's nice to meet you too, Alan," Mom gushed, smoothing her fitted, white button-down shirt self-consciously. "I'm sorry Sam is late." Now that we were out of the car and I could get a good look at Mom, I realized she had dressed up for this meeting. Gone were her usual working or weekend attire (suits or sweats and oversized tees, respectively) and in their place she had on tailored khaki capris and Coach ballet flats that didn't mask her height (5' 9½"), but did look nice. She was wearing makeup on her pale face and her brown hair, so similar to my own in all but texture, was its usual straight self.

"A few counselors are late and I suspect they're all in the same position," Hitch said and turned to me. "Sam, why don't you say goodbye to your mom, and I'll help her unload your bags so you can head down to the field and join the game. Ask for Alexis. She's my eldest daughter."

"Game?" I had only been here five minutes and I was already confused.

Hitch looked from me to my mother. "I find the best way to figure out which CITs belong with which counselors is to get them involved in teamwork. There's time to go over rules and paperwork during grub or campfires. Today they're playing dodgeball."

"Dodgeball?" I asked. I hadn't played dodgeball since the sixth grade and I wasn't good at it back then. I had a hard time playing any game that involved flying balls, which ruled out most gym activities and really aggravated my gym teacher, Mrs. Pepper.

"That's a wonderful idea," my mom gushed. Now that I'd met Hitch, I wasn't so sure he was my mother's type. Where he was all outdoorsy and tanned like a camp director should be, Mom's skin was milky white from too many hours at the office. The last time she did something outside, it was directing the guys from Crate and Barrel on how to unload her new dresser from the truck. Mom gave me a hug. "Well, this is it," she said, sounding choked up. "Have a great time and I'll talk to you in a few days, before I leave on my business trip."

"Thanks, Mom," I said, feeling awkward in front of Hitch. As I walked away, I could still hear Mom laughing at something Hitch said, but suddenly I felt very alone.

What was I thinking, going to camp? I had no idea what camp life was like, and I certainly had never flown solo before. I didn't know anyone on that dodgeball field. I didn't have a best friend to stand next to or even a semi-good friend I could chat with about stupid stuff. I was the newbie, and being the newbie was awkward.

Baby steps, I thought to myself. Just take baby steps. I breathed in the pine scent of the evergreens that lined the dusty dirt path that was spraying dirt all over my feet. One step. Two. Three . . .

I could do this.

When I got to the bottom of the hill, I could see the game had already started on a slightly muddy field that was boxed in by white spray-painted lines. Just a few yards away were the tennis courts and another field that had bags of athletic equipment waiting on it. There was an overwhelming scent of manure and I realized that to my left were the horse stables. I stood there, taking the scene in, and tried not to pass out from nerves.

That's when I saw him.

He was running across the field — shirtless, I might add — and he leapt in front of me and caught the dodgeball seemingly in slow motion. This guy was like an Abercrombie ad come to life. He was tall, but not so tall that I'd have to stand on my tiptoes to reach his lips. He had longish, dirty blond hair that would make Zac Efron's look lame, killer tanned abs that looked like they'd been airbrushed in, and eyes as green as my jade bedroom comforter.

"Hunter!" A pretty girl screamed as the guy threw the ball and it whisked by her face. "You almost hit me," she whined.

His name was Hunter. Hunter and Sam "LastNameUnknown." It had a nice ring to it.

"Sorry Ash," he said, out of breath. "It's a game. You've got to move or be moved."

At that moment Mr. Ab-solutely perfect, aka Hunter "LastNameUnknown," looked up and saw me. "Water break!" he announced, not taking his eyes off mine, which were blinking rapidly. "Hey," he said and smiled this absolutely perfect smile.

I looked around. Yep, I was the only one in this direction. My future husband was talking to me. ME! If I wasn't nervous enough before, I was ready to freak out now. My experience with guys was limited, but when they were that cute, I could barely function.

"You're the new CIT, right?" he asked.

"The new," I repeated dumbly. "You mean I'm the only new one you have?" The thought was terrifying. That meant everyone already knew everyone. I was the only new girl my age. The only one? How could that be? My lack of camp experience was going to stick out like a sore thumb.

He laughed. Not in a mean way, just loud and deep. "As far as I can tell," Hunter said. "What's your name?" he asked me as I tried my hardest not to drool over his sweaty torso. "You look familiar," he added.

Uh-oh. I knew that look. I really hoped to avoid this, but I guess that was asking the impossible. The Dial and Dash commercial was so popular it had aired on the Super Bowl twice and been dissected on everything from CNN to the pages of US Weekly. People at the Pines were bound to have seen it.

"My name is Sam." I couldn't take my gaze off his eyes. Up close I could see they were green with flecks of gold in them.

"Hunter," he said, revealing a mouth full of perfectly straight, white teeth. Any sense of recognition he had a moment ago seemed to vanish, thank goodness. "Join us for dodgeball," he suggested. "We're short on my side so I guess you're with me. You can stand over there." He pointed to a line of girls who were staring at me curiously.

In a daze, I walked over to my designated spot, trying hard not to slip in the mud that came from the week's worth of rain we had just had in the tri-state area. I smiled awkwardly at the girl next to me. She had red hair and glasses and was wearing a Hello Kitty t-shirt. I looked at her feet. She was smart enough to wear sneakers.

"He's hot, right?" she whispered and took a puff of what looked like an inhaler.

It didn't take a genius to know who she was talking about. "Yes." I sighed. "I'm Sam," I said shyly.

She smiled, revealing her braces. "Emily Kate. But you can call me Em. You're the new CIT, right?"

I guess it was true then. I really was the only new girl. "That's me," I said, trying to sound at ease.

Em nodded. "At the opening breakfast this morning they said there was one new CIT. Everyone else in the program graduated from campers. I'm a CIT too." Em stopped talking and stared at me curiously. "I'm sorry. It's just . . . have we met before?"

Stupid Dial and Dash moment. I couldn't escape it! "Do you live on Long Island?" I asked. I put a hand over my forehead to pretend to block the sun when I was really trying to cover up my face.

I heard a loud laugh and turned around. The pretty, whiny blond girl from earlier was flirting with my Hunter. Okay, maybe he wasn't mine yet, but a girl could hope! I watched as she touched his chest and pretended to push him. "That's Ashley," Emily told me. "She's a CIT too."

"Are they dating?" I had to ask.

"No." Em shook her head. "Hunter is a counselor. CITs can't date counselors. It's against the rules. Not that Ashley hasn't broken them before." Em grinned. "Ashley usually gets whatever guy she wants. They worship her."

It was easy to see why. Ashley looked like she belonged on *America's Next Top Model*. She had perfectly straight, non-frizzy blond hair, bronzed skin, and gray eyes. She was also super-skinny. She'd have to be to pull off that baby blue ribbed tank top she was wearing. I repressed the urge to hate her on sight. There was something very familiar about her. I felt like I'd seen her running across a field, or swimming laps in a lake. But how? "I feel like I know her or something," I said as several people started to take the field again. Water break must have been almost over.

"You probably saw her on the camp video," Em offered. "Ashley is the camp model. She's on the cover of the camp brochure, in the commercials, the camp video, all over the merchandise catalog. She's pretty much the Pines spokesgirl." I followed Em onto the field and waited anxiously for the game to start up again. I just hoped I didn't embarrass myself.

So that explained it! She's the one who told me and Mom — on video of course — that the Pines had world-class camping facilities and a list of activities to choose from that any camper would dream of. Before I could ask Em anything else, Ashley and a few other girls took places next to us and started talking.

"How was your year, Ash?" someone asked.

"Busy," Ashley said, with a flip of her blond hair. "I had to shoot a whole new line of stuff for camp, on top of the cheerleading calendar I agreed to do at school. My coach saw the Pines stuff and thought my face would so sell a charity calendar."

"Wow," a few girls said breathlessly.

"I met with some modeling agencies in New York too," Ashley added as she examined her bright pink nails.

"Did you sign with one?" another girl asked.

"Not yet," Ashley said quickly. "I'm still trying to decide who I like best. They all seem to want me, you know?" Ashley thumbed the girl next to her's blue shirt. "Cute tee, Candace!"

"Thanks," the girl said shyly. "You really like it?"

"Absolutely," Ashley said, sounding chipper. "Old Navy, right? I have the exact same one. Well, the designer version. Mine is Juicy."

"Hey," a blond girl said to me as she jogged over and stood next to Em. She looked buff and super tan, but I got the feeling it came from being the outdoorsy type rather than a tanning-bed queen. Her whole look screamed sporty. "I'm Grace," she said. "Are you the new CIT?"

"Yes, I'm Sam," I said.

Grace was staring at me intently. "Do I know you from somewhere?" she said. "Do you play field hockey?"

"That's exactly what I said!" Em nudged Grace in the ribs. "I feel like we've met before."

Oh no. They'd seen it. Any second now they were going to figure it out. I searched the group for Hunter. He was standing a few feet away throwing and catching the dodgeball into the air as he talked to a few other guys. Start the game, I begged him silently. Before they realize that I'm —

Grace gasped. "You're that girl from the Dial and Dash commercial!"

Shoot. I glanced around. Grace was so loud, people looked over to see what the fuss was about. Including Hunter, and Ashley and her group, who had turned around and were suddenly listening.

"That's right!" Em seconded. "I love that commercial."

"It's so genius," agreed Grace. "Your cell phone dies and you can't call your boyfriend to say good-bye before his trip," Grace narrated as a small crowd started to gather.

"And so you swim through that river, jump over a building, and steal a motorcycle all so you can get to a store that sells a Dial and Dash phone so you can call him immediately," Em finished excitedly. The two of them looked at me expectantly. "That was you, right? Did you do your own stunts?"

There was no denying it now. "That was me," I said and people began to murmur. "But I didn't actually leap over a building or ride a motorcycle."

Stupid Dial and Dash moment. There were hundreds of commercials on TV every day, but for some reason the one I made, stuck. I liked making video diaries that were just for me, or video messages for my friends. I never wanted to be the next Jessica Alba.

"That was the best commercial," Grace gushed. "So are you a model?"

"No," I said quickly and sighed. "It's a long story, but the short version is that I did this low-budget test video for my mom's company. It was part of an advertising pitch they were making to Dial and Dash Phone. The actress they hired dropped out last minute so my mom enlisted me. No one was supposed to see it but the Dial and Dash people. But when they did, they loved it so much they wanted to shoot the commercial for real. The catch was, I had to be in it. I can't even get up in front of class to make a speech or read a report so it was kind of terrifying. But it was the only way my mom's company could get the deal so I caved."

"Lucky you," Ashley interrupted. Her arms were folded across her chest and I could tell she was taking me in from head to toe. "I'm Ashley," she said with a bright smile. "I'm actually a *real* model and actress. I've done some commercial work myself."

"Sam," I said for what felt like the tenth time today. Ashley was staring at me so intently I felt uneasy.

"Ash, isn't that commercial the best?" One of her friends nudged her. "I loved the part when you jumped the building," she said to me.

"She didn't actually jump," Ashley interrupted. "Didn't you hear her?"

"Stunt double," I told the girl.

"Have you ever done anything else other than that *one* commercial?" Ashley asked. "Because the business is tough, you know. I've been working for years and —"

"You made a commercial, Ash?" her friend interrupted.

"For the Pines, yeah," Ashley snapped.

"But a national commercial?" the girl asked again.

"You guys ready to play?" Hunter interrupted the increasingly awkward conversation at the perfect moment. I had almost forgotten he was standing nearby the whole time. Now he knew my dirty little secret. Hunter had the dodgeball under his arm and he was grinning at me.

"Yes!" I said a little too loudly.

"Great," Hunter said. "I like a newbie who's ready for action." I tried not to blush.

Ashley and the girls dispersed after that, and I walked onto the field and continued to stare at Hunter and his cute, tight butt, covered in navy nylon shorts, as he walked in front of me. "Hunter, wait! Time!" A girl on the other team said and waved him over to talk. I stared at Hunter's bare, sweaty back as he ran. That's when I heard a low groan.

"Oh no. I know that look," a guy next to me said.

I looked left, then right, and then realized the guy was talking to me. "What look?" I asked him before I actually turned to face him, which was probably good considering he was beyond cute. He had slightly curly short brown hair that fell in his blue eyes and he reminded me of a Jonas Brother — tall, thin, and dark-haired. He was wearing red nylon shorts and a white t-shirt that was already muddy. I could make out the outline of his toned abs and muscles through the slightly sheer shirt and I quickly looked away and then couldn't help looking back again.

He gave me a sly grin, revealing a dimple in his right cheek. "The look that all the girls here get when they're falling for Hunter Thomas," he pointed out.

I inhaled sharply. "I'm not falling for Hunter." I folded my arms. "I was actually looking at the other team. I'm just trying to scope out our competition."

He laughed. "Whatever you say," he said. "I'm Cole, by the way, not that you'd notice when you're drooling over Hunter."

"I wasn't drooling," I said, feeling a swell of indignation. I had no idea my Hunter infatuation was so obvious. What if Hunter overheard Cole? I'd seriously pass out right there and they'd have to play over me. "I do not like him, okay?" I seethed.

Cole looked at me curiously. "Good," he said softly.

Wait. What? "Why? I mean, what do you care?" I asked.

Cole shrugged. "The truth is, a girl like you could do a lot better than Hunter."

"What makes you say that?" I had to know.

"Maybe I'm wrong, but you look normal. And nice." Cole said. He had an arrogant grin on his face that I wanted to wipe off. "Nice girls with potential acting careers have a lot more going for them than to spend their summer fawning over Hunter."

"I'm not an actress," I pointed out. I guess Cole had overheard our conversation too. "I'm anything but."

"You could be," Cole said. "People flipped for that commercial. I bet Hollywood came banging on your door."

"They did," I admitted without thinking. I usually didn't tell people that. "But I wasn't interested. I'm not. I really don't." How did I explain it? "I'm not one for being the center of attention," I said. "I like to help people, and I like to get involved, but I don't really want to be the star." Wow. I had never really told a stranger that before.

Cole shook his head. "I get it," he said, "but I have a feeling that you're going to be one around here. Hunter is going to be all over that."

We both looked over at Hunter, who had finished talking to the girl from earlier and was now leaning on two short CITs, laughing. Why wasn't he starting the game already? I wanted all these awkward conversations over with. "Don't get me wrong," Cole added. "I like the guy. He's a decent friend to other dudes, usually, but to girls, well . . ."

I was starting to feel defensive of my crush. "He's friendly," I said.

Cole sighed. "He is friendly. Too friendly, and I feel it's my duty to warn you that he's also a major flirt and a serial dater. He loves hitting on CITs because he knows it will never go any further than that."

I looked at Hunter again. I didn't see anything particularly flirty about him, even if he was talking to two CITs. Cole moved closer to me then and I took a step back. Wow, his eyes really were unreal. They were as blue as the cloudless sky, and he had long eyelashes that I would have killed for.

"Don't fall for Hunter Thomas, okay?" Cole told me, sounding serious, instead of just teasing, like before.

Em already told me we couldn't date counselors and besides, I hadn't come to camp to find a boyfriend. "Don't worry, I won't," I assured him.

"Good." Cole looked satisfied. But why?

"Game on!" Hunter yelled, interrupting my thoughts.

I hadn't taken more than two steps to get into position when the unthinkable happened.

BOOM!

The dodgeball smacked me in the face, dizzying me. The next thing I knew, my flip-flops were slipping on mud. I tried to regain my balance, but like a movie in slow-motion I felt myself slide backward. I was falling into the muddy grass below me and I couldn't stop myself. I felt a sharp thud, then blinding pain in the back of my head. I closed my eyes before the dizziness could take over.

What a way to make a first impression.

2

Home Sweet Home?

When I opened my eyes, the first thing I saw was Hunter.

"Hey, champ. That was quite a spill," he said as he leaned over me. "Are you functioning okay?"

I tried to speak, but all I could manage was a gurgle. Everything came flooding back. I got hit in the face with the ball and wiped out. In front of all the counselors. I'd only been at camp for an hour and I'd already made a fool of myself. Hello, bad camp nickname! Everyone was going to call me Slipper or something stupid like that all summer. I just knew it.

"Don't try to get up too fast," someone said, and I realized Cole was sitting next to me, cradling my head as he held an ice pack to it. He smiled down at me. "You hit your head on a rock. That must be some bump." It sure felt like it. The back of my head stung even with an icepack on it. I was suddenly aware that Cole's hands were on me and I struggled to get up. "Don't move. We're going to get the nurse," Cole instructed me.

"Samantha! Are you okay?" Ashley was standing over me

now, looking worried. "I'm *so* sorry. I threw the ball and I guess it went in the wrong direction."

Their faces kept coming in and out of focus and I could barely hear them my head hurt so bad. "It's okay," I managed.

"I'm just glad I didn't break your nose." Ashley clutched her chest.

Someone nearby snorted, and I could make out an African American girl in a tight black tank laced with bright pink ribbon, and short denim shorts, sort of laughing. Everyone looked at her. "Come on. You guys don't believe her, do you?" she asked incredulously.

"Nice, Courtney," Ashley pouted. "Trying to make the new girl hate me just because I *accidentally* hit her with the dodgeball."

While the two of them argued, Hunter spoke to me softly. "Do you think you can get up, champ?"

"Hunter, I think we should wait for the nurse," Cole said sharply.

"I can get up," I said and struggled to get out of Cole's reach. But everything went blurry and I had to let Cole's hands catch me. "Whoa."

"Cole's right, Hunter. She shouldn't walk right now," an older girl with brown hair and pretty gray eyes said. "Sam, I'm Alexis. I'm a senior counselor here. I think you should lie down and rest. We'll get you to your bunk. Your cabin is 8B."

"That's with us!" Em said excitedly. I didn't realize she was here. So was Grace.

"I think Meg, who is your bunk counselor, just got here so she's probably setting up her bunk," Alexis added. "I'll ask Nurse Nancy to stop down." I tried to lift my head again and Alexis grabbed my arm. "Don't move. You should be carried."

"I'll do it," Cole and Hunter offered at the same time.

NO WAY. "I can walk," I insisted, feeling my face get hot at just the thought of Hunter scooping me up and walking away with me, like a scene out of some romantic comedy I'd seen one too many times on TBS.

"Hunter, you take her," Alexis said.

I glanced at Cole and he gave me this weird sort of smirk. I looked away quickly.

"Sam, just rest," added Alexis. "Everyone will be heading to their bunks for a break after lunch anyway. We'll send food to you."

I was missing lunch? Not only was I late that morning, but now I had to miss more social time by being on the disabled list. Some first day it was turning out to be.

"Okay," I said, feeling weird as Cole handed Hunter the ice-pack and Hunter effortlessly lifted me into his arms. He had put his shirt back on, thank God, a gray one that hugged his chest. I might have imagined it, but at that moment, I thought I heard a few girls sigh. Now that I was airborne Hunter's face was so close to mine I wasn't sure where to look. Instead, I stared ahead at Em, who winked as Hunter carried me away.

This was awkward.

What do you talk about when a guy who is cuter than Orlando Bloom is carrying you across a field of sunflowers to bring you to your new bedroom? Especially when you look like I did at the moment — my face probably covered in dirt, mud all over my clothes and makeup melted off my face. I didn't even want to think about the weight issue. I always hated sitting on a guy's lap for a school group picture. And here was Hunter, having to carry me what felt like miles. My blush was never going to go away after this moment.

"So, champ, you didn't tell me your name," Hunter said suddenly. He wasn't even huffing or puffing and we were heading up a hill, walking past several old, worn wood buildings with signs that said POTTERY, NEWSPAPER OFFICE, and ARTS AND CRAFTS. They were nestled between lots of large leafy trees that the sun was poking through, sending bursts of light everywhere. None of the buildings looked modern. As far as I could tell, most of them didn't even have air-conditioning. This wasn't meant to be a tour of camp, I know, but my first thought was that the place was really pretty in a rustic sort of way.

I knew I told him my name earlier, but after all that happened, I wasn't surprised he'd forgotten it. "Sam," I said without looking at him. "Sam Montgomery."

"I think I prefer champ," he told me. I snuck a glance at him. Hunter's face was all sweaty, in a cute way. I wasn't even sure what to say to that so instead I said, "I'm sorry you have to miss the start of lunch."

"No biggie," Hunter said and shifted his hands under my body. His hand skimmed my butt when he did it and I couldn't help but jump slightly. "I'm sure Beaver — that's our cook — will make me a burger if they run out," Hunter added. "The most important thing is getting you back to your cabin in one piece. I'm sure no one's taught you how to ward off a wolf yet."

"You have wolves?" I croaked. "The brochure didn't mention wolves."

Hunter started to laugh. "I'm just kidding," he said and his hand closest to my arm tickled it slightly. "You should have seen your face!"

"It's not funny," I insisted. For weeks, I had a recurring nightmare that they ran out of beds and I was forced to sleep in the middle of the woods where I was attacked by a family of wolves.

"It's not funny," he repeated in a high voice. "I'm sorry. You're just adorable."

Adorable? How could Hunter call me adorable? Baby chicks are adorable. Golden retriever puppies are adorable. Fifteen-year-old girls like me are sweet, or smart, or any number of adjectives I couldn't think of at the moment because my head was on fire. Hunter had stumped me for a response again.

"Hey," he said, after he stopped laughing. "Look up there." He nodded toward the top of the hill and I could see what looked like several life-size wooden dollhouses. They were white with red porches and screen doors and red shutters. "That's what we call Candy Land," Hunter said. "Upper campus is where we house the senior campers, aka marshmallows, some counselors, and CITs. Lower campus, which we passed before, near the zip cord course, is dubbed Gumdrop Forest. That's where the peeps and pez sleep." He smirked. "That's where I sleep too. Senior counselors bunk with their charges and I've got peeps."

"Peeps, pez, and marshmallows?" I repeated.

Hunter grinned. "Cheesy, right? I know. They're all campers. Peeps are eight and under, pez are nine to eleven, and marshmallows are twelve to fourteen. The cabin division names are the only lame thing about Whispering Pines."

I tried to memorize the categories, but it was hard with a throbbing head.

"You'll get the hang of it." Hunter read my thoughts. "The most important thing you need to know is where I chill. That's the counselors' lounge." He nodded past the cabins and I saw a Swiss Alps–style wood lodge, the roof touching the ground, forming a large triangle. The building was surrounded by a huge porch. "I'm sure you'll get to hang out there sometime, if we counselors like you enough."

"I'm beginning to feel like I just parachuted into a foreign country and I don't speak the language," I admitted.

"Well, first things first." Hunter headed up the steps of a cabin that had a sign that said 8B. "Let's introduce you to your home away from home." The white front porch was adorable with red-trimmed windows and a red roof and three cute blue rockers waiting to be rocked in. The place looked like the dollhouse I had when I was little. I used to spend all my Christmas money sprucing it up. One year I even retiled the roof with real miniature shingles. They only lasted a month before my cousin Cara pulled them off one by one, thinking they were dominoes.

I reached out, since Hunter's hands were tied up, and pulled open the creaky screen door.

"Meg!" Hunter yelled. "You've got your first injury."

"What?" I heard a girl shriek. She ran out from the other room wearing a maroon Boston College tee and khaki shorts. She was pretty even with zero makeup, which let you see her freckles, and her blond hair was pulled casually into a loose ponytail.

"This is the champ — I mean Sam," Hunter corrected, giving me a lopsided grin. "She got slammed in the face by a dodgeball during the game and hit her head on the way down. Alexis wanted her to rest." He walked me over to the single in the room and gently placed me on it. I looked around. The room was full of black metal bunk beds, covered by saggy mattresses. The walls were made of — surprise — wood, that was decorated like the back of a bathroom stall. Etched everywhere were things like "Jess and Sara were here! 2006!" and "Kyle will love me 4EVR! — Sue '08." The room smelled faintly like bug spray.

"Are you okay?" Meg asked me worriedly. "I'm Meg Bauer, your bunk counselor. Do you want some ice? Something to eat? A magazine to read?" She looked around. "Your bags are probably in that pile over there." She pointed to a mound of duffels. I could sort of make out my oversized olive green sack on the bottom.

"Thanks," I said gratefully. "But I think I'll just lie here."

"Well, my knight in shining armor duty is over," Hunter said, bowing slightly. "I guess I'll see you at dinner, champ."

"Thanks, Hunter," I said awkwardly.

Meg sat down at the edge of my bed and waited for the screen door to slam behind him. "I have a feeling you're the envy of every CIT girl here right now," she said with a grin. "I could name a dozen girls who would kill for alone time with Hunter Thomas."

I blushed. I didn't know why the topic of boys was so foreign to me. I guess my lack of boyfriends was part of the answer. "He's really nice," I said.

"We'll see if you still think that way halfway through the summer," she said wryly. "That's the trouble with being the newbie. You don't know everyone yet. But I'm sure you'll catch on. Do you have any questions so far?"

"A million," I laughed. "But I guess Hitch will go over everything at orientation."

Meg nodded. "The most important stuff you'll pick up quickly. The camp is co-ed, which you know, and we have about 250 campers, most of which stay the whole seven weeks. Each bunk has six to eight campers and one counselor and either a CIT or a junior counselor. By the end of your third day here, Hitch will assign each CIT to a senior counselor. You'll work with that person all summer taking care of that one group of campers. You'll spend two sessions a day with them, and have occasional kitchen duty, but for the most part you'll still get to have regular camper privileges."

Meg went over more camp logistics — what the canteen was (the snack shack), what food to avoid (tuna salad was awful), and the best camp activity to sign up for (she swore by the hiking group that got to take an overnighter). Before we knew it, the nurse was there to bring me a plate of food (a hamburger with all the fixings and fruit salad) and check my head. ("Just a nasty bump," she decided, and handed me some packets of Tylenol.) Before I knew it, the screen door was bursting open and a group of girls was racing toward the bunk beds.

"I call this one!" I heard Grace yell as she zipped past me. "Em, I have our bunk!"

Ashley and two others ran by. One I recognized as the spunky girl who had the nerve to take on Ashley at the dodgeball game, and another I didn't recognize: tall, thin, dark tan, big chest, tiny waist, with perfectly curly, long light brown locks — looked like a model, too. The three of them stopped short at my bed.

"Did you already claim the single?" The brunette supermodel-in-training asked me icily.

"Gabby, I'll handle this," Ashley told her. She grinned. "I usually get the single," she said. "I don't know if anyone told you, but I'm the camp director's daughter, and the single usually goes to me."

"Give it a rest, Ashley," snapped the fiery girl, pulling angrily on the pink ribbon of her tank top. "You use that excuse every year. You're a camper just like the rest of us. It doesn't mean you automatically get the only single every season."

"Sam was here first," Meg tried to intervene kindly, but the way Ashley and the supermodel girl were looking at me, like I had a huge red bull's-eye on my forehead, made me instantly want to move. I hated being the cause of tension.

"That's okay," I said quickly. "I prefer a top bunk anyway."

The minute I slid off the bed, the three of them dove on top of the mattress. Ashley was on the bottom and she screamed triumphantly. "I was here first!" she said, sounding like a three-year-old. "This is mine."

Her friend dove on the bunk next to the bed, her chest cushioning her fall. "I call lower bunk! And since we're short one girl in here, this bunk is mine *alone*."

The African American girl with short brown hair, whose attitude was growing on me, looked disgusted. "Nice one, Gabby. I wouldn't do upper bunk again this year anyway. You snore." She looked at me and smiled. "I guess I'm going to be your bunkmate." She extended her hand. "Courtney, but you can call me Court," she said with a smile, and then leaned over and whispered in my ear. "To be honest, I didn't want the single. I just like watching Ashley squirm." I tried not to laugh.

"You're lucky you're with us, Sam," said Court as she looked over her shoulder at Ashley. "8A is super cliquish and they're stuck with Sara for a head counselor. She snores. Loud. Sort of like a few people in here." Ashley and Gabby glared at her.

"Girls, I'll give you a half hour to set up and then we can chat," Meg told us. "I'm just in the other room if you need me." Meg looked at me. "I share a room with Sara, 8A's head counselor. Our room bridges the two cabins." I nodded.

The other girls dove for their duffels and started pulling things out quickly. Within minutes, Ashley and Gabby were fighting over where to hang their Jonas Brothers poster — over Ashley's bed, or Gabby's bunk. Em was stacking what looked like romance novels on a shelf above her top bunk and the whole shelf looked like it was going to come crashing down at any moment. Below, Grace was hanging these inspirational sports posters that said things like COURAGE and BELIEVE IN RAW WILL.

Court laid her bright yellow comforter on the bed and fluffed a pair of royal blue pillows. They had bright shiny stars all over them. Then she started to decorate the wall behind our bunk with hot guys from every ad I'd ever seen in a magazine and a Chris Brown poster, and filled her half of the stacked egg crates next to our bed with US Weeklys and Cosmos.

How come all I brought was my dated jade comforter and my drab brown trunk? Everyone else was decorating with millions of cool stickers from camp, bands, and their schools. I made a mental note to call Mom and tell her to send some Carle Place stickers, Orlando Bloom pictures, and Magnolia Bakery cupcakes in her first care package so that I had some sugar to bargain with around here. Since I hadn't brought any decorations, the only thing I had to do was make my bed.

"Has everyone met Sam?" Ashley asked. "Gabby, you haven't, right?"

"Hey," Gabby said unenthusiastically, and looked at Ashley out of the corner of her eye. Gabby was just as pretty as Ashley, but in a more California-girl kind of way. She was wearing terrycloth shorts that had the word sweet embroidered across the bottom in hot pink, which matched her belly-baring tank top. Suddenly I wished we had to wear camp uniforms. We only had to wear our red Pines counselor tees on a few special occasions.

"So, Sam, other than the fact you're the Dial and Dash Phone girl, we don't know anything about you." Ashley was sitting on her fluffy comforter. "What camp did you go to last year?"

"Warning," Court whispered to me. "Watch your back."

"I haven't been to camp before," I said uncomfortably.

"Never?" Ashley's eyes opened wide. I shook my head, aware that everyone in the room's eyes were on me.

"Then how did you get picked to be a CIT?" Grace asked, sounding more than a bit miffed.

"I applied online and Hitch called me and did a lengthy interview," I explained. "I had to fax him all these recommendations from teachers and people I babysat for."

"So you got picked even though you've never done anything to prepare for being a CIT?" Grace looked baffled. "I thought Hitch had a strict system for picking his CITs. I wrote a thousand-word essay on my merits when I handed in my application."

Essay? What essay?

"That's because you're a psycho overachiever, Grace." Court rolled her eyes. "Hitch didn't even *ask* for an essay."

"Your campers are going to eat you alive," Gabby snorted. "They can spot someone who doesn't know what she's doing from across the lake."

"So what if Sam's never been to camp before?" Em sounded defensive and I couldn't help but smile at her gratefully. "Maybe she'll be better at this CIT thing than any of us because camp is all new to her." She turned to me and smiled. "I've only been coming here for five summers. Before this I went to Bellcrest, but they were super cliquish. The Pines is much friendlier. You're going to love it."

"Okay, lame-o, we get it, you want her to be part of your geek squad," Gabby said, sounding beyond bored. Then there was a knock on our cabin door. A group of girls walked in and rushed over to Ashley, talking a mile a minute about clothes, bunk groupings, and some sort of party they were all keyed up over. Each girl was prettier than the next.

"Do you think you'll get to have another sleepover at the ranch this summer?" a girl with a midriff-baring top asked.

"Absolutely," Ashley said. "I can only invite twelve girls, of course, but everyone will be considered."

I looked over at Court, confused, and she whispered in my ear. "Ashley has this invite-only sleepover at her dad's ranch, on the property, for her birthday every summer. Girls get desperate to be invited because then it means they're on Ashley's accepted list." She rolled her eyes. "Lucky them."

A girl who looked like Barbie stared at me. "Hey, you're the CIT who is in that Dial and Dash Phone commercial, right?" She walked toward me and the others followed. "That guy who played your boyfriend in the commercial was so hot and —"

"Guys?" Ashley interrupted. "I don't mean to be rude, but we have to finish unpacking. Catch you at dinner?"

As they filed out, I heard Court gasp. "I forgot! Everyone hide your cell phones," she warned as she started flinging even more clothes out of her bag looking for her phone.

"Meg will find it," said Em. "She can find anything. She once found the stash of chocolate I stuck below a cut-out in the floorboard. I wasn't allowed to go to the canteen for a week. She was so mad. She said I could have given the bunk termites."

"Why can't you have a cell?" I asked. I had to find a good spot to hide my video camera. I could go without my cell phone, but I was not giving up my palmcorder.

"No cells. It ruins the camp experience," said Grace without a hint of irony. "Camp would be lame if everyone was walking around with phones all the time."

"You are such a purist, Grace," laughed Court. "Sam, I hate to break it to you, your cell phone is a goner, but don't worry, you can use mine."

"Meg isn't taking yours?" I wondered.

"She's taking what she *thinks* is mine." Court held up a Voyager. "I'm giving in my old phone, which still works, and keeping my new one on me at all times."

"Nice," Em said with admiration. "Wish I'd thought of that."

"I'll let you eat up some minutes if you share some of those cookies your mom sends," bargained Court.

"Deal," said Em.

"That's my plan too," said Gabby, showing everyone two matching pink Coach cellphone cases. "I can't go a day without talking to Joshy. Have I mentioned my almost college freshman boyfriend?"

"Three times already." Ashley sounded annoyed. "While we were supposed to be talking about my prospects this year. And my theme for this year's sleepover."

"You have nothing to worry about this summer," Gabby pointed out. "I'm the one who has the major dilemma. Stick with Joshy or go after Gavin. He's so cute." She sighed and clutched her pink throw pillow to her chest. "I totally missed camp, but so much happened while I was away. My parents took us to the Greek Islands for Christmas and I got a killer tan. I went out with both Tommy Waters and Blake Edmonds, and then dumped them both when Joshy asked me to go to prom."

"And that's got to do with me, how?" Ashley looked bored. "We were talking about *me* finding a boyfriend. I've never gone a summer without one."

"It could happen this year," said Em, looking up from one of her books. She was holding one of those saucy romance novels that had a guy on the cover with a steriod-looking oiled bare chest and a loincloth as his only cover-up. "You've dated almost every guy here. There's almost no one left." Ashley glared at her and Em's face turned pink. "No offense."

"There are the counselors," Ashley reminded her. "Technically I am one so it's okay."

"Pul-eeze. You're a CIT and rules are rules," Courtney corrected her. "We may be almost sixteen —"

"I am sixteen," Gabby declared. "At least I am in two weeks."

"Well, the rest of us are almost sixteen and that means we're barely a step-up from a camper," Court corrected. "Not that I don't have my eyes on a counselor myself."

Gabby squealed. "Who cares about any of that! The point is we're back here. I've been counting down the days till camp for months. TGIH!" she said, breathing in deeply.

I looked at Em. "Thank God I'm Home," she explained. "Gabby likes to abbreviate everything. Or at least she thinks she is. Sometimes her made-up abbreviations are longer than the real words."

Ashley was sitting on top of a serene blue comforter and a mound of throw pillows. Behind her head was a black and white poster of two people kissing in the rain along with pictures of her with friends and guys. There was even a picture of her with Hunter and Cole. Cole looked really cute in a navy polo, his curly hair blowing in the wind. "Girls, this is going to be an amazing summer," she said confidently. "As long as you do things my way, of course."

Gabby laughed sort of uncertainly. Court rolled her eyes at me. Grace and Em just shook their heads.

Ashley caught me staring and smiled thinly. I got the feeling that the "you" she was referring to was me. And that what she wanted to add was: And Sam, don't you forget it.

♠ 3 ♠

Getting to Know You

After four hours, eight handouts, and a lecture on poison oak, Hitch used the second afternoon of counselor orientation for some "gender bonding time," as he called it. Grace said it was code for "matchmaking." The guys went sailing while the girls went on a hike. All three CIT bunks — 7B, 8A, and 8B — plus the counselors were going. Personally, I would have preferred boating. It was 95 degrees out and it was only 1 PM.

We were heading up the first trail and already I was behind. The 7B girls and some of the other counselors had shot ahead and I could see their dust and footprints on the pine-laden path. I could also see the outlines of Grace and Meg, both avid runners, at the front of our pack, along with Ashley's older sister, Alexis. Ashley, Gabby, and the CIT girls of bunk 8A were right behind them. It took all my effort not to laugh at some of the girls from 8A who were panting and sweating just to stay on Ashley's heels. They were hanging on her every (loud) word about filming the new Pines video. Somehow Court, Em, and I were the ones bringing up the rear. I wasn't sure if they were just as slow as I was or if they just felt guilty leaving the new girl on her own.

"You guys can go ahead," I urged them after I had stopped, yet again, to take a swig of water from my bottle. "I can manage on my own."

Court looked at me like I was crazy. "Don't be such a martyr. I'm not being slow on account of you; I am slow."

Em started to giggle. "Me too!" she admitted. "This is as fast as I go so you're not holding me up at all. I'm glad to have the company. Usually it's just me and Court and all she wants to talk about is boys." Court punched Em in the arm. Court had a habit of doing that. She told me the one sport she did like was kick-boxing and it had become a force of habit to use her hands.

"I thought you guys felt sorry for me because I'm as slow as a slug," I told them. "No one ever picks me first when it comes to team sports."

"Me either," Em and Court said at the exact same time. I smiled. I had a feeling the three of us would get along just fine. I looked up. I could hear someone coming down the path in front of us. It was Grace. She was sweaty, even down to her pony-tail, but she didn't look out of breath. She looked at me and smiled. "Another non-athletic type," she said. "Good. These two could use some company. Last year on one of our hikes, they were half an hour behind the rest of us. One of the counselors had to go back and check on them to make sure they were okay."

"We were enjoying the scenery," Em said, and took a puff of her inhaler. "Something you never do, Grace, because you go so fast."

There really was a lot to see up here. The air just smelled clear, like a fresh load of laundry, and I could hear every bird chirp and the crunch of dead leaves under my feet — something I never would have heard at home with all the street traffic and noise. From this spot on the hill, you could see the entire camp laid out below, like a miniature set, dotted with dozens of trees and tiny cabins. I still couldn't get over how large the Pines camp was. I'd overheard someone say it was about two miles wide. That was bigger than my whole town.

Grace gave Em a look. "Maybe today I will stop and smell the flowers, so to speak. I got to the end of the hike and then told Sophia I was heading back for you guys. I couldn't stand hearing about Ashley's latest camp video shoot one more time."

Court moaned. "I know. If I have to hear one more time about how she had her hair and makeup done professionally for the shoot I'm going to scream."

"Ashley offered to give me a makeover two times already," Em said, with a snort. "I had to keep telling her, nicely, that I only wear lip gloss, so a makeover wouldn't help me. She looked annoyed. I guess that means I'm off the sleepover list for sure."

"You didn't make it last year, so why would things change now?" Court quipped, but Em didn't laugh. "I'm sorry, Em. I didn't realize you were still bent out of shape over that."

"I'm not," Em said hurriedly. "I just, well, I was on the list, and then dropped off the A-list, I guess."

Court patted her shoulder. "Take it from someone who has never made the coveted list — you're better off."

"How did you fall from grace?" I asked, stopping to scratch my left calf. I had forgotten to put bug spray on and I was beginning to realize that was a huge mistake. "Is it a camp thing?"

"Last summer, I fell off the list the day before the party because I didn't lend her my brown polka-dot bikini," Em explained. "It was brand new! And my mom had just sent it and I didn't want to part with it." Em looked sort of bummed. "After that, Ashley would barely talk to me or Grace, who was sort of lumped along with me for the 'betrayal.' Two kiss-butt girls who are now CITs in 8A, Sierra and Delaney, took our places. Now Ashley barely speaks to us."

"Don't worry about it, Em," Grace said. "I've told you time and again it's not your fault. We're better off this way."

"Grace is right. You don't need Ashley," Court said. "You have me. And Sam here seems pretty decent, which means she's off Ashley's list for sure." She nudged me. "There is no way Ashley wants to compete with the Dial and Dash girl."

"So what's your reason for being anti-Ashley?" I asked.

"Two summers ago I caught her kissing my boyfriend, Paul Brock," Court told me, sounding not the least bit bitter. "Ever since then it's been war between us. Well, at least I pretend it is." Court giggled. "The truth is, I was totally over Paul by the time Ashley hooked up with him, but Ash was so freaked out that I caught her, I've been using it to my advantage ever since.

I'm repaying the torture she put me through my first year here. She pretended to be all nice to me at first and then she totally humiliated me. It's her MO."

"Hi, girls!" Sophia, a chipper senior counselor, jogged down the path toward us and we quickly stopped talking. "I know Grace came back to get you, but I just wanted to make sure everything was all right. We were worried you'd gotten lost."

"We're fine," the four of us said, in unison.

"I don't want any of you to push yourselves too hard," Sophia said, "but I am hoping you get to the finish soon. This hike is supposed to be about bonding with more than just your friends. We're trying to figure out who belongs with who and it's hard to do that with some of the CITs missing."

"You're right, Sophia," Grace said, looking determined. She turned to us. "Okay, girls, let's get a move on!" She sounded like a cheerleader. I had a feeling she would have hated it if she knew what she sounded like. Grace was not sideline cheering material. She was the girl on the field.

Em took a deep breath and tried to jog faster, but still looked like she was doing a slow crawl.

"That's good!" Sophia encouraged. "You too, Courtney! And Samantha. Let's get those legs in fighting form! It's bathing suit season, girls!" Sophia turned and jogged ahead. You could still hear her chanting mantras, but they were sounding farther and farther away. When I could no longer hear her, I stopped, resting my hands on my knees. It felt like my lungs were on fire and I hadn't gone more than three feet.

"Okay, we're safe now," Grace told us.

"I hate her," Court grumbled, out of breath. "What does running have to do with being a CIT?"

"I like running," Grace said, "but I hate when people make others feel bad that they can't go fast. Not everyone is a natural athlete."

"I hate jogging," I admitted.

"Me too," Em moaned. "I prefer swimming."

"I love to swim," Grace said with a smile.

"Me too," I said. "I've never swum in a lake though. I always wished I could have joined a swim team, but our school is so small we don't even have a pool. Sometimes I did laps at the nearby aquatic center, but it interfered with chorus practice and my friend Mal wanted us to do it together. I didn't have time to do both."

"But you liked swimming better," Grace pointed out. "You should have done what you liked, not what someone else did." I was about to say that Grace sounded like my mother when Court said it for me.

"Thanks, Mom," Court said, patting Grace on the back. "I'm planning on spending a lot of time at the lake this summer pretending I need help with my backstroke. I've got my eye on Donovan Mulcahy, the lakeside unit counselor. He's from Australia."

"An international romance," said Em dreamily. "In the new book I'm reading, Love Across the Shores, Amanda is an American peasant girl in love with a French duke who can't return her affections because he's betrothed to another. It's like you and Donovan being counselor and CIT! You can never be, but you can feel the heat."

"Speaking of heat, is anyone else ready to pass out?" I asked. "Or are some of you used to this weather?"

"Never. I still hate it," said Em.

"Me too," said Grace.

"I'm from Phoenix so I can handle it," said Court. "They don't have too many camps out west because who wants to play volleyball in hundred and ten degree heat?" I nodded. "My parents have sent me here the past three years in the hopes I'll become more responsible and less boy crazy." She rolled her eyes. "As if that would happen. At least this year I'm sort of no longer a camper. It will be kind of cool to boss around the younger kids."

"Where are you from?" asked Em.

"Carle Place," I said, feeling winded as we hiked up a steep part of the trail, past a few large boulders. "It's a small town on Long Island about fifteen minutes from Jones Beach and about forty minutes from Manhattan."

"Do you have a boyfriend?" Court asked eagerly.

"I've never had a legitimate boyfriend," I admitted, afraid to see their reactions. But when I looked up, I didn't see any pity, just piqued interest. "My last boyfriend was Bobby Shenowsky in seventh grade. Well, I guess he counts if holding hands as we walked from class and to each other's locker is a boyfriend. Guys at my school all tend to like my best friend Mal, which makes sense because she's pretty outgoing when it comes to boys."

"What does outgoing have to do with it?" Court wanted to know. "If a guy likes you, he likes you. They don't just go for the big mouths, even if I've always done well being one myself."

I laughed. "Maybe you're right. To be honest, I never felt like I needed a boyfriend. Mal and I did everything together. We had a tight group of friends who spent every weekend going to the movies, or having sleepovers, or going to dinner. I was so busy I felt I didn't have time for a guy." I sidestepped a vine in my path and then stopped to smell a group of wildflowers. "Then one by one everyone else got boyfriends till it was just me and Mal left. And then Mal met Mark. Within weeks everything kind of changed." And now . . . I didn't say this part out loud, but as annoying as Malomark was, seeing how happy Mal was with Mark made me kind of long for a boyfriend myself.

"Eww," said Court, disgusted. "I hate girls who drop their friends when they get a boyfriend. I've never been like that."

"She didn't really drop me," I insisted. Court crossed her arms. "I mean, okay yes, we don't get to hang out as much, but that's just because the relationship is still sort of new, right?"

"I'm kind of like you, I think, Sam," Grace said quietly, as she bent down to tie her well-worn sneakers. "I've always been too busy with my nine million after-school activities to date. But sometimes, I don't know." She looked wistful. "Maybe it wouldn't be so bad to be less busy and have time for a boyfriend, you know?"

"Do you miss hanging out with Mal?" Em asked.

"It was weird not being the first person she called anymore," I admitted. "Or the one she always hung out with on a Friday night. The two of us did everything together since we became best friends in fifth grade. And I mean everything. If Mal wanted to try out for kickline, I learned high kicks too. If Mal was doing poorly in Spanish, I took extra-credit assignments with her. It's just the way our friendship worked. Well, up until now. Now she calls Mark first. If he's busy, she calls me." I didn't expect to say that much, but it felt good to get it out.

"It sounds like you were kind of Mal's lackey," Court said delicately. "If Mal said jump, you said, 'how high?' Giving up swimming, taking kickline, waiting around for her on a Friday night. Your friendship was totally on her terms, huh?"

"It wasn't like that," I objected. "It just sounds like that because of the examples I'm giving you guys." Our friendship wasn't like that. Was it?

"Are you guys still close?" Em asked, stopping for a second to drink some water. The rest of us took it as a cue to do the same. It was so hot up here, I was afraid I'd burst into flames. Where exactly was the end of this trail?

I nodded. "Mal was upset that I decided to be a CIT this summer. We never do — or should I say did — anything separate so this move is sort of out of character for me."

"Smart one," Court said. "She deserves to know how it feels to be left out."

"I'm not trying to get back at her," I insisted. "I promised I'd . . . write . . . all the time. We're still really close."

Court looked skeptical. "This is what happens when some girls get boyfriends. They just disappear. My best friend Sasha has been dating a guy for the past six months and I'm sick of the public displays of affection. I've had a few boyfriends, but I like to keep my options open. I have a rule — break it off with any boy before summer so that I can be single for camp."

Em giggled. "You're so bad, Court!"

Courtney looked mock-offended. "What good is a summer away if you're tied down to a guy a thousand miles away?"

"Well, I hope when I meet a guy that I really like, I won't dump him because of a little distance," Grace said, swatting at a bee who had joined our group.

"Me too," agreed Em, who ducked to avoid getting hit by Grace's frantic arm motions.

"Em, you have to talk to a guy before you can go out with him," Court teased.

Em looked at me, embarrassed. "I don't know what it is, but the minute I get around a guy, I don't know what to say."

I thought about Hunter. "I'm the same way. I get all embarrassed and I'm lost for words. It's as if I've forgotten how to speak English."

"You and Hunter didn't seem to have any trouble communicating yesterday," Court said dryly.

"That was so romantic!" Em piped up. "Him offering to carry you all the way to the bunks."

I colored slightly. "Alexis asked him to take me back."

"He offered," Grace said. "I heard him."

"It was nothing." I stared at the pine needles on the ground. When I looked up ahead the rest of the counselors and CITs were sitting on a group of rocks waiting for us. We'd finally made it!

"There you guys are!" Ashley said, sounding exasperated. "We were getting so worried. We thought you got lost, but I guess you're just slow." Gabby and a few of her friends snickered.

"Girls, that's enough," Alexis told the group. "Being first isn't important. Having endurance is. Campers are, as you know, pretty full of energy and as a CIT you've got to keep up with them, not beat them."

Take that, Ashley, I wanted to say when I saw her smug face color slightly, and knew it wasn't just from the heat. Nowhere on the brochure did it say I had to be fast. I had to like athletics, which I do, but being good was a totally different thing. I caught Ashley's eye and she turned away.

"We've got a fun practice for all of you on the way back down the trail," Alexis continued. "We're going to pair each CIT with a counselor and you'll have to lead us down the trail on your own."

"But there are several paths," protested Court. "And I wasn't exactly paying attention to the route —"

"As long as you guys kept track of landmarks along the way, like Hitch explained in this morning's hiking orientation, you'll have no trouble," said Sophia smoothly. "The quicker you get back, the quicker you can go swimming or get a frozen drink at the canteen. They're on the house today. Now everyone pair up."

I stood frozen to the spot, watching some of the girls as they walked over to counselors. I didn't really know anyone that well yet other than Meg, and she was already standing with Grace.

"Hey," Alexis said with a bright smile. "Want to be my partner?"

I was about to say sure when I heard Ashley's voice. "Alexis?" We both turned around and Ashley was staring at me venomously. "I thought we were — you know, Dad said — we were —"

"I know, Ash," Alexis said. "But you're with Sophia on this trip. I'm going to head back with Sam."

I could feel all eyes on the three of us, watching, waiting for someone to say something.

"I'll switch with Ashley," I offered. I spied Court looking at me like I was crazy. "It's no problem at all."

Ashley's face clouded over, then quickly her sunny smile came back. "I'm fine," she said. "I love Soph! Right, Soph?" She ran over and linked arms with her.

Two by two the pairs headed down the first trail, leaving enough space between them so that no one could follow the group in front of them. Alexis made us go last. "After you," she said when it was our turn.

The first part of the trail was easy. I remembered a berry bush we passed right before we found everyone and then a tree that I thought was shaped like a Chihuahua. Alexis got a kick out of my reasoning for each turn, but other than that, I couldn't think of things to talk about. Alexis made me nervous. If she was anything like her sister, Ashley, we weren't going to get along. And for some reason, I kept hearing Gabby's catty voice and Ashley's snickering in my head: "You've never been to camp before? Your campers are going to eat you alive."

Alexis was the first to say something non-trail-related. "Sam, I hope you didn't think I was picking on you for being last," she said as she effortlessly navigated the steep path. I was already huffing and puffing. "As I said before, you don't have to be quick to do this. You just have to get the job done."

"I understand," I said, surprised at how nice she was being.

"I can definitely get the job done. I just might be a bit slower than some of the others. Speed is not my strong suit. That's why I never ran track."

"Track is certainly not a requirement for this job," Alexis said with a smile. "You have a lot of other qualities going for you. My dad was really impressed with your phone interview."

"He was?" I asked, surprised again. I mean, I knew he must have liked me if I got the job, but Hitch always sounded so gruff it was hard to tell.

"Absolutely," Alexis told me. "He wouldn't have hired you otherwise. He's pretty picky about taking on counselors who haven't been to camp before and he was doubly worried about finding someone to fill our vacant CIT slot. One of the campers we thought was definitely coming back this summer to be a CIT decided not to at the last minute and Dad was worried about replacing her. But he said your babysitting recommendations were top-notch and he liked your bubbly personality."

Bubbly personality, huh? That was cool. "I'm really excited to be here," I admitted. "I like the idea of being on my own and getting so many responsibilities. Usually my mom is hovering over me all the time."

Alexis laughed. "I know the feeling. My dad has been on his own for a few years so he's gotten rather protective. When I moved into my dorm freshman year it felt like I could finally breathe on my own. My mom passed away a few years ago," she added quietly.

"I'm sorry to hear that," I said and Alexis shrugged. "My parents are divorced and I'm an only child so it's just me and

my mom. She has to travel a lot on business and getting someone to stay with me is always tough. My mom's in advertising
and her new account is this stuff called Mouth Off mouthwash,
a freshener that supposedly keeps your breath minty clean for a
week with just one swig."

"That would come in handy," Alexis said with a laugh.

"I'm so glad Hitch hired me," I said. "Mom has to spend a
huge chunk of the summer doing focus groups in Brazil, London, Hawaii, and Mexico, and, of course, I couldn't go with
her," I explained. "I didn't really want to stay with my dad. He
runs a souvenir shop with my stepmom in St. Thomas and it's
tourist season so I'd just be in their way. And sneaking me into
Grandma's retirement vista in Boca Raton, Florida, seemed a little tricky. Plus, I'm not very good at Yahtzee."

Alexis laughed again. "Me either," she said.

After that, our conversation continued to just bubble over
like a shaken can of soda. Alexis told me about this cranky English teacher she had during freshman year of college — we
both loved writing — and I told her about the social studies
teacher who drove me crazy acting out scenes from history.
Then we started to compare favorite guilty pleasure TV shows.
Alexis's was *America's Funniest Home Videos*. Mine was anything on
E! Before I knew it, we had reached the final fork in the path.

"Which way, Sam?" Alexis asked me.

Good question. Which way was it? Okay, I needed to think.
Court had tripped over a stone that was right in the middle of
the path and that was the first time I'd realized it was just the
three of us in the rear. Whichever path had that stone was the

one we needed to go down. I walked over to one path and looked around. It was worn and littered with leaves, but there was not a rock to be seen. Then I looked at the other grassy area. There were rocks everywhere. "Court tripped over here and nicked her toenail polish so I know it's this way," I said. Alexis gave me a huge smile.

"You're right," she said and patted my arm. "I think you're getting the hang of things around here, Sam."

"I think so," I agreed, feeling proud of myself. Camp experience or no camp experience, I had a feeling I could do this.

4

Matchmaker

The third morning of orientation I woke up in a cold sweat. I wasn't sure if it was a dream or just my imagination, but I could swear I heard Mal from several hundred miles away asking her mom if I'd sent my first video message yet. Which I hadn't. In fact, I hadn't even *made* a video yet.

I had no idea orientation would be this busy! Between all the CIT/counselor bonding sessions and the group lectures on everything from what to do if you get poison oak to dealing with a homesick camper, I barely had a minute to myself. But I knew if I didn't get a tape for Mal done before the campers arrived, I'd probably have to wait several days to do one. So I got out of bed early, even though Hitch was giving us a pre-camper treat — we could sleep in till 8:30 — and headed down to the lake to film in private.

It didn't take me long to set up my camera on a large rock. I put batteries in the remote control and zoomed in on a shot of the lake for my background. The sun was just starting to peek over the mountains and it had cast a golden glow on the water. Even Mal would have to admit it was gorgeous here. It was eerily quiet, except for the sounds of songbirds and a faraway owl. I looked at my watch. It was only 7:30 AM. I figured I could probably get a video done for Mal and at least two more for my other friends. Then I wouldn't have to worry about doing more videos for at least a week. Now that I was at camp and saw all that it entailed, I was starting to think I had put my foot in my mouth by promising to send so many people messages.

I sat down on the sand and examined the image of the mini-me on the screen a few feet away. I actually looked really skinny on camera, which was a major plus, and I was wearing my favorite tank top — the green one that had a scalloped v-neck trim, and khaki shorts with flip-flops. (I figured I didn't have to start wearing sneakers till the next day when the campers arrived.) My hair was sort of curly now that I had taken the braids out that Court had given me the night before. All in all, I didn't look half bad. Satisfied, I pressed record on the remote.

"Hey, Mal, it's me," I said, trying to sound excited even though I was still half-asleep. "It is day three of camp orientation, our last day before the campers arrive, and I'm having a lot of fun already. My bunkmates seem really nice, well, most of them, and this place is gorgeous, as you can tell." I motioned to the lake behind me. "The only drawback so far is that I feel a little clueless about all this camp stuff," I admitted. "Someone needs to write a comprehensive camp manual for newbies. Hitch's lectures are helpful, but they're not giving me the big picture. For example, how was I supposed to know people decorated their bunks like they would a dorm room? The brochure didn't mention needing a Channing Tatum poster or Christmas lights for my bunk bed. We're here seven weeks. I figured all I needed was to pack my clothes, a toothbrush, and enough Secret deodorant. Needless to say, I unpacked in ten minutes — I basically stuck everything I owned in my trunk — while the others decorated for an hour."

Crunch.

I paused the video and shot up like an arrow. I had definitely heard something. I wasn't sure what, but it sounded loud, which in my book meant *big*. Was it a wolf? A bear? Hitch still hadn't given us any information on wolves, as much as I was hoping he would, so I wasn't sure what to do if I saw one. I stared at the woods for what seemed like an hour, looking for any sign of movement. There was nothing, so I sat down and hit record again. Maybe it was just leaves blowing in the early morning breeze.

"The chore wheel was another shocker," I added, looking at the woods again just to be sure. "I knew we'd have to clean up after ourselves, but scrub the toilets? EWWW! One of my bunkmates, this really nice girl named Em, must have seen my face turn green when our counselor Meg said that because she told me that sometimes people trade favors to get out of doing the more unseemly chores. Kitchen duty, which CITs have to do once or twice a week, isn't so bad, but I'd give all my canteen snack money to get out of cleaning the toilet. Then there's the problem with the showers. I'm wondering if bathing in the lake is a better bet."

Crunch. Crunch. Crunch.

I scrambled to my feet and looked around for the nearest branch or log to defend myself with. I wielded it like I was Obi-Wan Kenobi preparing for a duel. Out of the corner of my eye I looked at the video camera again. The red light was illuminated. I had forgotten to press pause. I burst out laughing. Maybe it was just a branch rustling.

"You must think I'm a total moron," I said to the screen. "I keep hearing noises and I thought it was a wolf. You know how that was my biggest fear about coming here? Well this guy named Hunter — who is really hot, by the way — told me that there ARE wolves here and I've been flipping out." I glanced around again, just to be sure, but I didn't see anything so I sat back down, keeping the stick handy. You know, just in case.

"Okay, now that the action part of this video is over, I'll re-turn to our regularly scheduled message," I joked. "I've decided there should be a warning on all camp info packages that says: CAMP SPIRIT REQUIRED. I've never seen such togetherness be-fore, Mal, and I know we come from a close-knit high school with fewer than a thousand students who all think 'Go green' means 'Go Carle Place!' Sure, we have pep rallies and sometimes people wear our school colors to a football game, but Mal, we don't break out into song at a moment's notice. I've already heard three chants of 'The Pines has spirit, yes we do! The Pines has spirit, how about you?' And we've only been here THREE DAYS. This other girl in my bunk, Grace, says camp solidarity is as big a part of camp as something called Color War. She said not to worry about that part yet or I might freak out. But the only thing I am freaking out about is this guy Hunter. He's so cute, Mal. He's older and a counselor so he's sort of taboo, but —"

CRUNCH! CRUNCH! CRUNCH!

The sound was louder and getting closer by the second. I grabbed my stick and started screaming, running over to the large rock my camera was on. I swung the palmcorder strap over my shoulder and jumped up hoping I'd be out of reach of a wolf. "HELP!" I called out. "If anyone can hear me, I'm being attacked by wild animals!"

Who was I kidding? Everyone sane was still asleep. I was done for.

"Sam?"

Huh? Since when could bears or wolves talk?

Walking out of the woods was Cole. He looked like he had been out for a jog. He was in sweats and a faded blue tee that was wet around his neck all the way down to his waist. The wet outline highlighted his abs. Cole's curly hair was matted to his head. He had a slightly comical expression on his face, and his eyebrows were raised. I could tell he was ready to burst out laughing at the sight of me, standing on a rock, holding a large stick, and screaming for help.

"I'd offer to rescue you, but the only thing in these woods are squirrels, and maybe an occasional jogger," Cole said with a wry grin. "That would be me."

"You scared me half to death," I said and started to climb down off the rock. Cole reached out his hand and, not thinking, I took it. His hand was warm and I held on as I jumped off into the sand. I slowly let go and folded my arms self-consciously across my chest. "How much of my conversation did you hear?" I asked nervously. I prayed he didn't hear me talking about Hunter.

"Not much," Cole admitted. "I thought I heard someone talking, but every time I got close, the sound stopped." Cole looked at my palmcorder. "So what are you doing with a recorder here anyway? Composing a love letter for Hunter?"

I pushed the palmcorder strap behind me. "It's none of your business what I'm doing," I said huffily.

"Yep, it's for Hunter," Cole said as if to himself.

"No, it's not," I said. I didn't know what it was about Cole, but for some reason, he seemed to get under my skin. "If you must know, I was sending a message to my best friend, Mallory."

Cole was stretching now and he put one leg up on the rock I was standing next to and leaned in. I couldn't help but stare at it. His calf muscles were huge. "Haven't you ever heard of a phone?" he asked me with a grin.

"We like taping our messages," I said as I tucked the palmcorder safely into my backpack. "It's more personal this way. Whenever one of us is on vacation, or grounded, this is what we do."

"That's cool," Cole said. "My mom's lucky if she gets two phone calls and a postcard all summer."

I couldn't help but laugh. "Well, my mom probably won't do much better," I admitted. "I promised Mal I'd video all the time, and some of my other friends asked for video messages too, so Mom has kind of been pushed to the back burner."

"Are you sure you're going to have time to do CIT duties with all your directing?" Cole questioned. "Sounds like you made an awful lot of promises."

In the distance, we could hear a trumpet blare. It was 8:30 AM. Our very own alarm clock was going off. I kind of preferred the sound to the old, annoying beep on my clock radio at home. The sound meant we had a half hour to get to breakfast.

"Are you hungry?" Cole asked. "I bet Beaver is already flipping pancakes. If we get up there early, we might actually get a warm breakfast this morning."

"Sure," I said awkwardly. I didn't know why, but I felt a little nervous. The two of us slowly started walking up the hill back toward the main part of camp and the mess hall. The camp was still pretty quiet. All of the action stations, like the arts and crafts cabin, were empty, and the only sound I could hear was birds and the faraway neighing of horses down at the stables.

"So, Sam," Cole said, looking at me as we walked past the camp vegetable garden, "I've done some checking up and here's what I know about you: You starred in the Dial and Dash commercial, you claim you wish you hadn't been in it, you're from Long Island, and this is your first time ever at camp, right?"

"How do you know all that?" I asked, surprised.

"I have my sources," Cole said cryptically. "But seriously, what brought you to camp? We don't get many stars up here, you know. Except for Ashley, who thinks she's one. No one has the heart to tell her that the Pines video won't win her an Oscar nomination."

I laughed. "I don't know," I said. "I guess I was looking for a change of scenery. I saw my summer in front of me and I didn't like it so I decided to try something new." I figured it was better not to tell Cole I was trying to get away from my best friend and her suffocating boyfriend. "Why do you go here?"

"I've been coming here since I was seven," Cole told me. "I couldn't imagine spending my summers anywhere else. My family lives and breathes camp, even all winter long. I'm the youngest of three siblings who are all Pines veterans. My brothers are always teasing me about whether I'll actually make senior counselor. I keep telling them I have to make it past CIT first." He grinned and I noticed that his teeth were all perfectly straight, unlike mine. Even after braces, my mom liked to joke that my eye teeth still looked like fangs.

"I'll just be happy if I survive being a CIT," I admitted.

"You'll be fine," Cole told me. "Everyone acts as if you have to be a lifer to do this job, but to be honest, you just have to be good with kids. The rest will come to you."

I smiled. "You know, you're not so bad, Cole, when you're not bothering me about what's-his-name."

Cole grinned. "We were just getting warmed up," he said. "So about Hunter . . ."

I groaned. "Why do you care so much if I like him?"

Cole's sunny face got a little foggy when I said that. But before he could answer me, I heard someone calling my name. Cole and I turned around and I saw Grace, Em, and Court hurrying toward us.

I grabbed Cole's arm. "Listen, they don't know about my palmcorder," I said awkwardly. "I know I'm not supposed to have one here, but it's more than that. I just . . . I just . . . I kind of . . ." We'd totally bonded, but my videotaping was something I felt was private. I wasn't ready to share it just yet. "I . . ."

Cole grabbed my hand and smiled. "It's okay, Sam," he said. "Your secret is safe with me."

"Thank you," I managed to get out before the girls were in front of us, all dressed in some variation of the standard camp outfit — a cute tee (in Court's case, one with a flashy logo. Hers said "Princess-in-training") and shorter-than-short shorts. I had a feeling I wouldn't be pulling the baggy gym tees I had brought with me out of my trunk all summer.

"Cole!" Court squealed, hugging him fiercely. "I feel like I haven't seen you yet. How was your year?"

"How was your year?" was a sentence I'd heard about a billion times already. I'd quickly learned that Pines lifers (as so many counselors call themselves) break their year into two categories: time at camp and time away from camp. Time away from camp seemed to be spent pining for camp, having reunions, or talking to other campers on the Pines MySpace page.

"Great," Cole said before hugging Grace and Em as well. "How are you guys doing? Who do you have your sights set on this year, Court?"

The rest of us laughed and Court looked at me mysteriously. She pointed to the two of us. "What are you two doing together?" she asked in a way that made me blush.

"We bumped into each other on the way to breakfast," Cole said smoothly and that seemed to satisfy Court. For the moment.

"So you guys heard the news then," Grace said breathlessly. "CIT assignments are going up this morning, not this afternoon."

Cole and I looked at each other. "Uh, yeah," we both said, but it was obvious to me that neither of us knew this.

"I have to get Colleen!" Grace said. "If not Colleen, then definitely Briel. Or Dana. Dana's not bad either, I guess. Hitch wouldn't DARE give me Melanie. I mean, Melanie doesn't even know what a soccer ball looks like. She's always like, 'Let's make a lanyard!' Hitch CANNOT give me Melanie."

Em giggled. "Can you tell she's a little worked up about this?"

"I'm not the only one," Grace said indignantly. "Ashley and Gabby sprang out of bed at eight and headed up here to wait for the posting. I wouldn't be surprised if they were at the mess hall right now." Grace rolled her eyes. "As if Ashley has a single worry about her assignment. She's obviously with Alexis."

Court shook her head. "It's so unfair. Alexis is probably the coolest counselor here. Ashley isn't worthy. Even if she is family."

"I take it you two still aren't getting along," Cole pointed out.

"What's there to like? Besides, Ashley isn't talking to Grace or Em either," Court said stubbornly. "And you can tell she doesn't like Sam."

"Court!" Em admonished and I laughed.

"Well, it's true," Court told everyone. "Anyone who competes with her star status is done for."

"Enough catching up," Grace said, tugging on Em's and Court's arms. "We have to get to the mess hall." The four of us started walking again with Grace leading the way.

"Is getting the right counselor that big a deal?" I asked as we headed toward the mess hall. Grace stopped and stared at me. "I mean, how bad could it be? CITs are nothing more than glorified campers, right? We help out a few sessions a day, and have rotating kitchen duty, but the rest of the time we have the same camp privileges as everyone else. Who cares if we don't love our senior counselor?"

"You don't want to get the wrong counselor, Sam," Grace said darkly. "Get a lousy counselor and your summer as a CIT could be hell. The right counselor will not only train you for next year, she can change your whole social status. The other counselors will respect you, you'll have a great recommendation for next year, and you'll get more free time."

"I know a girl whose sister got a lousy senior counselor her CIT year and spent the summer running a cabin of screaming kids while her leader was off with her boyfriend," Em added, her eyes wide. "Those kids almost got her expelled from camp after they set fire to one of the bunk beds when she went to take a shower."

Gulp. "I guess the right match is important," I said nervously. Who would I get? Sophia seemed a little high-maintenance. Dana wasn't that bad. Neither was Melanie, in my book. But sports weren't my strong suit.

"Guys, stop freaking Sam out," Cole told them. He looked at me. "I'm sure you'll like who you get. I know for a fact the senior counselors had a say in who their charges were so whoever picked you has to already like you." My shoulders relaxed a little.

"How do you know about the senior counselors having a say?" Grace demanded.

"I have my sources," Cole said with a twinkle in his eyes.

"He says that a lot," I observed.

Grace took a deep breath and I looked up. The mess hall was right in front of us. "Here we go," she said as she climbed the creaky wood stairs two at a time and hurried onto the wrap-around porch.

Now I knew why the campgrounds were deserted. Every CIT on campus was already here crowding around a large scroll of paper. It was like the tryouts for the school play. People were screaming and hugging, and the sound was deafening. Suddenly the crowd parted quietly and Ashley and Gabby pushed their way through. Ashley's expression was like steel and she strode purposefully toward the administrative buildings. When she saw Court, Cole, Em, and me staring at her, her whole look changed.

"Hi, Cole," she said, batting her eyes. "Hi, girls!" she added a little too cheerfully to be believed. "Exciting day, isn't it? Gabs and I are thrilled with our match-ups."

"We are?" Gab asked, and I saw Ashley stomp on her foot.

"Where are you guys off to? Aren't you having breakfast?" Court asked curiously.

Ashley looked taken aback for a moment. Gabby opened her mouth, but Ashley nudged her. "Of course. I'll catch you girls inside. I just needed some, um, air."

The rest of us looked at each other, and headed over to the list. The crowd had dispersed a bit and I noticed Grace was already scanning the names. Cole hung back to talk to another CIT named Dylan, who with his dark hair and tall physique, not to mention the Superman tee, sort of resembled a less dorky Clark Kent. Or from the look on Em's face, Superman himself.

"Oh my God!" I heard Court exclaim. Grace and Em collectively gasped. "Sam, you have to get up here." Their faces were anxious and they quickly made room for me.

How bad of a match could I have gotten? I put my finger on the list and scrolled through it. Grace got Colleen, just like she wanted, Gabby was with Melanie, Em got Briel, and Court got Dana. And I got . . . no. No way. It couldn't be.

"I got Alexis?" I said out loud. I checked the list again. How did that happen? But there it was in ink: Samantha Montgomery and Alexis Hitchens, peeps, ages six to eight, bunk 5A.

Yep, I had read it right. And then just to be sure, I looked up Ashley. She was with Morgan.

"This is priceless," Court laughed. "No wonder Ashley is acting freaky. Morgan is strictly by the book. There is no way Ashley is getting out of kitchen duty! You are so lucky, Sam. Usually the most promising CIT gets Alexis since she's Hitch's number two. That is so not Ashley, even if she's been bragging that it would be her for years."

"I adore Colleen, but you are in a great position," Grace told me. "They must really like you here. Already."

My stomach was fluttering wildly and I grabbed it instinctively, willing it to stop moving. "This is a disaster," I said. "Ashley must be furious." She already disliked me, between the attention I was getting for Dial and Dash and the fact that her sister picked me to be her partner on the nature hike. As much as I didn't think Ashley and I would ever be friends, I didn't want to be her enemy either.

Em patted my back sympathetically. "She can make a person's life pretty miserable."

"Who cares? She hasn't left me alone for years," Court says cheerfully. "Consider it an honor that you're her enemy. She only hates people she's really jealous of."

"Hey." Cole walked over with Dylan. "Do you two know each other?" he asked me.

Dylan shook my hand, but his eyes were on Em. "Not formally. Hey, Em," he said.

"Congrats on scoring Alexis," Cole said to me. "She's really cool."

"Thanks," I said distractedly.

"Are you okay?" Cole asked.

"She's afraid Ashley's going to flip out that Sam got her sister over her," Grace explained. The color in her face had returned now that she knew her assignment and it was the one she wanted.

"She's harmless," Cole told me, but I heard Em cough. "I don't know why girls get so worked up about her."

"Who'd you guys get?" Em asked the guys even though she was staring right at Dylan.

"Thomas," Dylan said with a shrug. "He's decent."

Cole glanced at me. "I got Hunter," he said and I looked down at my flip-flops.

Court squealed. "You're so lucky."

"Yeah, sure," Cole laughed. "I'm the one who is going to be picking up the slack with his peeps while he's off flirting with counselors. You and Alexis have peeps too, don't you, Sam?" he asked me. "I guess that means we'll be teaming up to do some activities together. " That sounded fun, doing group things with Cole. He was growing on me.

"I'm glad my marshmallows can go to the bathroom on their own," Court said with a shudder. "Who wants to deal with that?" Dylan had marshmallows too, while Em and Grace had pez.

Everyone's excitement over assignments and camper details helped me forget about Ashley. My friends were right — it wasn't my fault that I had been assigned to Alexis. Ashley had to know that. Right? I shuddered.

Suddenly my ears were ringing. Everyone was still talking so they didn't see me turn around. Just a few feet away were Ashley and Gabby, deep in conversation. Neither of them looked happy, but Ashley looked downright furious. Her skinny arms were waving wildly and her face was red. It didn't take a genius to know she was probably talking about me.

Gabby saw me looking and nudged her best friend, who spun around. Ashley didn't even try to hide her expression. Her eyes like slits, she stared at me coldly and then looked away.

"You okay, Sam?" Em asked me, putting a hand on my shoulder. I jumped.

"Yeah," I said with a small smile. "I'm fine."

I hoped.

5

They're Here

There was no need to panic. They were just kids, right? Sweet little adorable . . . yelling kids.

But I was still panicked!

There were busloads and busloads of them heading right toward me and I could hear them screaming even with the bus windows closed.

The first bus pulled up and opened its doors, and a sea of loud rugrats, dressed all in red, came running out. Two counselors anxiously rushed over to meet them.

Me, I was about to pass out.

That wouldn't have been good because I was lined up with the rest of the Whispering Pines staff to greet the campers. We were all standing there with big smiles, wearing our red Pines staff t-shirts, and everyone seemed really excited.

I would have been excited too.

If I wasn't completely petrified.

I wasn't ready for this! I'd only had a few days of training! I couldn't remember the rules to capture the flag. I still didn't understand what Color War was and I got lost on the way to the arts and crafts building. How could Hitch have thought I was a good match for Alexis or that I was in any way ready to be a CIT?

I stopped hyperventilating and looked around. Hmm. No one seemed to have noticed yet that I didn't belong. Hitch was belting out the camp fight song through his megaphone. Alexis, Sophia, and Gabby's crush, Gavin, were marking off clipboards with every camper's name on them while simultaneously talking to people on their walkie-talkies. Ashley and Gabby were greeting the first wave of girl campers, who all seemed pretty happy to see them. Hunter and some of the guy counselors were wearing red war paint, carrying camp banners, and cheering as obnoxiously as they could. I just stood there like a statue.

I was sure I was going to be sick.

"Are you okay?" Court asked, giving me an amused look. She was standing next to me. She'd cut the sleeves off her Pines t-shirt, added glitter to the Pines logo, and knotted her tee at the waist. Only Court could have made a boring baggy tee look trendy. I had a feeling she rocked at arts and crafts.

We were supposed to break off in a few minutes to meet with our counselors and then collect our campers and bring them back to their bunk. But I couldn't move. My feet were glued to the ground.

"I'm fine," I told her. "I'm totally ready for this."

"You look ready," Courtney deadpanned. She punched my

slightly swollen mosquito-bitten arm lightly. (I had made a mental note that morning: Put bug spray on at all times after dusk whether it seems buggy or not.)

I scratched my arm, which was lathered with dried calamine lotion. "I don't think I can do this," I groaned. "The campers are going to eat me alive."

"Your group is six, seven, and eight," Courtney pointed out. "They can't smell weakness yet. Although they do cry at night and wet the bed."

"Not helping," I moaned.

Em walked over to us. "Hey," she said. "How are you feeling?" I just looked at her. "That's what I thought," Em said. "Maybe this will help." She held out a card.

I opened it up and burst out laughing. On the front was a cartoon picture of two girls stuck up in a tree with a hungry-looking bear salivating at the bottom of the tree. Inside it said, "Sometimes at camp we do a lot of hanging around. Good thing friends like you keep life interesting." At the bottom of the card Em had written, "Good luck today, Sam! I know you're going to do great. Em." I was so touched I almost couldn't speak. Even Mal hadn't sent me off to camp with a card, though I had given her one before I left.

Court ripped the card from my hands, read it, and laughed. "You and your cards," she said to Em. "Is this from the Pines Country Store?"

"Where else?" Em asked. "They're the only ones that sell camp-themed cards."

I hugged Em. "Thanks," I said, and tucked the card into the pocket on the back of my shorts.

"Counselors, it's time," Hitch interrupted, yelling into his megaphone. I couldn't even see him in the huge crowd, but I knew it was him. "Find your troops and report to your bunks."

Court gave my hand a squeeze. "Good luck," we said at the same time, and then headed into the sea of people to find our counselors.

I only made it a few feet before I ran into a tiny, red-faced camper who was in tears. She couldn't find her counselor, so I wound up taking her over to Gavin, who had the master list, and then over to Morgan, her counselor. That's where I saw a boy trip and fall and bust open his knee in front of me. He was in Bridget's and Em's group, but since they looked so preoccupied, I offered to quickly take the kid to the nurse. After that I ran into Sophia, who was carrying an armload of unclaimed duffel bags and looked like she was going to be crushed under the weight. I offered to help her carry them to the administrative building.

When I came back, I couldn't find Alexis anywhere. The parking lot had become a total madhouse. Bus drivers were unloading duffel bags and putting them in a huge pile, counselors were holding signs with their bunk numbers on them, and everywhere I turned one camper was grabbing another camper and squealing some variation of "OH MY GOD! I SO MISSED YOU!" A few feet away from me I spotted Ashley and Gabby holding court with a few campers. Ashley saw me and waved, which was odd, but I guessed we were all trying to be on our best behavior.

I walked past their group, sidestepped a camper throwing up into a garbage bag that one of the counselors was holding, and bumped right into Cole.

"Hey," he yelled over the commotion. He was holding a tiny, sweaty six-year-old boy like a football with one hand and a nervous-looking little boy was hanging on desperately to his other. "Having fun yet?"

"Loads," I yelled back and added: "Have you seen Alexis?"

Cole shook his head. "Try by the duffels," he suggested and then disappeared into the crowd.

Where could Alexis have disappeared to? She said she'd find me as soon as Hitch gave the signal and we'd greet our campers together. But maybe I shouldn't have gotten so distracted. Just ahead of me, I saw Grace. I reached my hand through a group of crying girls having a reunion and grabbed Grace's arm. "Have you seen Alexis?" I asked, feeling myself start to panic.

"You mean you haven't picked up your campers yet?" she asked, sounding surprised. "I've found five of mine already."

What? How? They'd only been here five minutes. Okay, maybe it was more like fifteen at this point since I had gotten tied up doing other things. Now I was getting nervous. Where were my campers? I pictured Alexis on the other side of this crowd with all eight little girls lined up, saying, "What do you mean none of you have seen Sam? She was supposed to greet you." I felt a tug on the back of my shirt and turned around. A cute, brunette girl with an explosion of freckles on her cheeks was staring up at me. She looked the right age.

"Are you Samantha?" she asked nervously.

I nodded and kneeled down to her level. "Are you in my bunk? 5A? Are you a peep?" I asked, trying to think of every possible term she might recognize.

She shook her head. "I'm supposed to tell you that Alexis wants you to go to the west gate. She said your girls were dropped off there by accident and are waiting for you. She had to run back to the office to get something. She'll meet you there."

I hugged the girl. "Thanks!" I said, feeling relieved, and then turned back to Grace. "I found them! I'll see you later." I pushed my way through the crowd and sprinted to the main entrance. Then I stopped short.

Wait. This wasn't right. Where the heck was the west gate?

Okay, I could figure that out on my own. If we were at the main entrance and the camp was facing, um, it was facing . . . okay, where was the sun? Oh! Over there. Okay, so if the camp was facing north then that meant the west gate would be to my left. I think. It was probably on the other side of the tennis courts and that's why I'd never seen it. I took off running, as fast as my legs would take me, up the path.

I had no idea I could run this fast. I was going to make it to the west gate in no time. I'd get there, greet the girls and have them unpacking their stuff in the cabin before Alexis even got back from the main office. She'd be so impressed.

Wow, this was a really good workout. Maybe I was a natural athlete and never knew it. I should have signed up for more physical activity this session (right now I was signed up for as many crafts and non-sweating activities as they would allow). Next session I would take soccer and really wow Grace. Or sign up for the hiking group. Maybe I'd take up jogging with Cole. Wait. Why would I want to jog with Cole? I'd jog alone and . . .

Wheeze . . .

Trip . . .

Wheeze . . .

Were my lungs supposed to be burning?

I stopped and put my head between my legs, my hands firmly grasping my knees so I didn't fall over. I tried to catch my breath. I needed water. Was there a stream nearby? I thought Hitch had said something about the streams on campus all being clean enough to drink. Or was that, not clean enough to drink?

"Taking a little morning jog, champ?" I heard someone ask.

I looked through my legs. Hunter was leading a group of rowdy six-to-eight-year-old boys. I quickly stood up and then felt a little dizzy. Hunter reached out to steady me.

"Hold up, guys," he said to the kids, and then to me: "You look pretty flushed. It's me, isn't it?"

I could feel my face color. "Where's Cole?" I asked, trying to change the subject.

"We had a wetter," Hunter said, leaning into me. "Cole ran ahead with him so he could change and wouldn't be embarrassed." Hunter shook his head. "I would have made the kid suck it up."

Ouch. How could Hunter be so mean? I would have done the same thing Cole did.

"Don't look so wounded," Hunter said. "I'm half kidding. I don't want you to regret being happy to see me."

"I was on my way to the west gate to meet my campers so I should go," I said a tad defensively. He stared at me with those big blue peepers and a huge grin and it was making it hard for me to remember why I was here.

Hunter nodded. "The west gate, huh?"

"Yes," I said. I wished he'd stop looking at me. They needed an ordinance around here that said Hunter had to wear sunglasses at all times when he was talking to girls. "I should get going." The only problem was I still wasn't one hundred percent sure in which direction. I looked at him sheepishly. "Do you know which way it is?"

"Well, that all depends, champ," he said coyly. "What are you going to do for me if I tell you?"

I blushed. "I don't have time for games," I said, trying to sound composed. I wasn't used to guys flirting with me — if that's what he was doing. "Do you know where the west gate is or not?"

"I guess I could tell you for free, just this once," he said.

I waited expectantly. The minutes were ticking by. I was losing my lead time on Alexis. "Well?"

He looked at me. "Boys, tell the champ here where the west gate is."

"There is no west gate!" a slightly taller-looking boy in the back said first. "This is my second year here and I know the only gate is the main one." Two other boys muttered in agreement.

My heart felt like it just stopped. "But there has to be!" I freaked out.

Hunter shook his head. "I think you've just entered phase one of your initiation."

"My initiation?" I was confused. What was Hunter talking about? How could there be no west gate? That girl definitely said west gate. She said Alexis told her. Why would that cute little girl make that up?

ASHLEY.

Now it all made sense. This was payback. I felt like I was going to pass out. "You're not being funny."

"I'm not trying to be." He shrugged. "I knew there was no way Ashley and Gabby were going to let you waltz in here without one. You better watch your back, champ," he added with a smirk. "I think you should head back to the main entrance. I bet there's a group of crying girls waiting for you."

Oh God. He was probably right. I didn't even say good-bye. Or thanks. I just sprinted back to the parking lot, ignoring the fire in my legs and the dry feeling in my throat.

But there was no one there. Just a few bus drivers, still unpacking bags, and a few left-behind banners.

Oh no. This couldn't be happening. Where were my girls?

♠ 6 ♠
Meet the Peeps

It finally occurred to me that if the girls weren't in the parking lot and there wasn't a west gate, then they had to be with — gulp — Alexis. Which meant they were at our bunk already. Holding my aching side, I ran as fast as I could to the lower campus that housed the peeps and pez and raced up the steps to bunk 5A. I could hear kids chattering as I flung open the door.

"Sam!" Alexis said with a small smile. "Where were you?"

"Alexis, I —"

"We'll discuss it later," she cut me off quickly, but cheerfully. "Why don't you meet the girls? Girls, this is your second counselor, Sam Montgomery. Sam is a CIT."

"CV?" a cute little girl with braids asked. "What's that?"

Alexis laughed. "C-I-T. That's a counselor in training, which means Sam is my helper and she's going to help you guys too."

I looked at the group of eight little girls in front of me. They were so small I couldn't believe they were at sleepaway camp. Alexis had told me that three girls had been there last summer, but the rest were first-timers. Some were clutching dolls or old stuffed animals. One had her thumb in her mouth. And all of them had the look of kids who were dazed, slightly nervous, and ready to throw up or cry. I knew the look well from years of babysitting.

"Hi, girls," I said, sounding upbeat. "It's so nice to meet you. You know," I whispered as if I was telling a secret, "this is my first year at camp too."

"But you're big," a little girl holding a bear pointed out skeptically.

I laughed. "You're right. I am. But I've never been to camp before either so we'll have to figure everything out together, okay?" They nodded their heads slowly.

"Girls, let's play a game," Alexis told them. "Let's see who can take everything out of their duffel bag and put it on their bed first. I have to have a quick chat with Sam."

Uh-oh. I should have known I wasn't getting off that easily. I followed Alexis outside and waited till she shut the screen door. There wasn't much privacy at camp, but the girls were so loud, they probably couldn't hear us anyway.

"I saw you at the parking lot this morning," Alexis said quietly. "Then you disappeared. Where'd you go?"

"I looked for you, but it got so hectic that I couldn't find you when it was time for pickup," I explained helplessly. "I asked everyone and by the time I figured out where you were, it was too late."

Alexis seemed to be taking the story in word for word. "Why didn't you use your walkie-talkie to contact me?"

Gulp. The walkie-talkie. I forgot about that. All the CITs and counselors had one so they could communicate no matter how far away they were. "I left it back in my bunk," I admitted sheepishly.

Alexis looked at me. She didn't seem mad. Just disappointed, mystified maybe. And that was worse. I didn't want to let Alexis down. She had been so nice to me and I had screwed up already. "There has to be more to your disappearance than that, Sam."

Sigh. I had to tell her something. But what could I say? That I listened to a six-year-old and went looking for a phantom west gate? I could have ratted out Ashley, I know. But what good would that have done me? Ashley would have said I was lying and I had no proof anyway. I didn't even know where to find the camper that gave me the info in the first place. And at the end of the day, this was still Ashley's sister. Who was she going to believe? Maybe half truths would work.

"I got sidetracked," I admitted. "I helped a few counselors with their own campers and by the time I was finished, mine were gone."

"Sam, your first responsibility is your own bunk," Alexis said sternly. "You knew how important it was to get the campers this morning. These kids are practically babies and they're relying on us to show them the way," she said, her tone softening. "I had to oversee the camper checklist so when no one picked up our bunk, Mrs. Morberry sent for my dad," Alexis explained. Mrs. Morberry was the camp secretary. "He brought them to the bunk and then came and found me. The kids were really nervous that no one showed up. Thank goodness none of their parents were there to see what happened."

Double gulp. Now not only was Alexis upset with me, Hitch knew I screwed up as well. "It won't happen again, Alexis," I promised. "I messed up, but I really want to be here, and work with you, and I'll do a better job in the future. I swear. What can I do to make things up to you? Do you need help making the girls' beds? Helping them put away their clothes?"

Alexis smiled. "Let's start by getting back inside before the girls destroy the place." I turned to leave and she put a hand on my shoulder. "I know this can be hard, Sam. This is all new to you. But I see something in you that I see in me. That's why I picked you to be my CIT. I know everyone thought my sister was a shoo-in, but to be honest, as much as I adore her, I think she'd be better off with someone who can, um, tame her free spirit." Alexis smirked. "She'll learn a lot from Morgan. But you, you and I just clicked on that hike. You've got IT."

"It?" I asked.

Alexis laughed and I noticed she had a pretty smile. Ashley's mouth always seemed sullen, or in a permanent frown, but Alexis was always happy. The sisters may have looked alike with their blond hair and small waists, but in my opinion, Alexis's attitude made her ten times prettier. She also had Hitch's eyes, which were big and green. Ashley's gray ones reminded me of an impending thunderstorm.

"The camp spark, as Dad and I call it," Alexis explained. "The sign of a camp lifer — even if you did start a little late," she added. "It's something my dad said I've always had. I love this place so much I'll probably run it when Dad retires," she said with a laugh. "When I'm away at college, I miss it terribly. Unlike Ashley, who doesn't shut up about moving to New York City after she graduates high school and only returning to do her beloved camp videos and brochures."

Ashley had said that? All she talked about in our cabin was how much she loved the Pines. It was probably better not to bring that up.

"Anyway, I can tell when someone is going to fit in well here, and I think you will," Alexis told me. "You just have to stay sharp, and pay attention to everything going on around you. Especially with campers this little."

"I will," I vowed, feeling charged. Alexis had a way of making you think you could run a marathon — something she had already told me she loved to do — even when you weren't a trained runner. I didn't want to let her down again. I just had to make sure Ashley didn't botch things up for me.

The two of us headed back into the cabin and the girls all looked up expectantly. Their clothes were in large heaps on the beds. A few had posters and pictures with them, but no tape. Alexis and I quickly sprang into action. We showed the girls their beds (all singles because of their age), explained the shower situation, and helped them tape posters above their beds. Within an hour, the cabin looked like a Disney Store with all the *Hannah Montana* and *The Cheetah Girls* pictures, pillows, and bedspreads. When we were finished decorating, we sat down on the floor with markers and colored paper and helped each girl make a name tag to wear around her neck for the first day. You could tell the girls liked crafts.

"Sam?" Alexis said as I was helping Mackenzie write a z on her tag. Alexis was reading over a list of memos on her clipboard. I excused myself and walked over. "So it seems one of our campers, Mackenzie Hammond, has to take allergy shots every day. The nurse already has her medication, but we need to take Mackenzie down there every morning for her shot. Apparently Mackenzie hates needles and cries every time." Alexis frowned. "I guess I can get the girls up a few minutes earlier, and bring them all down there and have them wait outside."

"I'll do it," I said almost without thinking. I had to make up for what happened this morning, even though it meant I'd have to rise extra early to get Mackenzie to the nurse and then to breakfast on time. "It will be easier if you don't have to trek the whole bunk down there for the shots. I could take Mackenzie every morning before breakfast."

Alexis looked concerned. "Are you sure? That's a lot of responsibility. And I'd hate for you to have to get up extra early to do this."

"I don't mind," I said hurriedly. "It's the least I can do."

Alexis grinned. "Great then. That would really help me a lot." In the distance, we heard the trumpet signaling the end of the morning free period. "Okay, girls, we have arts and crafts this morning. Let's all put our shoes on and gather our name tags and we can walk over. Sam has to go to her own activity so we'll see her later."

I felt a tug on my shirt and turned around. Mackenzie was staring up at me. "I need my shot," she said.

Alexis frowned. "Didn't you have it this morning, sweetie?" she asked.

Mackenzie shook her head. "We left too early to do it. Mom said I would have it here." She was clutching a small brown bear in a red hooded sweatshirt and was stroking it nervously.

Alexis looked at her watch. "Okay, I guess we could swing by the nurse and just go over to arts and crafts late —"

"I'll take her," I offered, even though I was dying to get to the pottery class. I had grand illusions of making Mom a vase. "It's my job anyway, right? I can take Mackenzie there and then bring her to you for arts and crafts. I have pottery anyway and that's right down the hill."

Alexis looked grateful. "Thanks, Sam."

Mackenzie, her bear, and I headed down the steps of the cabin, and Mackenzie reached for my hand. Hers was all sweaty, but I didn't mind.

"Is it dark at night, Sam?" she asked me in a tiny voice. "I hate the dark. I brought a nightlight, but I wasn't sure where to plug it in."

"I'll help you find a spot," I offered. "But I do have a tip for you that should help. Your bed is closest to the exit sign. The exit sign lights up so think of that as an extra nightlight."

She smiled, revealing two missing top teeth. "I didn't think of that!" she said happily. "How did you?"

"Well, I've been here a few days already getting ready for you guys," I told her. We were swinging our arms now as we walked. "I have another secret to tell you — I was scared of the dark when I was your age too."

Her eyes grew wide. "You were?"

"Yep," I said. "And when I was little my class went on a week-long camping trip and I was really nervous about sleeping in the dark. That's when I discovered the exit sign. I slept in the bed closest to it so I wouldn't be afraid."

"Just like I'm going to do," Mackenzie said with a smile.

Within minutes we were at the nurse's station. "Here we are," I told Mackenzie and she clutched my hand even tighter. "You're going to like Nurse Nancy. She's sweet. She may even give you a lollipop when you're done."

When we opened the cabin door, I felt a rush of cool air. Ahhh, air conditioning. Maybe there was a benefit to taking Mackenzie to these daily shots. The nurse's office and Hitch's were the only two buildings on campus that had A/C units. Even five minutes inside would make all the difference on a 95 degree day. It was only late June, but already the temperature in the mountains was creeping up that high. Plus, the waiting room had a TV! It was the first one I'd seen in a week and I stared in awe at Rachel Ray making burritos. Maybe a news commercial would come on and I'd actually get a glimpse of the outside world. Camp was sort of like living in a bubble. I hadn't had a care package or letter yet so I had no idea what was going on off-campus.

"Hey." Cole and a small boy in a Mets t-shirt were sitting on the waiting room bench. "Did you get hit in the head again already?"

I laughed, surprised to see him. "I'm not here for me," I said. "This is Mackenzie and we're here to get her daily allergy shot."

Cole nudged the little blond-haired boy next to him. "This is Caleb. He's here for his shot too."

"Do you take them every day?" Mackenzie asked Caleb as she climbed on the bench next to him.

He nodded. "Every morning."

"Me too!" Mackenzie squealed.

"I guess we'll be seeing Caleb a lot," I told Mackenzie. I looked at Cole. "I'm on shot duty so we'll be here every morning before breakfast."

"That's pretty generous of you," Cole said. "I think I may have to volunteer for that job myself. A few minutes in this freezer is heaven. Now if I could just get a Mets score on TV I'd be all set."

Cole looked cute today. He was wearing his red Pines tee and Nike track shorts. The color looked great against his tan skin.

"What are you smiling about?" Cole accused me jokingly. "You're wondering how my CIT life with Hunter is, aren't you?"

"No I'm not," I said defensively.

"Yes you are," Cole teased. "Go ahead. Ask me how cute he is with the six-year-olds."

"I wasn't going to ask you that," I stammered. But come to think of it, I did want to know how he was with them. Was he like a big kid? I could picture him joking around with them and carrying them around on his shoulders. Sigh.

Static filled the air and Cole reached for his walkie-talkie. "Cole? Man? Are you there?" It was Hunter's voice.

"Speak of the devil," Cole said with a grin. He lifted the walkie-talkie to his face. "Yep, I'm here."

"Go to a private channel," Hunter said. "What's taking so long down there?"

"Nurse Nancy's already in with someone," Cole said, his eyes on me. "Some kid got stung by a bee."

Hunter groaned. "Really? That blows. I was hoping you'd be back here by now. I forgot what we have for the next period."

Cole looked amused. "Soccer, remember? I told you to take the soccer ball with you."

"That's right! Thanks, mate," Hunter said and paused. "Do you remember what the period is after that?"

I hoped my surprise didn't show on my face. How could Hunter not know his schedule?

"I think it's arts and crafts," Cole said to the walkie-talkie.

"Got it. Got it. I forgot," Hunter said. "See you soon."

Cole clipped the walkie-talkie to the back of his shorts. "So what do you think of your crush now?"

"He's not my crush," I said, even though I was blushing.

"For your sake, I hope that's true," Cole said quietly. "Because Hunter isn't a one-girl kind of guy, as you may have noticed."

The door to Nurse Nancy's office opened. "Who wants to go first?" she asked us as she walked out a sniveling little girl. I recognized a snotty CIT from 8A who was with her.

"Can we go together?" Caleb asked nervously, looking at Mackenzie.

Nurse Nancy smiled. "I don't see why not. Why don't you all come in?"

The four of us filed into the nurse's office. The room reminded me of the nurse's office at school. Everything was white and there were silly cartoon drawings on the walls with nurse humor on them. The room had three cots, all unoccupied. We helped Mackenzie and Caleb up onto the first one. Caleb's shot was over in less than a minute, but when it was Mackenzie's turn, she burst into tears.

"Mackenzie, it's okay," I said soothingly. "I'm here." I grabbed her sweaty little hand, but she just kept bawling and pulling her hand away. "Don't you want a lollipop?"

"I need you to keep her still," Nurse Nancy told me. I looked helplessly at Cole. He quickly knelt down in front of Mackenzie and stroked her teddy bear.

"So who is this guy, Mackenzie?" he asked her.

She seemed to calm down for a moment. "My bear," she said tearfully.

"I like his sweatshirt," Cole said. "Does this guy have a name?"

Mackenzie smiled. "Snooky."

"Snooky?" Cole said with a laugh. "What kind of a name is Snooky?"

Mackenzie laughed too. "I made it up."

"Well, I tell you what — what if I give Snooky a shot at the same time Nurse Nancy gives you yours? Would that be okay? That way you'll both get your shots done together."

Mackenzie looked thoughtful for a moment. "Okay."

Nurse Nancy approached again with the needle and I cringed, but Mackenzie focused on Cole. He grabbed another needle, still sealed, not that Mackenzie noticed, and put it to Snooky's arm. "It will be over in a second, Snooky," he told the bear. Mackenzie was so delighted, she barely flinched.

"Great job, Mackenzie," Cole told her with a smile. He whisked her off the table. "She's all yours now," he said to me.

I was at a loss for words. Cole was so cute with Mackenzie and I had to admit, it was really appealing. "You were great," I marveled.

Cole shrugged. "It was nothing. Listen, I better get Caleb back to the master." He grinned and I found myself staring at his lips. They looked soft. I felt like I could stare at them forever. "I'll catch you later?" Cole said, looking at me oddly.

"Uh-huh. Yep. Sure!" I laughed nervously and I wasn't sure why.

After dropping Mackenzie off at arts and crafts, I caught the tail end of pottery. Em and I were in the class together and she was already halfway through crafting her first vase. I didn't even have enough time to try the pottery wheel. Afterward we walked to the mess hall for lunch. I couldn't believe it was time for that already. Not that I was complaining. I was starved for anything — even runny mac and cheese.

"How was everyone's first morning as a CIT?" Meg asked as she joined us at the table with a plate of hot pasta. Since she was our senior counselor, she ate with us. I loved that we got to have lunch with our bunk instead of eating with our CIT charges. As a junior and senior counselor, you didn't have the luxury of dining with your friends.

"I've got an athletic bunch," Grace said excitedly as she

munched on her hot dog. "I'm so glad I got the pez. They actually know how to play games."

"The marshmallows rock," said Court, and took a bite of her mac and cheese.

"How was your morning, Sam?" Ashley asked innocently, and Gabby nearly choked on her bug juice. "Anything eventful happen?" Both of them had plates piled high with salad and nothing more.

"Take any walks near the *west* side of camp?" Gabby seconded, and Ashley laughed.

"What are you girls talking about?" Meg asked, confused. "Did everything go okay, Sam?"

Ashley stared at me triumphantly. I wanted to say something so badly, but I just couldn't. I didn't have the guts to deal with the grief that would go along with Ashley's vehement denials. "Yeah," I said, avoiding Ashley's glare. "My campers are adorable, and Alexis is awesome." I couldn't help giving a little dig at least.

"That's great, Sam," Ashley said, and took a sip of her iced tea. "I'm glad you're getting along with my sister. I wouldn't want to work with her, no offense. Don't any of you remember how she treated Patty last summer when she was her CIT? She ran her so much she didn't even have time for her hobby. She was so sick of Alexis, she didn't want to come back to camp this year."

"Didn't Patty decide to go on a European backpacking trip this summer?" Gabby scratched her head. Ashley gave her the evil eye.

"I think you were all given the perfect match." Meg smiled at me.

"I'll say," Ashley seconded. "It sounds like Sam's making a great first impression right out of the *gate*."

This caused Gabby to laugh harder. Everyone looked confused, except for Court. I got the feeling she knew something was up. She stared at me intently, almost willing me to respond to Ashley's taunting. But I couldn't. I didn't know how. Being obnoxious wasn't my strong suit. Helping my friends was. So instead I just stared miserably at my runny mac and cheese.

♠ 7 ♠

Arts, Crafts, and Confession

It was raining. Not that soft, misty rain that makes you want to run outside and twirl around in it. This was like a monsoon. Staring out our cabin window, I could see campers shrieking as they dashed through the large muddy puddles and held wet sweatshirts high over their heads. It was the first rainy day of camp that season — the most we'd had was an occasional passing thundershower — and the last thing I wanted to do was go outside.

I didn't really have a choice. It was free period and I had to finally finish Mal's first tape and drop it in the mail. I was already majorly behind in my video messages. Camp was a lot busier than I thought it would be. And even when it wasn't, I was having too much fun with Court, Em, and Grace to even think about sneaking off to make a tape. Not that I would ever admit that to Mal.

A clap of thunder overhead rattled my bunk bed. The storm was far from over, but I had to leave now if I wanted to get this done. I grabbed my green windbreaker and my backpack, slipping the palmcorder inside, wrapped in a sweatshirt. In this weather, the whole cabin smelled like wet wood. Grace had been on bug duty all morning — apparently this kind of weather draws them inside — and I moved out of the way as she used a fly swatter to squash another one.

"Gotcha!" Grace squealed. You could barely hear her over the sound of the rain hitting the roof. A strong wind blew open the shutters nearest Gabby and Ashley and they quickly ran to shut it. Grace groaned. "Meg, isn't there some way you can get us out of activities today?"

"I second that motion," Court piped up. "I say we head to the counselors' lounge and watch some soaps."

The counselors' lounge was a CIT/counselor privilege I was dying to take advantage of, but so far none of us had made it there. Set high on the hill above our cabins, the lounge had a huge TV with cable, which meant I might actually get to watch *Access Hollywood* at some point. The lounge also had the only video game system on campus (granted it was a PS2 and not a Wii, but at least they had *Guitar Hero*), big plushy couches, and free snacks.

Meg laughed. "I'm sorry, girls, but just because it's raining doesn't mean all activities are off. Obviously your outdoor ones are not happening, but there are alternatives today. There's a movie starting in the mess hall in an hour, and I think they're playing charades in the gym." Meg looked at Grace. "But you might get out of arts and crafts. I heard there was a leak in the roof this morning so no classes have been held there today."

Grace let out a whoop. She loved sports, but as I was quickly learning, papers, scissors, and glue were things she could do without. That gave me an idea. If the craft cabin was closed, I could sneak over there and film my video for Mal!

"Meg? Do you mind if I run up to the office? I'm expecting a package," I said.

My mom had sent a massive box yesterday with some cute throw pillows from Urban Outfitters, an Orlando Bloom poster, a sheet set, and a slew of candy. Thanks to her presents, my bed was finally starting to look like someone lived there and not like someone on a day pass. Seeing Mom's handwriting on her note made me a little homesick, I had to admit, but I was having too much fun to dwell on it for that long.

"Another one?" Gabby griped. "Haven't you been lavished enough already?" She was one to complain! Gabby was the first to steal candy from my stash. She gorged herself on the Milky Ways my mom sent and then groaned afterward about needing to exercise.

"If Sam wants to get soaked, I don't see the big deal," Ashley said, not looking up from her *CosmoGirl!*

"Maybe you should go with her," Court deadpanned.

"You can go, Sam, if you really want," Meg said. "But you're going to get soaked!" she added as a flash of lightning lit up the room. "Be careful. And meet us back here to find out if we have arts and crafts."

I nodded as I pulled my windbreaker hood tight over my head. "See you guys in a bit."

By the time I got to the craft cabin, I was drenched from head to toe. My coat did little to protect me from the driving rain and I was shivering. I pulled off the water-logged wind-breaker and wrung it out, sending puddles all over the cabin floor. The place was thankfully deserted, but part of me was annoyed I was even here. What was I doing heading out in this weather just to shoot a lousy video? Mal hadn't sent a video yet! And I hadn't gotten any letters from my friends, except for the postcard Piper sent from Great Wolf Lodge in Pennsylvania. Nevertheless, I was here. I quickly set up my palmcorder on one of the nearby tables and started recording.

"Hey, Mal," I said wearily. "Like my outfit? As you can tell it's raining and I got soaked sneaking out to send you this message. Anyway, I hope you're having a good summer. I'm liking it here and being a CIT is cool. I have the cutest little campers, especially this one named Mackenzie who I have to take to get allergy shots. She gets upset every time, but then Cole calms her down and she's fine. I don't know how he does it. Did I tell you about Cole?" I asked, trying to talk over the loud pattering of rain. "He's a friend of mine. He's Hunter's CIT. I already told you about Hunter, right? He's so hot, Mal, and such a flirt, but I can't help flirting back. I don't know what's come over me. You know I'm not the flirty type, but with him it's hard to resist. He's got these —"

SLAM. I whipped around. The door to the arts and crafts cabin had been thrown open and Court, Grace, and Em dashed inside, screaming as a clap of thunder burst. Court quickly shut the door behind her. I stood there frozen, unsure of what to do.

Court looked up and saw me. "What are you doing here?" Her

eyes trailed over to my video camera. "Were you just video-taping yourself, you dork?"

"What are you guys doing here?" I said in a high-pitched voice as I grabbed the camera and shoved it in my backpack.

"Meg got the info wrong," Grace grumbled. "Apparently the pottery cabin roof is leaking, not this one. We had to come to class."

"You didn't answer my question," Court prodded. "Why do you have a camera?" The three of them stared at me expectantly.

The door burst open again and in ran a bunch of girls from 8A. They grunted hello — our bunk was kind of rivals with theirs, especially since they're good friends with Ashley and Gabby — and headed over to their table to dry out. Ashley and Gabby didn't sign up for this class, thankfully. They picked archery so they could hang with the boys. Today that probably meant they were inside somewhere playing charades.

Our craft advisor, Cara, ran in behind the girls from 8A. "I'm glad to see you all made it in this weather," she said as another thunderbolt made us all jump. "I've got a fun project for you guys, but you'll have to leave it here so it doesn't get ruined."

"Promise you won't say anything," I whispered to them as we walked to our table. "I know we're not supposed to have cameras."

Court laughed. "Do you think I care if you tape yourself?" she whispered back. "But I am curious — what is that thing for anyway? You're not a camp spy, are you?"

That made me laugh. "No, I'm definitely not a spy."

"Today we're working on scrapbook layouts for July Fourth," Cara interrupted. She started explaining the project and I pretended to listen intently to avoid Grace's, Em's, and Court's curious stares.

When I saw the class options for older campers and CITs, I was a little surprised that arts and crafts were one of them. When I thought of arts and crafts all I could picture were glitter, glue, and lots of cotton balls. You know, grade school stuff. Kind of like the things I was making with the peeps. (They're making lanyards, popsicle-stick frames, and tie-dyed t-shirts.) But us? Cara was letting us make locker organizers for school, disco balls for our cabin, and scrapbook layouts for camp pictures.

Within ten minutes I had placed two twelve-by-twelve-inch red papers in front of me and started cutting blue paper mats for the page. I had my title glued down: Go Red, White, and Blue! I'd even added little silver fireworks that I made with glitter pens. It looked pretty good, if I did say so myself.

"How are you so good at this when this is your first time?" Grace grumbled. She was sitting next to me and so far all she had on her paper was a single blue paper mat that she kept moving around to find the perfect location.

"I don't know," I admitted, "but I like it. It's very relaxing."

"Who cares about layouts?" Court interrupted, as she shredded a piece of gold paper for her pages. "I want to know what Sam was doing with that camera." Her pages were really good. Some of the stickers on her page sort of popped off it and her title, FOURTH, was all sparkly.

"It's no big deal," I said quickly, not looking at her.

"Does it have anything to do with Ashley?" Court prodded. "Are you getting back at her for what she pulled the other day with your campers?"

I had told the girls what had happened on the first day of camp and Grace was livid. Court said that last summer Grace was kind of Ashley's lackey. She followed Ashley and Gabby around everywhere and they let her because Grace was obviously so good at everything. If Grace won capture the flag that made Ashley and Gabby look good because they were on the same team — even if they just stood there sipping their Snapples the whole time. Then Grace sided with Em instead of Ashley over the silly bathing suit incident and their friendship was done quicker than Lauren and Heidi's on *The Hills*.

"It has nothing to do with her," I said.

Court looked disappointed. "I still think you should get back at her with a raid." Her face spread into a devilish grin.

Grace groaned and Em took a puff of her inhaler. "We're too old to do raids," Grace told her. "We have responsibilities."

"Meg would kill us!" Em added. "She'd lock us in the counselor lounge and give us bread and water through a cracked window and . . ."

The rest of us stared at her strangely.

Em blushed. "Okay, maybe that's a little far-fetched. I was up late last night reading *Housekeeper of Love* and I think I might be getting those two worlds mixed up."

"Isn't a raid when you play tricks on someone else's cabin?" I asked. Court nodded eagerly. "How would we get Ashley if she's already in our cabin?"

Court frowned. "You've got a point. We'll have to figure out another way to get even with her. But that doesn't mean we can't pull it off! We're not going to get in trouble," Court added. "Everyone does them. It's a camp ritual!"

Cara cleared her throat, made the quiet sign, and winked at us. Cara was really laid-back. She let us put the radio on while we worked and let us bring snacks (even though we're not supposed to). She told us that the next session had a dedicated scrapbooking class. I was definitely signing up.

The four of us were quiet for a few minutes. You could hear scissors, glitter being poured, and paper tearing. I thought Court had forgotten about my camera.

"You were making a video for Hunter, weren't you?" Court whispered suddenly.

"No!" I said with a laugh. "Why would I make him a video?"

"I don't know." Court shrugged. "Maybe you were sending him some sort of sexy message."

Em giggled. "Sam was soaking wet. How sexy is that?" The rest of us laughed.

"Well, I'd make one for Donovan if I had a camera." Court sniffed. "I've already talked to him four times during free swim, and he told me that he's going to college in Australia to be a veterinarian. How hot is a guy who likes puppies?"

"Donovan has been good for you," Grace said. "I've never seen you work so hard to pass the swim test. Now you can finally go in the deep end."

"In years past, I hated getting wet so I was content to sit on the shore and tan, but this year, I had motivation," Court said proudly. "I took swimming lessons over the winter." Court turned back to me. "You've *got* to tell why you have that palmcorder."

I sighed. "You're not going to give up on that, are you?"

Court smiled. "Nope."

"You guys are going to laugh," I said, feeling suddenly embarrassed by my pastime, but they all voiced some version of "no we're not!" I took a deep breath. "Okay, the truth is, I was taping a message for my best friend, Mal. You know, the girl I've mentioned —"

"Like a thousand times already," Grace interrupted. "Yeah, we know who she is."

I ignored her sarcasm. "Anyway, it's something we do whenever we're apart. I'm supposed to be taping her these messages almost every day telling her about camp and what I'm doing. Kind of like a diary. But I haven't had the time. That's why I lied about going to mail call. I'm so behind on all these videos I promised that I needed to get Mal's done so I can do the rest."

"What other videos are you doing?" Em wanted to know.

I blushed. "I promised all my friends I'd send them a video." Court opened her mouth to speak, but I cut her off. "I didn't realize how busy we'd be! I barely have time to finish one for Mal and hers is the most important. She's going to kill me if she doesn't get one soon."

"You're insane!" Court told me. "You do too much for that girl. And your other friends too. Have they sent *you* any messages yet?"

"No," I admitted sheepishly.

"I don't think it's so strange," Em said. "I think it's kind of cool. It's like you're making a video diary of your camp experiences, except you're sending them to someone else to watch instead of keeping the record for yourself. Oh." She frowned.

Hmm. I never thought of it that way, but Em had a point.

"It would be better if you kept the tapes," Grace suggested. "Then the rest of us could be on them too. I've always wanted a record of me on the high-ropes course so I could show my mom how good I've gotten."

"And I could have a tape of myself being all super-responsible with the campers so my parents won't think I'm boy crazy, even if I really am," Court seconded.

"But we're not allowed to have electronics at camp," I reminded them. "That's why I've been sneaking off to tape without you guys knowing."

"Oh," Court said regretfully. The group of us were quiet again and I could hear other tables working diligently on their layouts. Scissors were working a mile a minute, I could hear glue bottles sputtering, and someone had just spilled glitter all over the floor. Cara rushed over with a dustpan.

"You know what I like about your videos, Sam," Court said quietly, "you can tell the video your deepest thoughts and no one else has to hear them. It's sort of like confession. Or a CIT guide to camp life. Much better than the manual Hitch put together anyway. If we were really brave, someday we could sell the tapes to prospective CITs and make a fortune."

"I'm not sure about that part, but I think we should make our own video!" Em said. "Come on, Sam," she begged me, "this could be fun. Think of it as your camp video scrapbook. What better memory could you have of your first summer here than that?"

"I'd do it," Grace surprised me by announcing, "but only if I got my own copy to watch at home. Or at reunion. We could get together this winter and watch it together."

"I love that idea!" Court said. "I'd save my copy to show my future kids how cool I was."

"I'm not so sure this is a good idea," I said uncertainly. "I've never let anyone else be on the video with me. Besides, I still have so many tapes to do for my friends first."

"That's lame." Court pouted. "You shouldn't waste your summer sending videos when you can live your summer making great tapes with us. I thought you said this summer was about you standing on your own and doing something new? This is something new."

Court was making sense. And it did sound different. Mal never wanted to make videos with me. She just preferred if we sent them to each other when we were apart. This was something I could do with my new friends together. And did I really need to make all these videos for my other friends? They hadn't sent any, had they? I could send everyone a postcard and if they were annoyed, then tough. This was my summer and I shouldn't let it fly by because I was too busy concentrating on life at home.

I looked at the girls and smiled. "Okay, if you guys are that into the idea, I guess we can try it."

Court dove over the table and hugged me. Em did too.

"So when do we start?" Grace asked and grabbed a piece of paper to start jotting down notes. "Do we need to rehearse first? Because I don't want to say anything goofy."

"We can't censor ourselves," Em objected. "These tapes are our chance to blow off steam, you know? They can be our sleepaway camp confessions or something."

"Oooh, I love that," Court agreed.

"But to be on the safe side, we should have a code word for when we want to make a video since we're going to have to be alone to do one," Grace suggested. "We need a name that only we would understand."

"Boy crazy?" Court suggested. Grace made a face.

"I've got one," Em said. "What about the sleepaway girls? That's what we are, aren't we?"

Sleepaway girls. I kind of liked that. "Works for me," I said.

Court grinned. "Well, sleepaway girls, I have a feeling this is the start of something amazing."

8

Fireworks

"Ready, set, go!" Hitch yelled through his megaphone.

On "go," Court and I started, hobbling madly. One of each of our legs was tied together, and we were making our way toward Em and Grace, who were waiting anxiously at the designated relay station.

"Faster!" Grace egged us on loudly. "They're gaining on you!"

My hair was whipping my face, but I managed to catch a glimpse of our competition — Ashley and Gabby. The two of them were wearing pink pinnies, and Ashley had a look of fierce determination on her face. The pink pinnie looked great against her tan skin, while my bright green one, layered over my red Pines t-shirt, made me look like a Christmas tree in July.

"If they beat us, I will kill you," I could hear Ashley yell at Gabby. She was pretty loud considering I could hear her over the screaming campers cheering on the sidelines.

It was July Fourth, and all regular activities were canceled to make way for a special Fourth of July celebration. Hitch had planned a field day with races, a special barbeque dinner at the lake, and fireworks to finish the night. (What I mean is, we could see the fireworks from the lake, which bordered the town park on one side, where they were having a display.) For the game part of the day, everyone got to pick teams and then as the day progressed, we'd face different groups, partner up with younger campers, or face off against the boys. Grace said that bunks usually teamed up, but Ashley and Gabby ditched us for their friends in 8A. When Meg said our teams were unfairly balanced, the 8A team forced two sad-looking bunk-mates to join us remaining 8Bs. They hadn't spoken to us all morning.

"Move it, Sam!" Court hollered. "I'm not coming in second."

I was hopping as fast as I could, but it was hard when you had someone else tied to you. Ashley and Gabby were inching closer and closer so I picked up speed. By this point, Grace and Em were so close I could see them sweating. Four more steps, three; Gabby and Ashley hopped closer, two more steps and —

"YES!" Grace screamed as we reached our team first. Court and I untied the ribbon in one swift motion; Grace and Em grabbed it, tied their legs together, and headed toward our team-mates from 8A.

"What are you two standing there for?" Ashley snapped as she passed the ribbon to the next two girls on her relay team. "GO! Get them!"

"They'll never beat Grace," Court told me confidently. "She's the fastest girl at camp."

Court was right. Grace and Em had reached our third and final relay stop when the pink team was only halfway to theirs. We were going to win! But then — I could see Grace barking at our teammates, but it didn't make them move any faster. One yawned. Another bent down to retie her Lacoste sneakers. Within seconds, the pink team's second leg was at the finish line and handing off their ribbon to the third group of teammates.

"GO!" I heard Em yell. "We're going to lose!"

"They're doing it on purpose," I realized. "They want us to lose."

Two minutes later, we did, and Court and I stormed over to our 8A teammates. Instead of apologizing to us, they were high-fiving the opposite team!

"How could you do that?" Grace demanded.

Ashley stepped in front of them. "Can they help it if they're slow?" A few girls snickered and Ashley stared at me sweetly. "Too bad you don't get to play the guys next. Enjoy the sidelines, ladies." I held Court back.

"We'll get them in the next round," Em declared, sounding irritated.

Meg approached us. "Good effort, girls," she said cheerfully. We all just looked at her with raised eyebrows. Meg blushed. "Let's just try to enjoy the day, shall we? Since you guys are sitting the next round out, I thought you could help your senior counselors for a bit. What do you say?"

"Fine," Grace said, sounding as deflated as some of the

balloons that were drooping at the nearby picnic tables. Beaver and the cafeteria crew were already setting up for that night's dinner.

"Grace, you know we're not winning a trophy for today, right?" I asked as we headed down the dusty path to meet our senior counselors. They were playing games on the great lawn. The day was just as hot as the days before — about 95 degrees — and the air was so thick and humid it felt like you could cut it with a knife. Whoever said Florida was hot hadn't spent the summer in the New York Catskills. I had expected it to be cooler up here than it was at home on Long Island, but it was turning out to be anything but. People told me it was a freak heat wave. Figured the year I came, that happened.

"I hate losing," Grace grumbled. "We had her. We were in the lead and then —"

"There's nothing we could have done," Em pointed out.

"Maybe if *some* of us were less tired this morning we would have had a better chance," Grace mumbled under her breath.

"Hey!" Court said. "I was out late on important business. Donovan and I were at the boat house listening to some of his emo-rocker ballads on his iPod after lights out and I told him I'd give him feedback. He's going to audition for *American Idol* this year," she added proudly.

"You keep sneaking out like that and you're going to get caught," Em warned. "We should be saving sneak-outs for our first sleepaway girls —" She paused just in time.

Hunter was walking toward us. I inhaled sharply. It may have been hot, but he looked cool, as usual. He was wearing a royal blue pinnie with nothing underneath, and you could see his well-defined biceps. "Hi, ladies," he said with a huge grin. "Nice pinnies." Em took a quick puff of her inhaler. "I'm in a bit of a bind." Hunter was staring directly at me. "My buddy hurt his ankle during our last round and I'm partner-less for this game. Mind if I borrow the champ?"

"What?"

"We're supposed to meet our senior counselors," Grace said, sounding like the perfect schoolgirl.

"We have a few minutes," Court interrupted and pushed me forward. "But only if we can we stay and watch."

"Sure," Hunter said. "Let me just go tell the guys." He jogged over to a large group of counselors and CITs. Some were wearing blue pinnies, and others were in white and sky blue. Their younger charges were with them, sitting cross-legged on the sidelines.

I hit Court's arm. "What did you do that for?" I complained.

"I'm doing you a favor," she said. "Hunter likes you, and you're into him. It's time you made a move. Be bolder than your mom and Hitch and do more than just talking!"

I blushed. Ever since I told the girls that my mom had admitted that she and Hitch were "phone-dating" I hadn't heard the end of it. Court thought it was hysterical.

"We can't date counselors, remember?" Grace said.

"We're not," Court said innocently. "But there are no rules against flirting. Now why don't you and Em wait over by Dylan and Tim. This game will be over before you know it."

I knew Em liked Dylan, but Grace hadn't said anything about liking Tim, another CIT. It was obvious from her shifty attitude and bright-pink face, however, that she most definitely did have a thing for him.

"I guess we won't be missed if we're just five more minutes," Em said. "It's not like our counselors know we're coming anyway."

"Fine," Grace said, trying to sound grumpy, even though I knew she wasn't.

That's when I noticed Cole walking our way.

"I hear you're filling in for Albert," he said. He was wearing a light blue pinnie and his curly brown hair was matted to his head. It looked like he had just showered, but I knew it was the heat. "Lucky Hunter. Or should I say lucky you?"

"Neither," I mumbled, feeling weird.

Hunter joined us. "So after this, champ, I thought we could head over to the canteen and get some Slush Puppies. My treat."

"Aren't we supposed to take the kids down to the lake for canoeing?" Cole asked.

Hunter frowned. "I forgot the little guys were waiting on us," he said and waved to them. They let out a big cheer. "They're awesome, aren't they?" he asked me. "I can't get enough of them."

So Hunter *did* like his charges. He wasn't here just for the girls! Seeing Hunter smile so brightly at the mention of his bunk made me feel warm and fuzzy. And not just because it was hot out.

"How about a rain check?" Hunter asked me. He grabbed a burlap bag from the ground. "Ready to play, champ? This game is simple. The two of us hop in this sack here and have to jump our way to the finish line together. Piece of cake."

WHAT? Of all the races to have to do with Hunter, I had to do one where I was sandwiched next to him in tight quarters. I wasn't sure I could handle it.

"Good luck," Cole said.

I stepped forward and grabbed a piece of the bag. Hunter leaned over and whispered into my ear. "These guys think they have you beat since you're a girl, so we have to prove them wrong, okay?"

I couldn't breathe, Hunter's mouth was so close to mine. He smelled like pink bubblegum.

Hunter and I walked to the starting line and that's when I noticed who our competitors were. My heart sank. Next to us were Cole and Dylan. Cole winked at me, but I felt strange winking back. My body began to feel uncomfortable, like it knew it was about to do something it shouldn't. Why did I feel so weird about being with Hunter in front of Cole? Our other competition wasn't nearly as bothersome. Donovan and this tall, skinny counselor everyone called the Bean were team three.

Hunter stepped into the large bag and held it out for me to hop in. He was smiling. I got the feeling he knew I was intimidated. I stepped in next to him. The bag wasn't as roomy as I thought. We were side by side, but there wasn't even room for air between us. I could feel Hunter's thigh touching mine, and his light blond hair tickled my arm. I felt like my face was on fire. I stared straight ahead at the finish line, avoiding Hunter's gaze.

"Comfortable?" Hunter's voice drifted over to me. I couldn't look at him. I just nodded.

"GO!" Someone blew a whistle and we were off. I could hear Grace and Em screaming, and Court chanting Hunter's and my names. Hunter was fast and I did my best to keep up, but I was distracted. Our bodies kept bumping into each other and each time it happened it sent a shiver down my spine. Hunter finally put one arm around me and grabbed my side of the bag. I was now sandwiched in his arms, which made my breathing even more shallow than it already was from all the running we were doing. I glanced to my right. Cole was neck-and-neck with us. Bean and Donovan were in the lead, but we were gaining on them.

"You've got it, champ," Hunter encouraged me. "Keep it up." Bean and Donovan came close to us, and Hunter yelled, "Hold on!" Then I felt him push with all his might and I saw Donovan's bag hit the ground with a thud. Hunter laughed. "Got them! Now it's just us and them," he said, referring to Cole.

I was sort of dumbfounded. It was just a game, wasn't it? Was he going to do that to Cole too? I really didn't want him to. Right then and there I decided it was better to beat Cole than see him land in the mud. I hopped faster, but Cole was just as quick. Seconds from the finish line, we were in a dead tie. Everyone was screaming.

"Jump, champ! Jump!" Hunter growled as Cole and Dylan closed in on us. With a sudden lurch, I felt our bag plunge forward.

Our only chance of winning was to dive and Hunter knocked us to the ground. I screamed as I saw the dirt and grass coming up to meet us. Then THUD! We were on the ground, and Hunter had one hand on the finish line, and was laughing. He was also lying practically on top of me, his Abercrombie-model-worthy chest pushed up against my heart-pounding one. Hunter's face was inches from mine. His lips were within reach.

Hunter was on top of me. Hunter was on top of me. Hunter was on top of me!

I started to squirm out of the bag, but it was tough with Hunter's weight on me. "Hunter and Sam are the winners!" I thought I heard someone announce.

"He cheated!" I heard Donovan yell.

"Way to go, champ," Hunter told me as he pulled himself into the push-up position, allowing me to get out. I tried to avoid his gaze as I shimmied. The whole time I felt like my heart was going to leap out of my chest and smack him in the face.

"Need help?" Cole was standing over us and he had his hand out to help me up. I was out of the bag and sitting on the cold ground and I reached up quickly.

"I've got her." Hunter was faster than me, and he pulled himself out of the bag in one quick move. Then he reached down with two hands and practically swung me into the air, making me giggle. "So what are you doing right now?" Hunter asked me.

"I should get going," I said and grabbed a cup of water from the nearby oversized water thermos. "My bunk is waiting for me. I need to help Alexis."

Hunter nodded. Then he leaned and kissed me on the cheek. "I'll see you tonight at the fireworks, okay? I'll be looking for you so don't disappear."

I instinctively grabbed my cheek, and then realized what I was doing, and remembered Cole was standing right there, and I put my hand back down. "I'll be there," I said, shaking slightly.

As Hunter slipped away, I heard Cole laugh quietly. "Congrats, Sam. I guess you got what you wanted."

I turned to yell or say something sarcastic back, but I realized two little boys from his bunk had run over and were holding each of his hands. Cole was still staring at me and I felt the need to look away. "See you tonight," I said quickly. Then I headed over to Court, Grace, and Em.

We were halfway down the path before I screamed — part joy, part frustration, part confusion. My cheek felt like it was still tingling from where Hunter had kissed me and I kept replaying the moment over in my mind.

"Hunter is so into you!" Court said wistfully. "I wish Donovan was like that. I got excited when he let me borrow his demo tape. I never got a kiss on the cheek."

"I'm never washing this cheek again," I joked, and Em laughed.

"This sort of thing never happens to me." Em sighed. "Can I touch your face?" she asked suddenly.

The only one who wasn't laughing was Grace. I figured she was just tired. The rest of us kept talking about Hunter and my near-kiss, about how Em could talk to Dylan at that night's barbeque, about what Court was going to do next about Donovan. As we reached the clearing where the pez and some of the marshmallows were competing, Grace finally opened up.

"I know Hunter's hot and all, but did you guys see what he did to Donovan?" she asked quietly. "He pushed him so he and Sam could win. It was a silly sack race. There was nothing riding on it, but he still couldn't play fair. Something about that rubs me the wrong way. And another thing, have you noticed how Cole is always the one with his bunk? Hunter is never around. He brags about loving his kids, but he's always off flirting with some girl instead and Cole has to pick up the slack." None of us said anything.

Deep down, I knew there might be truth to what Grace was saying, but I didn't want to believe it.

"Hey, Sam!" Mackenzie came racing toward me and enveloped me in a big hug. "Are you here to play with us? The bubble yum team is winning three to two!"

I squeezed her hard, trying to force Grace's words out of my head. "I'll catch you guys at the barbeque," I said to the girls.

"Sam," Grace said awkwardly. "I didn't mean —"

"Don't worry about it," I called back as I took Mackenzie's hand and headed toward the girls of bunk 5A. I forced a smile. "I'll see you later."

The rest of the afternoon moved quickly. Alexis and I participated in a kickball tournament with the girls, decorated July Fourth flags with them at the craft station, and took our little winners for some celebratory cotton candy at the booth set up near the mess hall. I met up with 8B again for a dodgeball game, and took a break for some ice cream, which melted faster than I could eat it. I had to take a quick detour to the nurse's station when one of my charges, Serena, skinned her knee during a race, but other than that, the afternoon was incident-free. The girls couldn't wait to get to the campfire, and despite Grace's observation, I was itching to see Hunter again.

"Sam, we're sitting over here!" Serena tugged on my t-shirt sleeve. I had taken a few of the girls up to the barbeque line for dinner and was pouring myself a glass of fruit punch — or should I say bug juice, because that was the weird name everyone called the ever-changing colored drink. My plate was piled high with mashed potatoes, barbeque chicken, roasted corn, and cornbread, and my mouth was watering from the smell of dessert: warm apple cobbler. Believe it or not, this was a five-star meal at the Pines.

Since it was a special occasion, we were eating outside on the picnic tables by the lake. Someone had hung up twinkling white Christmas lights on the trees surrounding the tables, and it looked like thousands of fireflies lighting up the sky. The tables even had red and white paper tablecloths on them, and Beaver had set up a stereo near the buffet area that was playing light music. As hot as the day had been, the night had turned fairly cool, not that any of us were complaining. You could still wear shorts and t-shirts, but the light breeze gave me a slight chill every once in a while.

I didn't see Meg or my bunkmates yet, so I decided to sit down with Alexis and help her with her bunk meal ritual — cutting people's food. The girls were still small enough that this was sometimes necessary, especially if you wanted them to eat something sticky, like barbeque food, and I felt bad letting

Alexis do it alone. The whole time I was cutting, I was looking around for Hunter, but I didn't see him anywhere.

"Do you guys mind if we join you?" Cole asked. He had a long line of kids behind him and I realized it was his and Hunter's bunk.

"Sure," Alexis said, wiping her sauce-covered mouth. This meal was definitely not flirt-friendly. "We can scoot over. Where's Hunter?"

I thought I saw Cole's face change slightly, but if it did, he recovered quickly. "He had to check in with the main office."

"Is that who that girl was? She works in the office?" a little boy asked.

"That was his girlfriend, silly," Caleb corrected him. "That's why he kissed her!"

Cole looked at me quickly and I tried to fake a smile.

Hunter was kissing another girl? He asked *me* to meet him here, didn't he? He said he was going to be looking for me. Didn't that mean something? Or did I get excited over nothing? My heart was pounding and I felt slightly sick. I pushed my food away. Maybe I had misread him. Why would Hunter, the hottest guy at camp, like me? I had lost my appetite. If I hadn't been sitting with everyone I might even have gotten a little weepy.

"I hope he gets here soon," Alexis said lightly, "or he'll miss the roasted marshmallows and the fireworks."

Hunter didn't show up in time for the marshmallows and when that happened, I wanted to call it a night. But Cole convinced me to stay so I could see his top secret trick. When Hitch passed out a bag of marshmallows to each table, we followed

Cole over to the barbeque pit, which was still illuminated lightly. I could smell the charcoal and I inhaled deeply. It reminded me of barbeques at home. Mal's family had huge ones every summer and the two of us religiously made s'mores. I could almost taste the melted chocolate on my lips and for a minute I felt homesick. I stared at the red-orange embers sadly.

"Watch this, Sam, or you're going to miss something cool," Cole nudged my arm. He was grabbing a handful of marshmallows and one by one he put them on his stick. I couldn't quite believe my eyes when I realized what he was doing. He could somehow melt the marshmallows just enough to shape them into birds or snowmen. Alexis and I couldn't stop laughing, and our bunks were fascinated.

"I know what it is! That's a mouse," one of our girls said excitedly as Cole took a gooey marshmallow and put it on top of another one that was almost completely melted. He used an extra stick to poke the figure and shape it.

"That's not a mouse, it's a canoe," said one of the boys indignantly.

"You're both wrong," Cole said, concentrating on his sculpture, which was growing taller and skinnier.

"I've got it," I said. "It's Hitch." Alexis burst out laughing.

"It does kind of look like my dad, doesn't it?" she said. "Cole, don't forget to add his megaphone."

"It's not Hitch," Cole said with a laugh. "It's Beaver. Don't you see the fry pan on his head?"

"Um, not really," I said. "It looks like a pile of marshmallow to me."

Cole looked mock-insulted. "I'd like to see you try this insanely difficult trick."

"I think I need to practice first," I told him.

"If I could get everyone's attention, I'd like to make an announcement," Hitch said to quiet the large crowd. I looked around. *Still no Hunter.* I saw that my friends were seated with their own bunks, and Ashley and Gabby were sitting with some guys on the other end of the campfire. The night was perfect for a campfire under the stars. When everyone had settled down, Hitch continued. "I hope everyone enjoyed today's Fourth of July festivities," he said to loud applause. "As is tradition, we're going to watch the town fireworks, which you can see from here. They'll start in five minutes and when they do, the lights here will dim so that you can see them. I ask that everyone remain seated till the end for safety. If any of the little ones get scared, you can sit up on the hill with them. Enjoy the show!" Everyone cheered.

"Sam?" Alexis leaned over to me. "You don't have to sit with us for this. If you want, you can sit with your friends, or maybe Cole." She gave me a look.

"Cole? No, we're just friends," I said, confused.

She smiled. "Cole looks like he wants to be just friends," she said. Her lip curled slightly.

"Hey." We looked up. Hunter was standing in front of us in a hooded sweatshirt, his hands in his pockets.

"Hey," I said and jumped to my feet. My head felt like it was going to explode with emotion. Part of me was angry, the other part wanted to do flip-flops I was so happy to see him. Maybe I was being too hard on him. It's not like we were going out. He hadn't even said he liked me, even if my friends thought he did. "Where were you?"

"I had some business to take care of," he said, "but I made it, didn't I?" He sat down. "Do you want to move closer to the lake to get a better view, champ? I know the perfect location."

"I'll bet," I thought I heard Alexis mumble. "Hunter, aren't you supposed to sit with your bunk? I think Cole's held down the fort long enough tonight, don't you?"

I glanced at Cole. He wasn't saying anything. He was doing a magic trick for a few of the boys, who were mesmerized by his every move.

"Absolutely," Hunter said to Alexis. "I forgot. Thanks."

"I'm going to move onto the hill with the girls, Sam," Alexis said to me. "You enjoy the fireworks."

When she was gone, Hunter asked me again. "So do you want to get closer to the lake?"

"But your campers," I pointed out, feeling suddenly uncertain. I thought he adored his bunk. Now here he was ditching them, and dumping more on Cole, for some time with me.

Hunter rolled his eyes and sighed. "Listen, champ, if you don't want to watch the fireworks with me, I can think of a few other people who would."

I winced. "Cole has been here all night and —" The lights were dimming and I could hear the crowd growing excited.

"Cole, you don't mind watching the fireworks with them, do you? I want to give Sam a better view," Hunter said.

"I think they'd prefer you," Cole said to my surprise. His eyes locked with Hunter's. The awkward mood was interrupted by a small cry.

"I don't want to hear the noise," a little boy named Lucas cried. "I want to sit on the hill."

"Lucas, you'll be fine," Hunter insisted as Lucas sniffled. "No one else wants to go sit on the hill. You don't want us to all go to the hill, do you?"

Lucas just cried more and Cole went over and put his arm around him. "I want Hunter to sit with me on the hill," he sobbed. I looked at Hunter. He rolled his eyes again.

"Lucas, buddy, I'll take you," Cole said soothingly. "Can I tell you a secret? It's a better view up there anyway. That's where I always watched when I was your age." I smiled. Cole had such a way with kids.

"But I want Hunter!" Lucas continued to wail.

"Guess what?" Cole tried again. "I have some cotton candy stashed in my backpack to share with you guys if we head up the hill."

"I'm not missing the fireworks." Hunter sounded frustrated. "Cole, you deal with him." He turned to me and grabbed my hand. "Ready, champ?"

Suddenly everything seemed clear. As the first rocket sent a glow over the lakefront, I knew. Hunter was a hottie, yes. He was picture perfect on paper and every time I saw him my eyes watered, my heart leaped, and I felt like I could faint. But standing in front of him, watching him act the way he did with his campers and be so shady about his conquests, I knew I couldn't like someone like that.

I dropped Hunter's hand. "Nope, sorry, I'm not ready," I said. "I'm going to sit on the hill with Lucas, Cole, and the kids."

Hunter shook his head. "Suit yourself," he said, and then he slipped away in the dark, presumably to find someone else to sit on that rock with.

"Sam," Cole started to say, but I stopped him. Another firework exploded overhead, illuminating the serious expression on Cole's face.

"Come on, guys," I said to the boys. "Everyone take someone's hand and Cole and I will lead you up the hill so you don't miss anything else."

We had them settled in minutes, tucked in beside Alexis and the girls, on the cool, damp grass. I could smell gunpowder in the air, and the sky was growing smoky from the explosions. Mackenzie saw me and smiled. She and Serena scooted next to me. Next to them was Cole, with Lucas under his arm. He had calmed down and was eating cotton candy happily.

"I didn't mean for things to get weird back there," Cole said.

I shrugged. "You didn't make things weird," I pointed out. "At least now, I won't waste any more time . . ." But I couldn't finish the sentence. I couldn't say "having a crush on Hunter" to Cole. I always seemed to have a hard time with Cole teasing me about him. "It's fine. Really. I'm glad things turned out the way they did," I said instead.

"You are?" Cole asked, and held out some cotton candy.

"Yeah," I said, and I meant it.

Cole smiled. "Good. Because like I said that first day, you can do much better."

I looked at Cole and I smiled. "I know I can," I agreed. And I was starting to think I knew exactly where to look to find him.

♠ 9 ♠

Reporting for Duty

I'd been this close to Cole dozens of times, but this time it felt different. The two of us were on kitchen duty that morning and even though we had to show up at 7:30 AM, Cole looked amazing, and I noticed it right away. His hair smelled like mint, and he was wearing yellow nylon shorts and a navy tee that looked great against his summer tan. I couldn't stop staring at him.

Truthfully, I hadn't been able to stop staring or thinking about Cole since the Fourth of July. I didn't know how I hadn't seen it before. I always thought Cole was cute, but suddenly I noticed how charming he was, how witty, and how amazing he was with his bunk, which made him all the more appealing. Em said I needed to get Hunter out of my head to realize all this, and that's what had happened. The downside to this revelation was that our comfortable banter had become awkward — on my end. Because now, it wasn't just conversation, it was me, talking to the boy I realized I liked. And I sort of felt guilty about it because I hadn't noticed I liked him till I realized I didn't like Hunter.

"Are you okay over there?" Cole asked me with a wry smile.

I was so freaked out when I saw Cole this morning that I set up my pancake batter post on the other end of the kitchen where my view of Cole was partially blocked. That way Cole couldn't catch me staring. "Um-hum," I mumbled.

Not knowing Cole was on duty with me, I had shown up in my pajama pants, like my bunk and I always did for breakfast. MY PAJAMA PANTS! My pink heart patterned pajama bottoms and a red tank top. If I wasn't embarrassed before, I really was now.

"Earth to Sam! Come in, Sam!" Beaver, our head chef, was waving his hands in front of my face and motioning wildly. "You've been stirring that batter for ten minutes. Don't tell me it's still lumpy."

I handed over the bowl and smiled sheepishly. "I guess I lost track of time."

Beaver looked at me skeptically, took the bowl, and handed me a new one filled with pancake batter powder. "Let's try to keep this for less than two minutes so that everyone can have pancakes this morning, okay? The natives are getting restless out there." Beaver was kind of scary in that I-ride-a-Harley-and-could-whip-your-butt-in-a-fight kind of way. But when kitchen duty was done, he seemed sane. (At our cookout the other night, he even did some karaoke.) This being the start of breakfast duty, Beaver was in crazy mode.

"No problem," I told him sweetly.

Cole came over to my table and I stood up straighter. "Let me help you," he said. "I finished my job already." Cole took the bowl from my hands, added some water, and began whisking like a maniac. All without looking at the directions on the batter box.

"How do you know how much goes in there?" I wanted to know.

Cole shrugged. "I make these all the time at home. I like to bake." He blushed.

A boy who liked to bake? Could Cole get any better?

Cole's face was deep in concentration, but then for some reason, he looked up and gave me this smile that, if I were pancake batter, would have made me ooze all over the floor.

"Sam!"

Uh-oh. That was Beaver again.

"Yes?" I said.

"If you've got someone else doing your battering, then maybe you could get some more OJ out to the tables. A few have already run out." He pointed to the pitchers nearby.

"OJ, sure," I repeated. I mouthed "sorry" to Cole, grabbed two big pitchers, and used my butt to push open the kitchen door. The smell of syrup wafted into my nose immediately. The clanking of forks and plates scraping made me want to cover my ears.

The difference in the noise level between the kitchen and the mess hall, even at 8 AM, was deafening. The place was packed and kids were either running around to different tables, or singing (they did a lot of singing in this place) while they waited for Hitch to do the morning announcements (which would lead to more singing of the "announcements" song). Once Hitch entered the room, the place quieted down while everyone ate, and then everyone got rowdy again when it was time for mail call.

I dreaded mail call.

Not because I didn't get mail. Mom sent two more care packages, one with these amazing tank tops she got me in Paris — she was in Europe with work at the moment — and Grandma sent this sweet care package with all these cookies and chocolate — that Ashley saw and tattled on me for having, but only after Gabby had already stolen some — but I STILL hadn't gotten anything from any of my friends, or Mal for that matter. It was really starting to bother me. I had sent Mal two videos and the rest of my friends postcards (that was all they were getting, I had finally decided). But I had gotten nothing in return. I was thisclose to asking Court to borrow her secret phone so I could call Mal just to make sure she was still breathing.

Thump. I put down the first pitcher of OJ at a table full of rowdy boys. I was about to put the next pitcher down at a table of peeps, when I heard my own bunk whining and yelling my name. The benefit of being a CIT instead of a full-fledged counselor was that you still got to eat most meals with your own bunk rather than your charges.

"Thirsty! I'm dying of thirst!" Courtney motioned to her throat and pretended to be choking.

I brought the pitcher over and placed it by Court, Grace, and Em.

Gabby moaned. "No fair! I want it first."

"Ew," Ashley said. "Sam brought us one with pulp. I would

never drink pulp," she complained. "Bring me another pitcher." Ashley had on cool pajamas. Hers were these cute boy shorts and one of those fitted logo tees that said "Everything in Miami is Hotter." Why didn't I have pajamas like those to wear for kitchen duty?

"Ash," Meg warned, "this is the OJ we have today. If you don't like it, drink milk."

"NW," groaned Gabby. "I'd rather drink H2O. It's better for you, anyway."

I gave Meg an appreciative glance, then crouched down next to my friends. They leaned in closely.

"I'm on kitchen duty with Cole," I told them quietly. Em squealed.

"It's a sign!" she said dreamily. "You have to tell him you made a mistake and you don't like Hunter, you like him."

"That will look good, Em," Grace said sarcastically. "Cole, I know I never actually admitted I liked Hunter, but I've decided I don't like him now, I like you!"

Em and Court glared at her, but I groaned. "Grace is right. There is no way to tell Cole without it sounding bad."

Em cleared her throat. "Maybe it's time we had a longer conversation about this," she said empathically. "One with the sleep-away girls."

"Huh?" At first, that statement didn't make sense to me. Then I realized what Em was talking about. We needed to have a sleepaway girl taping to discuss my Cole problem. It would be our first one.

"It's definitely time," Grace said excitedly.

"I smell a midnight sneak-out," Court whispered. "We could do it Wednesday night when the counselors have their weekly meeting."

"I don't know," I said nervously. "What if we get caught?"

"We do it every year," Grace told me. And if Grace was that calm, then maybe it was not as big a deal as I thought it was.

My stomach growled and Em laughed. "That hungry, huh?"

I nodded. "I'm starving and it all looks good today." I was dying for some pancakes.

Court pushed over a plate piled high with eggs, bacon, pancakes, and fruit. "We saved you a little of everything." She looked guilty. "But I'm having a hard time resisting the pancakes. They're calling my name and they're the last ones."

"You can have them if you want," I said without thinking.

"Sam, you haven't had any yet!" Grace pointed out. "Court's already had three."

"But I'm still hungry," Court whined.

"Take mine," I insisted. "There's plenty of other stuff I can eat."

"Here she goes again," Grace muttered.

"What?" I asked.

Ashley interrupted our conversation loudly. "Meg, isn't Sam supposed to be on kitchen duty, not talking to people?"

She smiled nastily at me and I gave her a dirty look. As much as I wanted to do otherwise, I was still choosing the non-confrontational route when it came to Ashley. I let her have her digs, but I never came back at her. I was terrible at arguments and my skills hadn't improved much at camp.

"She's right, Sam," Meg said. "You should finish up in the kitchen and we'll save you some breakfast."

"Not," I heard Gabby say.

Finish up in the kitchen? Oh God. Work! I left Cole in there with the batter and I still had all that OJ to bring to the tables. "I've got to go," I told the girls.

"Wednesday," Court mouthed to me as I backed away toward the kitchen and plowed right into Hunter.

"Cute PJs, champ," he said with a wink.

I walked quickly past him with my head down and rushed into the kitchen to collect more OJ, but it was all gone. Gulp.

"Hey," Cole said, coming up behind me. "I finished the batter — and told Beaver you did it. And I hope you don't mind, but you still had a lot of OJ to deliver, so I took all of it out for you. You just have one pitcher for your peeps left."

I was so grateful, I threw my arms around Cole's neck. "Thank you!" I gushed. Then I realized what I was doing. My arms were around Cole's neck. His neck that smelled deliciously like soap. I could have breathed in that aroma all day. I felt Cole's hands tighten around my waist and I tensed up. Normally, I wouldn't think twice about hugging Cole, but that was B.C. Before I liked Cole. Now . . . what was I doing? Cole wasn't just my friend anymore, he was the guy I liked, and I was thisclose to him. I backed away and I could see Cole was blushing.

"Good thing Hunter didn't see that," Cole said, not looking me in the eye.

"I don't like Hunter," I said quickly and firmly and Cole

looked up at me curiously. "I told you already. You were right about him."

"Nice to hear you're thinking clearly," he said and sort of smiled. My heart felt like it was going to leap out of my chest and my mouth felt unusually dry. "So I was going to ask you, does this mean . . ."

"Lovebirds," Beaver interrupted, yelling from the edge of the stove, where he was flipping more pancakes. I jumped, hitting my knee on the wood table next to me. Ouch.

"Yeah, I mean you two," Beaver said. "You're off-duty. You can join your bunks."

Nooooooo! What was Cole about to say to me? But it was too late. Cole and I looked at each other awkwardly. Then we looked around. The other CITs and counselors were already at their tables. We kind of mumbled good-bye to each other and then turned toward the door, knocking into each other. I remembered I still had to bring Alexis's bunk their OJ so I grabbed the pitcher on the way out.

"Sam, there you are," Alexis said when I got to the table. Our peeps could be kind of wild, but Alexis always looked calm. "I was beginning to think you forgot about us."

"Sorry, Alexis," I apologized.

"It's okay," Alexis told me and nudged me in the side. "I always moved slower during kitchen duty too. I hated it."

My eyes widened. Alexis hated something about camp? I couldn't believe it. I wanted to hear about this one. "Really?" But before I could ask Alexis our whole table started to shake.

The jelly jar started bouncing toward me, the pancakes were popping off the plates and the syrup was sloshing over the table.

"EARTHQUAKE!" A few of the peeps screamed at the top of their lungs. They were holding the edges of the table and shaking it for all it was worth. I tried to steady my side, but I was no match for eight little girls.

"What are you doing?" I asked, alarmed, when they finally stopped shaking the table and burst out laughing. Alexis was laughing too. "You almost gave me a heart attack!"

"It's called earthquake," Mackenzie said proudly. "We saw the pez do it."

"Classic camp mess hall game," Alexis told me in confidence. "I was a master at it. I could shake the whole table by myself and never knock over a single glass."

"Good morning, Whispering Pines!" Hitch broke through the sound barrier and made the girls' earthquake seem tame. "How is everyone doing?"

"I still don't think I'll ever get used to your dad using the megaphone before 9 AM," I told Alexis. She laughed.

"I have a few announcements to make this morning," Hitch said happily. "Today is supposed to reach ninety-five degrees so we will be forgoing third period so that you can all have an additional free swim." A loud cheer erupted. "If the weather continues, we'll do the same thing tomorrow," Hitch added. "I also wanted to tell you all about an exciting new craft activity for session two . . ."

I stared across the room at Cole's table. He was sitting with his bunkmates, but one of his peeps, Caleb, was on his lap. He had the little boy in a playful headlock. He was so cute. How did I not realize this before?

". . . and finally the talent show auditions will take place in two weeks." Another loud cheer from the mess hall went up. "If you're interested in signing up, there'll be a sheet outside the mess hall doors."

"I wonder what you'll be doing for the show," Alexis said.

"Me? No, I don't perform," I told her. "I'm more of a behind-the-scenes kind of girl than an actor."

"Your bunk is always in the show," Alexis told me. "My sister always cooks up something for the group to do together. I'm sure you won't be able to get out of it."

Yikes. I was about to say I wasn't doing it when our table started shaking again.

"AFTERSHOCK!" the peeps yelled.

This time I was prepared and I didn't fight it. Alexis started shaking the table as well while I sat back and watched. This was so silly. But I guess it was sort of fun if you were six. Oh, what the heck. I started shaking the table too and screamed "Aftershock!" Then the OJ pitcher fell over and the ice-cold juice spilled all over my pajamas. I jumped up and screamed. I must have been loud because everyone looked at me. From across the room, I could hear Gabby and Ashley cackle.

"Oh, Sam!" Alexis said. She was laughing, but not in a mean way. "At least you didn't get dressed yet." She blotted my pants for me. Serena guiltily handed me some napkins.

My pink heart pants were practically see-through and I was wearing purple underwear. Thank God my butt wasn't wet, but still. I had to get back to the bunk and change. "Can I . . ." I started to say.

"Go," Alexis finished. "We'll meet you at the arts and crafts cabin after your chores."

I was walking out of the room when I heard Hitch start to do the mail call and call my name. I almost fell over. One of the campers ran over to me carrying a small brown padded envelope. One big enough to carry a videotape. I felt the package. It *was* a videotape and it was from Mal!

Now I didn't care that I was wet. If I wasn't, then I'd have to go back to the bunk with everyone else and I wouldn't be able to watch my tape. Now at least I would have a chance to start it. Mal's and my tapes were always at least thirty minutes long. I was halfway out the door when I heard my name again.

"Samantha," Hitch said in his typical gruff manner. He strode over to me and smiled. "How are you?"

"Fine," I told him. Ever since Mom told me her and Hitch were "phone dating" I'd felt a little awkward around him.

Hitch nodded. "Good. Good. I promised your mom I'd keep a close eye on you," he told me and patted me on my shoulder. "I'm sure your mom is upset that she has to miss visitors' day."

I knew Mom probably wouldn't be able to make parents' day. Her work trip was extended at the last minute. At first I thought it would be weird having no one come see me at camp — it's not like Mal was going to take a day off from Malomark time to get her parents to drive her two-plus hours — but Em's parents weren't coming either (she sort of talked them out of it). Most of our bunk was parentless for the day — like Ashley (since Hitch and Alexis were busy running visitors' day) and Gabby (whose parents weren't flying in from California for what they called a "four-hour H and G" — hi and goodbye. Now I knew where Gabby got her weird abbreviations from). Court's 'rents were stopping for a few hours before they caught a flight to Miami.

"I knew my mom probably wasn't going to be able to make it so I'm okay," I explained to Hitch.

He nodded. "I know she really wanted to come see you."

This was awkward. Me talking to my mom's potential boy-friend who happened to be my camp director. Weird! I had to get out of here. "I should get changed," I said, pointing to my pants.

Hitch blushed. "Absolutely, talk to you later," he said.

I ran all the way back to the cabin to save time and when I arrived, my PJs were dry, but pretty sticky. (It was THAT hot out.) I fumbled through my trunk for my backpack and unzipped it to get to my camera. I was moving so quickly I practically dropped the tape as I tried to jam it in the recorder. I pressed play and waited anxiously. The first thing I saw was Mal.

She was sitting in her backyard on a lounge chair, wearing her big faux Chanel sunglasses and she was wearing the Donna Karan black bikini we found at TJ Maxx back in April that would have made me look huge, but looked perfect on her. Her long, dark brown hair was soft and sort of curly at the ends, and her tan had deepened to a bronze. She waved to the camera.

"HI, SAMMIE! I MISSSSSSS YOU!" She yelled. "CP just isn't the same without you. I ran into Mrs. Gisondi in Waldbaum's and she says hi. So does Mrs. Macario. I told them we didn't like

English class as much this year without them. Piper, Bridget, and Ivy send their love and said thanks for the postcards."

I breathed a sigh of relief. I guess the others had forgotten I even said I'd send them tapes. Which made me stop and think — was it them who suggested I send them videos or was it me being me, agreeing to do too much without thinking things through?

"I'm dying of boredom around here," Mal continued. "If it wasn't for Mark and the Mineola Pool I would be completely lonely . . ." Mal told me about our friend Piper's new boyfriend, and a funny story about our friend Audrey's summer job. She talked about her annoying little brother and how her parents gave her a later curfew for the summer. I was feeling homesick until she said something that made me flinch.

"So like I was saying, it's really boring here so thank God for your tapes," Mal said and then made a nervous face I recognized. It was the one she used anytime she had screwed up. "It's just that . . . um . . . don't be mad, but I'm not sure . . . it's just . . . I don't think I'm going to have time to make another one. I want to! It's just, well, I'm so busy with Mark that I don't have a moment to myself."

Wait. Didn't she just finish saying she was bored? How could she not have time to make any more tapes? It got worse.

"I even had to have Mark tape this video for me," Mal confessed, anxiously. "Mark, put the camera down and come say hi to Sam," she instructed her off-camera boyfriend.

What? Allowing boys or anyone else to watch or view our transmissions was strictly prohibited in our video code.

The camera view shook for a moment and I heard Mark

place it on what must be the patio table. He walked around the camera and sat at the edge of Mal's lounge chair. He looked the same. Tall, rail thin, with almost shoulder-length thick brown hair and a tattoo of a pirate on his right arm that he always showed off proudly. He was one of the few guys at our school who actually had one. Mark seemed to think it made him a bad-ass. He swung Mal up and she squealed as she jumped on his lap. I rolled my eyes. I hated how gushy Mal was when she was with Mark.

"Hey, Samantha," Mark said. He's probably the only person my age I know who calls me by my full name. "Mal told me you've got your eye on some guys there. Come home with a boyfriend so we can finally double date, okay?" The two of them laughed and I cringed.

Mal broke both video rules? She let him video her message and told him what I said in mine? Mark knew all of my fears about camp, my gushing about Hunter and my last confessional about liking Cole? How could she do that to me?

"Sam, please, please pick Hunter. He sounds beyond hot," Mal seconded.

"Baby, are you saying someone is hotter than me?" Mark cooed.

I rolled my eyes again.

"No one is hotter than you," Mal baby talked back to him. Then the two of them started kissing.

I fast-forwarded a few seconds till Mal finally came up for air and spoke again. "Sorry about that, Sam," she giggled. "I'll try to call you soon. I miss you and I'm sorry for my lack of tapes. I'll try my hardest to send you another one, but I'm not sure if/when I can. I can't wait for your next video though! I like hearing what you're up to. Oh! And before I forget, I wanted to tell you that I don't think we should try out for cheerleading this fall. I think we should do kickline instead. Mark says the routines are hotter. I'm also thinking we should try out for the school play instead of doing chorus. I'll talk to you about it when you get back. Have a great summer!"

The screen faded to fuzz. I looked at my watch. FOUR MINUTES? That's how long the tape was? Just four minutes? My tapes were each at least thirty minutes long and I had already sent two!

I pulled the tape out of my palmcorder and threw it in the bottom of my trunk.

Mal was in for a rude awakening if she thought I was sending her another tape anytime soon. I had better things to do with my summer than just please her. Leaving my friends and becoming a CIT was the first independent thing I had done in a long time, and yet instead of embracing it, I'd been spending all my time worrying about my friends back home. Enough was enough. I had to make time for me and my new life.

"Hey!" The door to the cabin slammed shut. Court was the first one back from breakfast. We had chores and a bunk inspection before our first period. She frowned when she saw me. "What's wrong?"

"Nothing," I said. "I'm just really glad I'm here."

♠ 10 ♠

The First Meeting of the Sleepaway Girls

The first thing I noticed was a bright light in my face. It was kind of hard to miss.

"Are you awake?" Court whispered. She'd climbed onto my bed and was leaning over me with a flashlight that was practically burning my eyeballs.

"Yes," I told her, even though I was actually falling asleep. Meg was at her "counselors' meeting" (or more likely hanging out at the counselors' lounge AFTER her meeting. She generally didn't check in on us on Wednesday nights) and lights-out was supposed to be at eleven. I knew we were sneaking out at 11:30, but I had drifted off.

I threw back my covers and pulled off my pajama pants and top (I had kept my real clothes on underneath). My hands were shaking as I did it. I'd never snuck out of the bunk at night, but Court, Em, and even Grace looked like pros. The girls were dressed and waiting by the cabin door. The only sound I could hear was Em using her inhaler. I winced. Just the thought of Ashley and

Gabby waking up and seeing the rest of us gone made me want to throw up.

I grabbed my backpack with my recorder, and walked briskly to the door. The four of us managed to get through the screen door without it making a single squeak. Once we were several yards away from the cabin, Court let out a small squeal.

"I told you that would be a piece of cake!" she said. It was so dark it was hard to see her.

I still wasn't used to getting around camp at night. There were lights on the paths and the buildings, but it was still pitch black. While the camp was inviting and fun during the day, at night it reminded me of a horror movie. Sure, there were counselors on patrol, but I still had never run into one. The place was eerily quiet, except for the sounds of crickets or the occasional owl. When it was breezy and the wind blew a few dead leaves across the dirt paths, I always jumped. A wolf could sneak up on you and you wouldn't have a chance. Suddenly I heard a noise and gripped what I hoped was Grace's arm.

"Would you stop worrying about the wolves!" she admonished. "I told you I've never seen a wolf here."

"Even if there are no wolves, there are counselors roaming about," Em warned. "I'm sure they're all at the counselor lounge, but we should move quickly if we don't want to bump into one of them."

"What happens if Ashley and Gabby wake up and see we're missing?" I asked.

"They won't wake up," Court said firmly. "And if they do, I

have something over on them — I was awake when they snuck out on Monday night and I didn't say anything. If they tell on us, then we tell on them."

A little blackmail never hurt anyone, I guess. "So where are we going?" I wanted to know. "It's kind of dark to record here."

"That's why we're going to the mess hall," Court said matter-of-factly.

"The mess hall?" I squeaked. My voice bounced off the nearby buildings.

"Keep your voice down," Grace hissed.

"It's the safest place to go," Court explained. "It's not like anyone is there at night and besides, we can get a snack."

"I wouldn't do it if I thought we would get caught," Grace assured me.

That was true. Grace was like the model Pines camper.

Ten minutes later, after we were safely inside and had closed the blinds in the kitchen, I pulled out my recorder. The mess hall was equally eerie at night. The hum of the refrigerators put me at ease, but it was strange seeing the kitchen look so neat and tidy when I knew for a fact it looked anything but during food service. We decided to hang out in the kitchen rather than the mess hall table area because that had too many windows and we had turned on two of the lights so that we could see. We were sitting on one of the stainless steel tables eating popcorn, some leftover cake from the Fourth of July — it was sort of soggy at this point — and apple slices Em had found in the refrigerator. Court had turned on the radio they kept in the kitchen and was playing it low. I was still a little freaked out about being in here, but I tried to relax.

"Do you think we should have snuck over to Hitch's place first to tape him on the phone with your mom?" Court asked. Everyone laughed.

I groaned. When I had made my weekly phone call to Mom from the main office yesterday, she had broken the news that she and Hitch were trying to find a way to go on a real date. She wasn't sure if Hitch was going to come down to Long Island on a day off or if Mom was going to drive up here. "Between Mal's lousy tape and my mom admitting she and Hitch were trying to plan a proper date, it's been some week and it's only Wednesday."

"I think it's kind of sweet," said Em. "The idea of people the age of Hitch and your mom finding love again is rare. Even in my romance novels."

"Em, it's not sweet if I have to move to the boonies and I'm stuck with Ashley as my stepsister," I moaned.

Em picked up the recorder and was examining it. "What about Mal? Have you made another video for her to tell her how you feel?"

I shook my head. "I'm not really in the mood."

Court grinned. "Good! So let's get started with our video then. How do we do this?" she asked and swiped the camera from Em.

"I'm not really sure," I admitted. "I've never taped anyone other than myself before."

"Maybe we should just say what's on our minds," Em suggested.

I picked up the recorder and pressed record. Then we just sat there staring at each other.

"I feel weird," Grace said and laughed nervously.

"Me too," admitted Em.

"Maybe it would help if we asked each other some questions to loosen the mood," suggested Court. She looked at Grace with a serious expression. "So Grace, how are your CIT duties going?"

Grace perked right up. "Excellent. I love having marshmallows. They're so mature. I mean, when they're not fighting over which Jonas Brother is hotter or what the it-song of summer is." She grinned. "I like working with Colleen. She's really taught me how to give each kid individual attention."

"That's so important," interrupted Em and I focused on her. "Even with the peeps. I find they function better when I give them all one-on-one time, whether it's working on a craft or just helping them write a letter to their parents. Speaking of which, I still have a few who are pretty homesick."

"Me too," I said and Court grabbed the camera from me. We were going to have some shaky camera angles with all the moving around. "I have this one little girl, Serena, who Alexis says still cries herself to sleep at night. Poor thing. I had her tape her family's photo to the wall behind her bed so she could see them at night."

"That was smart," Grace said admiringly as Em trained the video on her. We seemed to be getting the hang of the taping thing and everyone looked more relaxed. Every time someone new spoke, another person grabbed the camera. "Is it working?"

"Sort of," I said. "I just wish I could do something more for her. At this point she should be having fun, not worrying about home, but then again six is young to sleep away for a summer."

"It helps build character," Court said defensively. "Seriously, my parents used to ship my brother and me away to California for a month every summer from the time I was five to stay with my grandparents."

"Whoa," said Em. "You didn't cry?"

"Nope," Court said. "I liked it. And besides, that's what they've done every summer since. That's the real reason they send me to camp, you know. They send me to Pines and my brother to a music camp, and then they're off to Europe or wherever without us. They like it better that way. I, on the other hand, wish I could see Europe, or go on a month-long cruise, with them. I've hinted, but they always say I'm better off at camp." She looked suddenly sad.

"Court, that's awful," Em said.

"I'm used to it," Court said with a small smile. "There are benefits to having parents who are MIA all summer while you're at camp. When I get in trouble, Hitch can never find them."

"I have a little girl in my bunk that I think wants to get in trouble just so she can go home," Em admitted. "I feel so bad for her."

"I have this one little girl, Mackenzie, who seems to like being away," I told the rest of them. "Even though she has those allergy shots every day, she loves being with the bunk and doing activities. I shouldn't admit this, but she's sort of my favorite. She has this tiny voice, and big eyes, and she always wants to hold my hand and asks me cute questions like 'Why does thunder have to be so loud?' She's adorable."

"Don't let Alexis hear you say that," Grace warned. "We're not supposed to show favorites."

"I don't," I said quickly. "I guess I feel responsible for her in some way since I'm the one who takes her for those allergy shots. I'm not the one who keeps her from crying though. That's Cole. He always manages to make her smile."

"Aww," Em said. "You really like him, don't you?" She grabbed the camera and started taping me.

Suddenly I was the one who was nervous. I wasn't used to someone *else* taping me talking about something this important. I taped myself. And retaped myself. That way I could edit out anything I said that I hated. This time I couldn't edit. I had to be totally honest with my friends, and myself, in one take. I took a bunch of apple slices and started shoving them in my mouth. "I do like him, but it's complicated," I mumbled.

"Swallow," Em instructed me.

"I've told you guys this," I lamented. "I feel weird telling Cole I like him because of the Hunter thing. He used to tease me about Hunter all the time. I don't want him to think he's taking second place to Hunter. If I had paid attention to all the signs maybe I would have realized Cole was the one from the beginning. The more time I spend with him, the more I find his sort of flirty, sort of cranky attitude appealing. And now I can barely speak in front of him," I admitted.

"I'm so relieved you don't like Hunter," Grace said. "But that aside, I think with Cole you just have to get back to being Sam and Cole, the way you were before you had the crush. You can't have a relationship with a guy you're always intimidated by."

"I know," I moaned. "It's just that I've never been good at talking to guys. Mal was good at that. I don't know how to let Cole know I like him as more than a friend."

"I think we need a flirting course from Court," suggested Em.

"Step one is to actually act interested," Court explained. "You three always clam up when boys talk to us. Laugh! Flirt. It won't kill you."

"What's flirting?" Em joked.

"You guys have to start acting like you *want* these guys to like you back," Court told us. "That's what I do with Donovan."

"But what if guys have never seen us as girlfriend material?" Grace asked pensively. She took a handful of apple slices and dipped them in a caramel sauce she had found in the fridge. I wondered if anyone was going to notice food was missing. "It's fun being the girl everyone wants on their team, or the first one picked for Color War challenges. I've wanted to be Color War captain since I was six, and this is the year it could happen. It means a lot to me, but sometimes I wish certain people would see me as more than just a potential captain, or the best freestyle swimmer at this camp," Grace said quietly. "The guys here want to be my teammate. I'm always just the friend and I hate that."

We were quiet for a moment. I knew Grace loved sports, and she couldn't stop talking about Color War. It sounded liked some sort of school field day amped up and held over several days.

The camp was broken up into several teams and each team had a color. People took it pretty seriously, I was told. Close-knit bunks were known to have huge fights with each other if they wound up on opposite teams. Grace lived for it, apparently. But I wasn't used to hearing Grace admit there was something she wasn't good at — even if it was boys, something I was terrible with as well.

"Did you ever think guys are intimated by you?" Em asked. I grabbed the camera and turned it toward her. "You know, because you're so good at everything you do? Maybe guys think they can't compete with that."

"I'm not going to apologize for being good at sports," Grace pointed out.

"And essays, and being a CIT, and everything else," Court added. "Boys get nervous around girls who can do it all and who are as confident as you, just like we get nervous around so-called 'perfect' guys. I'm not saying you should change who you are, I'm just saying it wouldn't hurt to admit you're not perfect at everything you do. If you miss a goal during a soccer game, don't say, 'Oh, I could have gotten that, but the wind pushed the ball.' Guys appreciate honesty. I'm sure Tim would."

Grace blushed. "I guess I could try that."

"Me too," said Em. "Not the honesty thing. Just the talking to guys thing." I barely heard that last part because she said it as she yawned.

It must have been contagious because I started to yawn too. I looked down at my watch. Was it really 1 AM already? We had to be up in six hours. Gulp.

"Em, I think your problem is you're too busy reading about romance to notice a real one blossoming right in front of you," I told her. "Dylan likes you."

Even in the low light, I could see Em's face turn red. "I don't think so."

"He does, Em!" Grace agreed. "He's always buying you stuff at the canteen."

"He said he's got all this money to spend and he won't be able to finish it," Em protested. "He bought Court a cone last week too."

"That's only because I begged him to," Court pointed out. "He offered to buy yours. Talk to him, Em. He won't bite."

Em shook her head. "How do you know so much about boys?"

Court shrugged and took a piece of apple. "Boys and friendships are the only things I'm good at."

"I don't believe that." Grace spoke with a mouth full of cake. "I think you pretend your life is all about boys because you don't want anyone to see the real you. You've got talent, Court. I've seen it. The year you designed our costumes for the talent show was our best year ever. And the murals you painted last summer were gorgeous."

"I was just playing around," Court mumbled.

"There's nothing wrong with being known for more than one thing," Grace said lightly. "You might surprise yourself."

"Okay, you're bringing me down," Court said with a sigh. "We're supposed to be having fun, not analyzing each other."

She cranked up the radio and started singing along with Danity Kane.

"Dishing about our issues is important," Grace said loudly.

I heard a door slam shut and I let out a scream. The four of us looked at each other nervously. Em dove under the table. Court shut off the radio. Grace started clearing the food. I fumbled to put my recorder away. I zipped it into my backpack just before the kitchen doors swung open. If it was Hitch, or Beaver, or even Meg, we were so dead.

"Up kind of late tonight, ladies?" Hunter said with a sly grin. He was in a thick navy hoodie and jeans with flip-flops.

Hunter! He didn't look mad, but still. We'd been caught after curfew breaking into the mess hall. The color drained from Grace's face. My hands felt clammy.

"Are you going to turn us in?" Em asked as she slowly came out of hiding.

Hunter laughed. "For what? Doing what I always do? Nah. But I would suggest you pick someplace other than the kitchen for your next girl talk. This is kind of an obvious meeting place."

Court raised her eyebrows and looked at me. "Girl talk?"

Did Hunter hear us? Did he hear me talking about Cole? I felt my face get hot.

"No problem," Grace said as she quickly tidied up and pushed Em and Court out in front of her. She motioned to me to move. I was still rooted to my spot. "You won't even know we were here. And thanks, Hunter, for not telling on us."

Hunter grinned and then took the leftover bowl of apples from

Grace's hands. "Don't mention it. Oh, and a word to the wise —
when you sneak back into your cabin tonight, try not to let the
porch door squeak. That was always a dead giveaway for me."

"Got it," Em said nervously.

The four of us filed out. I was the last one to walk past Hunter.
I tried not to make eye contact with him, but I could feel him
staring and I looked up. He winked at me.

"Sweet dreams, champ," he said. "I hope they're of me."

11

Swimming Lesson

Taking my campers to the lakefront for swimming lessons should have been the easiest CIT assignment I had. What could be better than spending a hot afternoon in the water? But when you're dealing with six-year-olds, nothing is ever easy.

"SAM! Serena said she gets to jump in the water first, but you promised yesterday that I could," whined Mackenzie as we threw our beach towels on the hot sand and everyone began pulling off t-shirts and flip-flops.

"It's not your turn, it's my turn!" said Bridget, who proceeded to clench her fists into tight balls. "You're a fibber!"

"If Mackenzie goes first then I get to be the first one Donovan practices with," complained Serena, who stomped her feet in protest.

"Donovan said, Donovan said, I, I, n-need ex-extra help practicing my b-breathing!" interrupted Callie, a redhead whose face was as tomato-colored as her swimsuit. When she was nervous she stuttered.

Suddenly all eight peeps were yelling at once, and then they started shoving. Serena grabbed Mackenzie's pigtails and began to pull.

"Not again," I groaned. Yelling at the girls never worked. I needed two people to break up a fight, and Alexis was at the main office dealing with some paperwork. What was I going to do? I heard someone laughing and turned around. Donovan was standing two feet away. That gave me an idea. I ran over.

"Hey, Sam," Donovan said, chuckling. "Having a rough day?"

Court's crush was cute, and the Aussie accent only added to his dreaminess, but I didn't have time to drool. I reached for the whistle around his neck, pulled him toward me and blew into it as loudly as I could, trying not to laugh at the shocked look on Donovan's face. The girls stopped their fighting at once.

"If you guys don't cut it out immediately then NONE OF YOU are going swimming today," I told them sternly. Serena immediately started to sniffle. Swimming was her favorite activity and she would hate to miss it. Everyone else was quiet. "That's more like it." I smiled. "Now if you all file behind me, we'll head down to the water and all walk in at the SAME TIME. Then Donovan will decide what activity you do first. Understood?" They all nodded.

"Nice one, mate," Donovan said admiringly. "I can take it from here."

"Are you sure? I know there are a lot of them," I told Donovan. "If you want me to help you I can." Even though Donovan ran the class, I always offered to help out. I felt guilty sitting on the sand watching him work.

"I've got it," Donovan insisted. "I'll call you over in a minute." He smiled. "Oh, and if you see Court later, tell her I said hi."

"I will." I tried to suppress a grin. Court was going to flip when she heard that.

I walked back toward the pile of my peeps' discarded towels and began to tidy up. After I laid them all out on the sand, I pulled off my sweatshorts and tank top. I had my shirt over my head when I heard voices.

"Thanks so much for the invite, Ash," someone said breathlessly. It sounded like one of the girls from 8A. "I'm beyond excited!"

"This is going to be your best sleepover ever," said another. "I can't believe your dad is letting you hire a DJ and we're playing *Guitar Hero* and having mani/pedis done."

"Since I'm stuck with a lame January birthday and you guys aren't around, Daddy had to do something spectacular to make up for it," I heard Ashley say. "But remember — my sleepover is supposed to be hush-hush. Daddy doesn't want people to feel left out."

I had to stop myself from laughing. Court said Ashley used this excuse every year and then she proceeded to tell everyone at camp about her party anyway.

"So how many girls were invited?" someone asked.

"Ten," Ashley said. "You girls in 8A, of course. A few marshmallows who are so eager to come they'll do all the grunt work for the bash, and then Gabby."

By this point, I had my shirt off, and was trying my best not to be noticed. I was halfway to the water's edge when I realized I had forgotten a hair tie and had to go back.

"You didn't invite your other bunkmates?" I heard a girl ask.

"Are you kidding me? Those geeks? I barely speak to them," Ashley sniffed. "Especially since, you know, they have so many issues."

"What kind of issues?" another girl asked.

"I shouldn't say." Ashley sounded serious. "It would be rude of me to talk behind their backs." The girls started to beg. "Okay, but this is strictly confidential," she said not a second later. "Courtney has daddy problems and is always sneaking out to hook up with guys. Grace is on the verge of a nervous breakdown. She so can't handle the strains of being a CIT. And Emily Kate, well, let's just say she's too boring to even discuss." Ashley laughed. "Then there's Sam. She's bizarre. She's always going off on her own and no one knows where she goes. She's trying to fit in, but the truth is no one in our bunk even talks to her." Her voice dropped to a whisper, but I could still hear her. "She's a complete outcast."

My blood was pumping. I didn't want an invite to Ashley's stupid party, but when she blatantly lied about my friends, I had to say something. Ashley was still talking when I approached her group and the girls saw me before Ashley did. "Hey," I said, startling her. I was smiling broadly. "How are you doing, Ash?"

"Oh, hey, Sam." Ashley looked nervous. It was the first time I'd ever caught her off guard.

"I thought I'd see if you wanted to borrow any sunscreen." I held up my bottle. "We all know how red you get if you don't put it on." I looked at the other girls. "She looked like a lobster the other night and we did all we could with concealer, but it didn't help." I was surprised at how good my jab sounded.

"I've got my own sunblock, thanks," Ashley snapped and gave me a tight smile. "But since we're being all friendly, I should probably tell you something." She looked me up and down. "I think your bathing suit shrunk. It's kind of tight around the belly." She made a face. "Unless you've gained weight. I mean, you have eaten an awful lot of carbs lately. It's not surprising. Since it's your first year at camp, you don't know how to eat right, but don't worry, sweetie, I'm sure no one other than me even noticed your tire." A few of the girls giggled. My face flushed.

"Sam? I could really use your help over here," I heard Donovan yell from the water. The girls were all splashing around so much I could barely see him.

"Sure," I said, not looking at Ashley. My brief moment of confidence was gone and all I could do was meekly retreat. "Talk to you guys later," I mumbled.

"I hope so!" Ashley sang.

As I approached the water, I turned around and saw Ashley and her posse huddled deep in conversation on their matching hot pink towels. Court called Ash's friends the Beach Blanket Brigade because they always placed their towels on the same spot on the beach, and if anyone else tried to sit there, they threw a fit. Apparently the location of towels was pretty important at the lakefront. Me, I could care less where I threw my towel, just as long as it was there when I got back.

"So what are we doing?" I asked Donovan when I had made my way into the water. The girls were all holding on to the dock as they waited for further instruction. There were ropes that enclosed the shallow and the deep ends and two lap lanes were roped off for free swim. As much as I liked doing laps, I couldn't face the thought of doing them in a lake with water so murky you couldn't see the bottom. Grace swore the lake was clean, but I was freaked out by the possibility of brushing against a fish while I swam.

"Practicing our breaststroke," Donovan said, and made the motion with his muscular arms. Even the six-year-olds took notice. "Why don't you start working with each girl one by one?"

"Sure," I agreed.

The class moved quickly. I helped Mackenzie practice floating on her back, worked with Callie on swimming underwater, and helped Serena with her breaststroke. Donovan used me as his assistant to teach the girls what to do if they were having trouble in the water and how to signal him. Then Donovan pretended to rescue me and bring me back to shore. I couldn't help but keep looking back at Ashley and her buddies, but it was growing harder and harder to see them. The lakefront had gotten pretty crowded with other classes and even the roped-off section of the water was full with other lifeguards teaching lessons.

"I think you guys are getting pretty good at your breaststroke," Donovan told the peeps. "I want you guys to remember we're having a swim test next Friday." The girls groaned. "I'll be around during free periods to help anyone interested in practicing for the exam." This caused Mackenzie to giggle. The girls may have only been ages six to eight, but they could spot a hottie when they saw one. Donovan looked at his watch. "We have ten minutes left. Want to play a game of Marco Polo?" Everyone cheered.

"Mind if we join you?"

I turned around and Cole was wading into the water. He was shirtless and wearing navy swim trunks. I tried not to stare, especially since Cole seemed to be staring at me too. At least I thought he was. The thought of that only made me blush more.

"The more the merrier, mate," Donovan told him.

"We're a little early for free swim," Cole said as he strode over. "Hunter is on his way down, but it's just me and the rugrats right now." Cole's peeps were already splashing rowdily behind him.

"No worries, join in," Donovan said.

"Hey," Cole said to me. There was something about being in a state of undress and standing next to Cole that was making me really nervous. "How's your day going?"

"Good," I managed to say. "Yours?"

"Better now," he said with a sly smile. "Have you been over to the arts and crafts shack with the peeps yet?" I shook my head.

"Warning," Cole said ominously. "They're using glue today, and lots of it. Caleb dumped a bottle all over the floor."

"I don't know why they let them do projects with it at this age," I said. "Last week, Serena glued her hand to the table. I had to find nail polish remover to get her loose." Cole laughed.

Once Cole and I started talking about anything other than us, our conversations flowed. That sometimes made me think it would be easier if I just thought of Cole as a friend, but I couldn't. I was starting to like him. A lot.

"I'm It first," Donovan interrupted. "Game starts now!"

Marco Polo was always fun to play, but it was especially fun now that Cole was in the game. When it was his turn to be It, he tackled me in the water and all I could do was laugh. When I was It, I actually managed to get Donovan. A few of Cole's peeps were really good too — either that or they were cheating by keeping their eyes half open — while only one of my girls (Serena) managed to avoid being It.

Afterward, our whole group headed back onto the beach to dry off. Cole's group had lessons, but Donovan needed a five-minute break to make a phone call and no one was allowed in the water without a lifeguard present.

The girls ran for their towels, but stopped short when they saw Ashley and her posse sitting nearby.

Serena pointed at Ashley and stared. "You're the girl in the video."

"That's me. How are you doing?" Ashley said in her friendliest sugary-sweet tone. It always made her sound like she was campaigning for office.

"You're on all the camp stuff my mommy showed me at home too," Callie said in awe. You'd think they'd just met Hannah Montana the way they were staring at Ashley. All of my girls crowded around her. Ashley started to get up and stuffed her towel in her beach bag. She threw a cranberry-colored terry-cloth dress over her bathing suit.

"I do the video every year," she told the girls. "I'm actually an actress/model."

"Have we ever seen you on TV?" Serena asked.

Ashley stuttered for a moment and a giggle escaped my lips. She glared at me.

"Sam's been on TV," Mackenzie piped up and Ashley only turned redder. "She's been in a commercial and everything. She's famous. Everyone at camp knows her." I was trying not to laugh. I glanced at Cole and he winked at me.

"So I've heard," Ashley snapped and quickly put on her flip-flops.

"The Pines video isn't on TV, but Sam's commercial is," added Callie. "Sam told us all about how she made it so I know."

A smile spread across Ashley's lips. "Did she now? Then I'm *sure* Sam told you how she was *cast* in the commercial."

I just looked at her. What was she getting at? Cole was toweling off behind me and I was trying not to get distracted.

"It's not like Sam was hand-picked or went to a huge audition and was discovered," Ashley said solemnly. "Unlike *me*, who producers and casting directors *ask* for."

"Producers are asking for you?" One of the girls from 8A asked. Ashley ignored her.

"Sam was in that commercial because her mommy works for Dial and Dash Phone," Ashley told my girls.

A sickening feeling took over my stomach. I'd always been

honest about this. Maybe too honest. I had told the whole story to Ashley myself on the first day of camp. But with my peeps I had glossed over this detail, mostly because it seemed too complicated for them to understand. Cole knew the truth, but I hated having him hear it said in such an ugly way by someone as vindictive as Ashley.

"I guess the company didn't have the money to hire someone on their own so they wound up using the demo they shot with Sam for the national commercial."

"That's not true," I said shakily. I hated bragging about Dial and Dash, but I wasn't going to let Ashley drag my name through the mud in front of my peeps.

Ashley continued to ignore me. "You guys have seen the other Dash commercials, right?" My girls nodded. "Why do you think Sam isn't in them? They didn't *want* her."

"That's enough, Ashley," I said. "That commercial was a hit. They *did* want me, but I didn't want to do more commercials." Even if I wanted to say something cold about Ashley's career at that moment, I couldn't do it in front of my peeps and she knew it. Ashley had the upper hand once again.

"You don't have to be defensive, Sam. I'm just telling them the truth." Ashley shrugged. "That's what a good counselor does. They don't *lie* to their charges." She grabbed her beach bag and pulled it onto her shoulder. "See you, girls." She walked away with her friends. I could hear them laughing.

"Is that true, Sam?" Mackenzie asked. "They didn't want you for more commercials?"

"It's complicated, Mackenzie," I said, grabbing her towel

and handing it to her. "But the short version is that everyone liked the first commercial a lot and I had a lot of fun making it."

"Just ignore Ashley," Cole whispered in my ear and I felt my body stiffen. I could smell his gum. Today it was grape. I breathed it in. "She thrives on being evil."

"It suits her well," I said. I was afraid to move.

"You can't let her get away with it," Cole added.

I shrugged. "I can't do mean as well as she does, so what's the point?"

I moved away and handed the rest of my girls their towels. I made sure everyone had their beach cover-ups and sunblock (something they seemed to lose on a daily basis). Then it was time for me to get dressed. I looked around. My towel and clothes were MIA. "Has anyone seen my stuff?" I asked the girls. They shook their heads.

We all searched, even Cole, thinking maybe my stuff had gotten mixed in with his peeps', but my clothes were nowhere to be found. Then it dawned on me: Ashley. She and her minions must have grabbed them when I was in the water.

"Can I borrow someone's towel?" I said.

Cole stripped off his, standing there in his swim trunks, and held the green towel out to me. It smelled like Downy. I tried not stare at Cole's abs as I took it and wrapped the towel around my chest.

"Ashley took your stuff, didn't she?" Cole asked.

"It looks like it," I said wearily.

"Sam," Cole started to say something and I was sure it was about taking on Ashley.

"Cole, I just don't even have it in me to fight her," I said. "Thanks for the towel. I promise to return it later."

Then I trudged up the hill behind my peeps, in my bare feet, clutching Cole's towel. All I could think about was the fact that Ashley had humiliated me yet again.

♠ 12 ♠
Talent Show-Off

"Come on, people, I don't have all day!" Ashley snapped. "I'd like to actually go swimming this afternoon. It's boiling out."

We were back in our bunk midday — a rarity — to have an Ashley-mandated bunk meeting about the talent show. But no one was paying attention to Ashley except, well, Ashley. Everyone was still keyed up from yesterday's Parents' Day visit. Since Mom wasn't coming, I had offered to help Alexis with the peeps. Em thought I was crazy. She was making an appearance with her bunk, like all the CITs had to do, but then she was taking advantage of being visitor- and activity-less and was spending the day at the lake reading her latest novel, *London Lovers*. But me, I felt guilty letting Alexis handle everything on her own, so I offered to help her make special snacks, signs for the parents' arrival, and crafts for the girls to give to their parents. I had worked till nine last night and today I was exhausted.

"Gab, are you getting off the phone or what?" Ashley's eyes shot daggers at her best friend.

Gabby was talking to her boyfriend, Joshua, on the phone she had hidden from Meg. She liked to check in with him from time to time to make sure he still missed her — even if she was flirting with Gavin behind his back. "Pooks, I have to go," Gabby cooed, making me want to gag. "TLF, sweetie. TTYL."

She even abbreviated words to her boyfriend! I wondered how he could stand it.

Gabby snapped the phone shut and glared at the rest of us. "Guys, WAYWF?"

"Huh?" Even Grace was confused.

Gabby sighed. "I said, 'What are you waiting for?' Let's pay attention to Ashley, okay? She's trying to tell us about this year's beyond brilliant theme."

"Yeah, about that," I piped up, feeling slightly brave. "If we're performing as a bunk, shouldn't the theme be a bunk decision?" Court snorted and her ice tea came shooting out of her nose.

Gabby practically shot venom at me with her eyes. "Ashley's always picked it."

"Because I'm the one with the good ideas," Ashley added icily. "I have a background in acting, you know." She paused and looked at me, as if daring me to say I did too. But my moment of bravery was gone. "If you don't like it, you can sit this out. The routine I have in mind would work better with five girls anyway."

The girls looked from me to Ashley. "No, I'm in," I told her. I had promised the sleepaway girls I would be part of the show even though I didn't want to do it. And besides, I didn't want to be the only CIT not part of a routine.

"Fine," Ashley said, waving a paper fan in front of her flushed face. "God, I need air. Let's take five." She stomped out of the cabin, the door slamming behind her and Gabby followed.

"I know this sucks," Em told me gently. "I don't like working with her any more than you do. None of us do! But this is tradition, and on the upside, her number is always the most popular one," Em said brightly. "When it comes to the talent show, you can't cross Ashley. She'll make you wear a cow costume."

"A cow costume?" I asked, trying not to smirk.

"Two years ago, when I was 'in' with Ashley, I questioned her song choice — we did 'Milkshake' by Kelis. Ashley got mad and made me wear a cow costume for the routine. I was mortified."

I wanted to laugh at the image, but I knew I shouldn't.

"I just wish someone around here — someone who isn't afraid to stand up to Ashley — would come up with her own talent show number and take over the routine," Grace said, and looked directly at Court.

Court sighed. "Grace, I appreciate the vote of confidence, but it's too much work! I can't spend all my free time ogling Donovan *and* plan a talent show number. I vote for letting Ashley do the heavy lifting like always."

"Come on, Court," Grace begged. "Remember last year when you thought of doing a funnyordie.com-type spoof of camp life? Your ideas are brilliant. Ashley's may be popular, but yours would be the talk of the show."

Court didn't get a chance to respond. Gabby had slammed the door loudly and marched in front of us with Ashley at her side.

"Everybody finally ready?" Ashley said, looking at me. "So this year, since it's our last year we're officially in the talent show, I thought we should go out with a bang. We need to make this performance as memorable as possible so they'll be talking about it all winter. I want something sexy, something daring." She looked at Gabby. "That's why I've decided that this year's number will be 'Big Spender' from *Fosse*." Gabby clapped enthusiastically.

"Hasn't someone done that already?" Em asked slowly.

Ashley rolled her eyes. "A few girls *tried* to do it last year, but it stunk so bad they weren't even picked. They just lip-synched to the song. We'd actually sing it. And we'd dance. Most people don't do both. And our costumes would be killer. I'm thinking black bra tops, tight spandex pants, and tulle skirts."

There was no way I was going up onstage in front of the entire camp in a bra and spandex! Especially when I didn't have a stomach as flat as a surfboard like Ashley.

"Isn't that song kind of old-school?" Court asked skeptically.

"And kind of racy for camp?" Grace added. "I don't think I want to sing that in front of Hitch."

"We'll change some of the words," Ashley said dismissively. "I've already got our background all picked out. We're going to paint a bar scene and have bar stools and pick one of the hot counselors to sit in the middle of the stage and be our 'big spender.'"

"Oooh, can we pick Gavin?" Gabby asked. "Or Donovan?" I glanced at Court. She looked like she wanted to tackle Gabby.

"I was thinking Patrick," Ashley said. "I'm sure he'll say yes when he hears it involves *me*." She looked at the rest of us and smiled. "So it's all settled. We'll start practicing right away since auditions are in two weeks. And we'll have to get our costumes. They shouldn't take too long to order from Victoria's Secret. Well, if you can all squeeze into spandex." Gabby giggled. "Maybe we should have a bunk diet — for you guys, of course. Gabs and I don't need one."

"That's it." Court stood up. She looked angry. "Your idea reeks! It's been done before and I am not spending my last talent show in spandex! If you want to do this number, then perform it at your lame sleepover party. We're not doing it!"

I beamed at her proudly. Why didn't I have the guts to stand up for myself like that?

Ashley's jaw dropped and hung there for a moment. "And you think you have an idea that is better than mine?" Ashley's eyes were slits. "Let me remind you that I have come up with our talent show idea for the last six years."

"Six," Gabby repeated loudly. She stood next to Ashley in solidarity.

"And every year the whole camp has told us how *amazing* our number is," Ashley added.

"Amazing!" Gabby seconded.

"As long as I'm being honest, I have to say last year's number was kind of silly," Court said, enjoying the effect she was having on Ashley. "I mean, Kanye West's 'Stronger' was played out by the time you made us dance to it in those silly military costumes, which by the way, were a direct rip-off of Janet Jackson's 'Rhythm Nation.'"

Ashley gasped. "They were not!"

"They were too!" Court said. "You copied some of the moves verbatim. I know that video because my older sister was a Janet freak."

Gabby looked confused. For once, she didn't come to Ashley's defense.

"Well that's got nothing to do with this year," Ashley snapped. "This number is totally original and this is the one we're doing."

"Says who?" Court was standing eye-to-eye with Ashley now. I thought I saw Ashley flinch. I looked at Grace, alarmed. She was smiling.

"If this is a bunk decision, then *everyone* should vote on it," Court said matter-of-factly. "The Pines is a democracy, not an Ashocracy."

Em laughed. Ashley spun around and shot her a look.

"Everyone who thinks 'Big Spender' is not the way to go, raise their hand," Court said, and raised her hand. Obviously Gabby and Ashley didn't, but Grace's hand popped up, mine followed, and Em joined us. "Hmph. Four against two," Court said triumphantly. "Looks like 'Big Spender' is out."

"Fine, we'll do it without you," Gabby spat.

Ashley leaned over and whispered loud enough that I could hear her. "Idiot, we can't do it with just two girls. We'll look lame." Gabby's face fell. Ashley turned to Court. "So what's your brilliant idea, Court?" The way she said it, you just knew Ashley didn't believe she had one.

Court looked at me. For a split second, I thought she was nervous, but then she spoke. "I agree with Ashley on two things:

our last year should really be spectacular, and since everyone in this room has a crush on someone this summer, I think the number should be sexy." She took a deep breath. "So here is what I think. I think we should do a cowgirl theme. We could take worn pairs of jeans and make them into daisy dukes. We could get those red button-down shirts and tie them above our waists and we can try to find cowboy boots. I was thinking our background could be a western town or look like a horse ranch or something."

"No one's done a western," Em pointed out to the rest of us.

"Background and costume is one thing, but do you actually have a song in mind?" Ashley smirked. "Because obviously the song makes the whole number."

"Well, I'm not sure if we should just dance or if we should sing as well," Court said thoughtfully. "I guess it depends on our voices. But we could definitely dance. We're all good at that."

"HELLO! Ash asked you about the song," Gabby snapped.

"The problem with doing anything too current is that our song could be played out and by next summer our number would be long forgotten. But if we pick something that is classic, we can get away with using it and making it look hot." Everyone nodded in agreement, even Gabby. "I didn't want to do anything too trendy, so I was thinking, 'These Boots Are Made for Walkin',' the Jessica Simpson version."

"I love that song!" Grace said enthusiastically.

"It is kind of fab," Gabby admitted.

"It's not cooler than 'Big Spender'!" Ashley sounded shrill. "Jessica Simpson is so country now."

"True, but her version of that song is pretty decent, and we could easily come up with dance steps," Court said.

"I could make us daisy dukes," I piped up. "I fray my shorts all the time. And I know you're great at murals, but I could help. My art teacher in Carle Place said I had a real eye for scenery. I could help you work on the choreography too!"

Grace looked at me strangely. "You realize there are other people willing to help, right? You don't have to do it all."

"I know," I said, embarrassed. "It's just, I like helping."

"So we've noticed," Court said dryly.

"I hate this whole idea!" Ashley shrieked, but no one was listening.

I looked at Court. It was her turn to smirk. "Well, since most of us hated your idea, and you hate mine, I guess you could sit this one out."

Ashley made a face. "We'll join 8A's number."

Gabby whispered loudly. "Ash, you know your dad likes bunks to perform together. If we bail now, we'll have nothing and be stuck working backstage. Eww."

Ashley screamed in frustration. "What is up with you guys this summer?" she complained. "Ever since *she* got here, you've been acting weird and annoying."

I assumed by *she*, Ashley meant me.

"It's like you guys think you call the shots now or something," Gabby seconded.

"Sam has upset the balance of everything around here, and I hate it," Ashley said, stomping her feet like a little kid.

"Thanks," I said. It was kind of exciting to know I had this much of an effect on her. Maybe I needed to use it to my advantage and finally stop getting picked on.

"Well, I love that Sam came to the Pines," Court countered. "She's made this place ten times better and if I have to choose who is going in this number, obviously Sam is my choice over you. So like I said, you're welcome to sit this one out. Maybe you could do a solo."

Ashley began to look nervous. Em had told me that Ashley loved attention, but one of her biggest fears was having the spotlight to herself. She always needed an entourage.

"FINE," Ashley said. "I'll do your stupid rehearsals. But if our number stinks and we don't get into the talent show, we're reverting back to my idea. I'll beg Daddy to let us re-audition. That's the least he could do for me."

"Deal." Court held out her hand to shake Ashley's. Ashley left her hanging.

"I'm going to the lake to cool off," she said. "I'll meet you guys fourth period."

She headed into the bathroom with Gabby close behind her. When I heard the faucet turn on, I jumped on Court.

"You were amazing," I said. "I wish I could be like that with her."

"I'm so proud of you," Grace agreed.

"Your idea is so much better than Ashley's," Em added. "I can't believe she actually agreed to do your song."

"That's what scares me," Court said darkly. "She is definitely going to get back at me for this, I know it."

"I wouldn't worry about it," Grace said, and just then Ashley and Gabby stormed past us, wearing their beach cover-ups. They didn't even look our way. The door slammed extra loudly behind us. "As I said, they'll get over it." She started to giggle.

"I think this calls for a sleepaway girls briefing," I said, checking quickly to make sure Meg wasn't coming before I pulled out the recorder. The group of us huddled into the bathroom. I pressed record and Grace told Court's victory story with Em giving background commentary. Court was really pumped.

"Now that I've totally found my inner grrrl," Court growled, "you guys have to too. Who's up first? Grace?" Grace blushed. "Don't you think it's time you talked to Tim about something other than sports?" Court turned her gaze toward Em and me and I knew I was in trouble. "And you two — stop whining and tell Dylan and Cole you like them."

I sighed. "It's not that I don't want Cole to know."

"Me either," Em interrupted. We looked at each other. "It's just . . ."

I finished her sentence. "I've never told a guy I like him before," I admitted.

Em looked relieved. "Me either!" She turned to Court. "I know you tell guys this sort of thing all the time, but not all of us are as confident around them as you are."

"Or as big of a flirt," Grace pointed out.

Court gave us a smarting look. "There's always a first time."

"It's not that easy," I protested.

"I don't think I could stand face-to-face with Dylan and admit I like him," Em said nervously. "I couldn't handle him staring at me as I said it. Sometimes I think it would be easier if Court told him for me. Sort of like *Cyrano de Bergerac*."

"I'm with you," I agreed.

"Who?" Court looked confused.

"You don't read at all, do you?" Em scolded. "Cyrano is this guy who wants to tell Roxanne that he loves her, but he's scared, so he helps this gorgeous dude named Christian do it instead." She frowned. "It sort of backfires, but the idea of helping someone else say the words you're scared to say has always seemed so romantic."

Court put down the camera for a moment and Grace took over videotaping. "You've given me an idea," she said looking pensive. "What if you could be like Ciro?"

"Cyrano," Em corrected.

"Whatever." Court waved her hand. "What if you could tell the guys you like them without actually saying it to their faces?"

"You mean you're going to tell them for us?" Em asked hopefully.

Court shook her head. "They're going to be in disguise and so are you!"

"I don't get it," I said, but Em gasped.

"Do you mean during the counselor hunt?" Em asked. Court nodded.

"What's the counselor hunt?" I demanded.

"It's this game the counselors and CITs do every year," Court explained. "The counselors and CITs wear costumes and hide all over camp. Then the campers have to go find them. The winners of the contest get free canteen snacks or something. It's a lot of fun. Anyway, if you guys are in costume, then Cole and Dylan don't actually have to see your face and you don't have to see theirs when you tell them you like them. That would make you less nervous, right?"

It was pretty genius. Em and I looked at each other.

"Court, this might be your best idea ever," Grace said.

"Well?" Court asked.

I inhaled sharply. Court was right. We had to tell the guys we liked them. The summer was half over. It was time. "Well, Em, I guess we have to get some really good costumes."

Court lowered the palmcorder from her eye and grinned. "Girls, don't worry about a thing," she said confidentially. "I'll teach you everything you need to know."

♠ 13 ♠

Playing Games

The kitchen grill went up in flames. Sadly, I was secretly excited.

I had quickly learned that people did not come to camp for the food, especially when most nights it was burgers or hot-dogs. The night of the grease fire (which was so bad the fire department showed up), Gabby was on kitchen duty. Rumor had it she was so busy flirting with Gavin that she forgot to take a few burgers off the grill. I had the feeling Beaver wanted to fry Gabby for supper.

Thankfully, the damage wasn't that bad. Hitch said the kitchen would be open the next day. And on the upside, because of the fire, Hitch ordered the whole camp pizza. Real pizza. Not those little frozen ones that tasted like cardboard. While we waited, the younger campers were watching a movie in the auditorium and some of the off-duty older campers and counselors were playing games on the great lawn. The sun was finally lowering behind the trees, which made the weather much more bearable, and it wasn't dark yet, so the mosquitos were still at bay. After Alexis reassured me that she didn't need me to sit with the peeps in the auditorium, I decided to play Capture the Flag with my friends. The game was really growing on me, mostly because it didn't require me to throw a ball or catch one. All I had to do was run.

Court somehow made sure Em, Grace, and I were part of the same game as Donovan, Dylan, Cole, and Tim.

Playing on Cole's team sounded like a good idea at first, but once we started playing, I found it kind of distracting. Just the night before, Em and I were freaking out about the Guess the Counselor game again. Court told us we had to chill. "It's so easy," she said. "You walk up, tell them, and take off your mask for a kiss!" Great idea, if you had the guts, which I was starting to think I didn't. If I did, I would have casually mentioned the camp-wide dance to Cole by now. I hadn't. The problem was, I couldn't just blurt out "Cole, I like you." Just looking into his eyes made me dizzy.

"Court? Hello, Court?" Donovan waved a hand in front of Court's face. Sweat was beading down his chest. Donovan and Hunter, who were also playing with us, had taken off their shirts about twenty minutes ago and wrapped their opposing team pinnies around their waists. "Heads up out there. You don't want to get captured!"

"Captured is bad," Court said in a trance. I'd never seen her like that. Grace stepped on Court's foot and she yelped. "What was that for?"

"Will you get it together?" Grace whispered heatedly. "We're getting killed out there because you're too busy staring at Donovan's abs." She glared at Em. "And if you say, 'It's just a game' one more time, I'm putting you in our own jail."

"Look who's all huffy," Court pointed out. "Grace, remember: You don't have to win every time. Just have fun."

"And you promised not to make us practice for the talent show so much my calves would hurt," Grace complained. "I can't be worn out before Color War. What do you think these kids will think if I lose today? They might think I'm not a worthy Color War captain candidate."

Court flashed her you've-got-to-be-kidding-me look. "You're going to win captain, okay? And besides, the practices have been paying off, haven't they?" Court asked. "Our number rocks. Even Ashley didn't have a nasty comment to make after yesterday's practice."

We had decided to go with "These Boots Are Made for Walkin'" and it was coming together nicely. We borrowed cowboy boots from the theater department to use in rehearsals. The drama teacher said no one had done a western-themed act in years.

"I still don't trust Ashley," Grace worried. "She is not going to take this loss lying down. She and Gabby will get you back somehow, Court. We already know they're out for blood with Sam and now you too."

"Tell me about it," I grumbled. Seriously, Ashley's attitude was the only sore note to this whole perfect summer experience. I'd gotten over missing Mal (especially since she didn't seem to miss me enough to send more videos). I'd made a bunch of new friends. And being a CIT made me feel like an adult. But

Ashley's attitude and her comments were getting old. I didn't know how much more of them I could take.

Cole jogged over. I was a little disappointed that he didn't join the other guys in the shirt removal trend. "Why do you guys look so down?"

"Because we're losing!" I complained. "We've got five teammates in jail and *someone* on the other side seems to have it out for me and Court."

"She's got a point," Grace agreed. "We've had to rescue Sam and Court from jail six times already."

I rubbed my sore elbow. I felt like I was playing football, not a mindless camp game. Every time I crossed the dividing line I was tackled. So was Court. Every time, by the same two burly marshmallows. I wanted to blame the smackdown on Ashley, but she wasn't even in the game we were playing. I hadn't seen her since Gabby's fire was put out.

"I don't mind," Court said with a sigh. "Donovan has come to my aid every time I fall."

"That's great, Court, but my welts are starting to add up." I glared at the opposing team. "It's those two guys over there." I pointed to two marshmallows that were covered in mud and grass stains. "They're not even trying to capture the flag. They just want me and Court."

"You do seem to be getting banged up out there," Cole agreed. "Do you want me to talk to them?" I shook my head. "Are you sure they're after you in particular? We lost Colin and Joyce on that last round. Maybe you're just not very good." He smirked mischievously and I felt my heart skip a beat.

"I am too good!" I said defensively. "Maybe if you were paying attention to the marshmallows instead of yelling out fake code words to me, Joyce and Colin wouldn't be in jail." I tried not to laugh. Cole was always yelling things like, "Sam, forty-eight, twenty-two — go left!" Or "Sam, initiate Operation Storm Shield!" I had no clue what a storm shield was, but he made me laugh anyway.

"I'm trying to distract the other team," Cole protested. "They don't know the codes are fake." Cole's face was sweaty and there was a huge smudge of dirt on his forehead that I hadn't told him about. He looked cute like that.

"Are you done writing your surrender speech yet?" Hunter yelled from across the dividing line.

"God, he looks good," Court whispered to me. I glanced quickly at Cole. I didn't want him to hear Court say that. I was already sensitive about the fact that he thought I used to lust after Hunter. Hunter did look good, I had to admit. Was it okay to think that? He had his hands on his hips and there were grass stains all over his white nylon shorts and mud splattered across his chest.

"You're the ones who need the pen and paper, my friend," Cole yelled back.

I wasn't sure I believed the threat.

Donovan joined our huddle, putting his arms around Court and me. Cole then put his arm around Grace and me. All I could think about was the fact that Cole was touching me.

"Team, forget the flag," Donovan instructed us. "We need manpower. Cole and Sam, I need you two to distract some of the girls while Court and I make a run for the jail to get some of our teammates back. Grace, you tag out as many people as you can. The rest of you, keep Hunter and the marshmallows running in circles." We placed our hands in the circle and chanted our battle cry ("Bleed Red or Die!" which didn't make sense to me, but I guessed it was a boy thing).

"Don't worry," Em told me. "If those guys come after you again, I'll put them in jail so that you don't have to worry about them anymore."

"I'll help you," Dylan offered. Em looked panicked and took her inhaler out of her pocket. I coughed loudly. Dead giveaway, I wanted to tell her. Thankfully, Em seemed to get the point.

"Thanks. I could use some help," she said shyly.

"Me too," Grace said loudly. "I know I'm fast, but sometimes I get confused when so many people are charging at me." She looked at Tim out of the corner of her eye.

"I'm with Donovan," Court announced before hurrying to his side.

"Ready, partner?" Cole nudged me.

"Ready, sir." I saluted. I took my mark on the matted-down muddy grass and stared menacingly at the two guys who kept going after me. Bring it on, baby, I thought. Bring it on. I was determined not to go down again.

"Game back on," yelled Donovan and we were off.

The scene reminded me of *Gladiator*. Both sides started charging at each other and screaming. The muddy field, already squishy from last night's rain, was splattering all over the place as both teams stormed the dividing line. Our jails were supposed to be quiet, but you could hear captured teammates on either side screaming for release or cheering their teams on. Cole was fast so he was already several paces ahead of me. A girl lunged at him, but he was too quick for her.

Their jail was straight ahead of me and I could see the flag. A girl in a red pinnie was waving it listlessly. I knew I wasn't supposed to, but I was sure I could reach her. I started running and I was getting pretty close. Maybe those guys were going to leave me alone this time. They would have tackled me by now if —

OOOF! In an instant, I got sandwiched to the ground and I felt the mud squish into my blue pinnie and white shirt. Eww! Both of my legs hurt and I could swear I felt my back snap when I went down. I pushed with all my might and heard Donovan calling a time-out. From my position on the ground I could see Court down a few feet away. Donovan was helping her to her feet. Right away I knew it was the same two guys who tackled us last time. I tried to stay calm. I was a CIT and they were campers. I couldn't yell, but I was angry. "Guys, I know you're into the game, but do you think you could quit the tackling?" I asked one as I dusted off my shorts. "We don't tackle in capture the flag. You're supposed to capture me, not kill me."

The guy shrugged and smiled at his friend. "We're just playing the game."

Cole made it to me first. "Are you okay?" he asked and I nodded. He turned to the two campers. "Guys, take it easy on her okay? This is just a game." Then Cole turned back to me, looking worried. "Are you sure you don't need ice? Where does it hurt? Can you move your knee?"

"Cole, I'm okay," I promised.

He looked skeptical. "You're out of this next play. You shouldn't be running."

"I'm playing," I said and I meant it.

"If you hurt something you need to tell me now." Cole touched my shoulder gently and I felt a tingling sensation.

"Whoa." Court was standing behind me. "Cole is like your own personal bodyguard," she whispered in my ear.

Watching him get all protective of me was pretty cool.

"Isn't getting hurt great?" she asked me, linking arms. "Donovan helped me up." There was blood dripping down her arm.

"Court, you're bleeding!" I told her.

She pointed to my knee. "So are you," she said. She shook her head. "If we keep getting nailed like this there is no way we'll be able to practice tomorrow and we need a few more practices before our audition."

"I think you should go to the nurse," Cole said to me.

"Cole, it's just a little scratch," I told him. "I'm okay, really."

"Everything okay over here?" Hunter asked.

"We're just going over the rules of the game, right, guys?" Cole said to the marshmallows. "No tackling allowed."

"Guys, what are you doing?" Hunter asked, sounding stern. "Cut it out or you're out of the game and I'll have to write you up. Got it?"

The two campers mumbled some form of "got it" and walked back over to their places. I couldn't take my eyes off them. They were whispering to each other and looking back at the woods next to our field. What were they up to?

I didn't have a chance to find out. I got back to my spot just in time for the game to start again. We'd gotten one of our marshmallows back during the last round, so we were up a person. This time, Grace flew past me on her way to tag out some more people. Tim was at her side and I heard her asking him for help. Court was shadowing Donovan's every move and Em and Dylan were working together. I headed straight for the jail, following Cole's backside. Hunter jumped right in front of me. I stopped short for a second in a total panic. He was trying to capture me and I didn't want him to. Even if he did have amazing abs.

"You're mine, champ," Hunter growled.

"Sam, RUN!" Cole bumped Hunter out of my way. I moved just as Hunter weaved left to nab me. Hunter started chasing Cole and he left the jail unguarded. Now was my chance. Closer, closer . . . I could feel someone brush against my pinnie, but I kept going. Just a few more feet and I'd be able to rescue Colin and Joyce and

Boom! I was down again.

You've got to be kidding me! I felt the pain shoot through my right leg. This time I was hurt and mad. I looked down at my knee and it was covered in dirt and gushing blood. I looked around for Court. She was a few feet away lying on the ground. Donovan was leaning over her. She said something I couldn't hear and he helped her up. The two of them hobbled over to us and I noticed Court was limping.

I knew I was a CIT and I was supposed to set an example, but this was ridiculous. "Guys, we went over this," I complained to the misbehaving marshmallows. "What are you doing?"

"Sam, you're bleeding a lot!" Em freaked.

"I think Court sprained her ankle," Donovan said as he helped her over to us.

The marshmallows didn't answer me. Cole and Hunter came running over. Grace, Em, Dylan, and Tim were right behind them. A crowd was beginning to gather.

"You two are out of here," Hunter told them. "I'll be talking to your senior counselors and you'll be sitting out all of tonight's and tomorrow night's activities. Go to your cabins and wait for instructions."

They didn't look too upset. One of them actually looked like he was going to laugh.

"Do you think you can walk?" I heard Donovan ask Courtney.

She nodded. "My friends can help me."

"I think I should take you to the nurse, Sam," Cole said. "You shouldn't walk on that knee." He looked so concerned. Even though I was bleeding, I was secretly swooning.

"Thanks," I said breathlessly. I pictured Cole carrying me through the woods.

"The girls can help you and Court get there, right, champ?" Hunter asked. He put his arm on me. It felt warm and sweaty. I wiggled away.

I looked at Cole and realized he was looking at me. Did he

want to see how I reacted to Hunter? He needn't worry. "Guess I'll check on you later," Cole told me.

Grace helped me and Em put her arm around Court. We hobbled off the field. It didn't hurt too badly, but the blood had dripped onto my socks and was ruining my Pumas.

We were halfway down the path to the nurse's office when Em stopped. "Guys, do you see what is going on over there?" She dragged Court over to a nearby tree where another game of capture the flag was in progress. Court started motioning wildly and waved Grace and me over. I peeked over her shoulder and that's when I saw the commotion.

Ashley and Gabby were standing on the sidelines of the game talking to the two marshmallows who had given Court and me a beating — and they were all laughing! This was no coincidence.

"They are so dead," Court said, practically breathing fire.

The group of us did our best attempt to storm over.

Ashley saw us and elbowed Gabby, but the two guys looked nervous. They pretended to be watching the game. Ashley, on the other hand, looked ready for the confrontation.

"Hey, girlies. What's up?" She looked down at my knee. "Oh, did someone get hurt? Too bad. Gee, I hope this doesn't mess up the talent show audition. I'd *hate* for you two to be out of the running. If that happened, we might have to go back to my idea."

"You're unbelievable," seethed Court. "You got Sam and me beat up just to avoid doing my number for the talent show audition? We could have gotten really hurt!"

"I didn't say I did it," Ashley said, looking innocent. "I just said it would be a shame if this messed up the audition, which it looks like it might have seeing as how Court looks like she has a sprained ankle." Gabby was doubled over in laughter.

My blood was boiling as the two of them continued to make fun of us. I had had enough. "I'm sick of this. We should go to Hitch," I said to my friends.

Ashley just laughed harder. "Who do you think he's going to believe, Sam? You or his daughter? And don't even think of trying my sister. She may like you, but I'm still family. All you'll do by tattling is wind up getting yourselves in trouble." She looked at my knee. "You guys better hurry. I wouldn't want Sam to bleed all over her no-name sneakers." The two of them giggled.

"This isn't over," I said. "Actually it's far from it. You have no idea what you started." For a split second, Ashley actually looked worried, but then she started to laugh again. "Let's get out of here," I said to my friends, feeling disgusted. "She makes me so angry," I complained when we were far enough away.

"You were really good back there," Grace said admiringly. "I think Ashley looked a little nervous for a change. What made you finally speak up?"

I shrugged. "I think I've finally had enough."

"It's about time," Court said. "I think it's time for a little payback. The sleepaway girls have to have a meeting about pranking Ashley and Gabby."

"I can't believe I'm saying this, but I agree with Court," Grace seconded. "Ashley has gotten away with being queen bee around the Pines for long enough. She deserves a taste of her own medicine." I guess I must have looked surprised at Grace's unsportsmanlike behavior because she added, "You don't think I'd do this if I thought it would cost me Color War captain, do you?" Grace had put in her name for the job last week and voting was going on now.

"You're right," said Em, sounding charged up. "I'm in."

"Okay, we're agreed then," I said, then paused. "Not that I know what we're actually doing. How do we get her back?"

"Don't worry about that," said Court with a sly smile. "I'm a pro at a little camp mischief. We'll meet later during our next camp confessional and figure out the logistics."

"Works for me," I said. I looked back at Ashley. She was still laughing.

Enjoy it now, Ash, I thought. You won't be laughing for long.

Game on.

14

Gotcha

"Watch it," Grace whispered.

"Sorry," Em mouthed.

"Shh," Court and I told her. Then Court started to giggle and I kicked her.

"What?" Court said. "It's not like she is going to wake up. She got an hour's sleep last night. Listen to her snoring. She could saw wood."

This made all of us laugh.

"Shh!" Grace admonished us even though she was laughing herself.

Court was probably right. Last night was Ashley's sleepover party and according to Ashley, who had dark circles under her eyes at breakfast, she and her friends had "the most awesome time anyone could ever have" and barely slept a wink last night. I was glad we didn't do our prank during her sleepover. We'd thought about it and realized the culprits would be too obvious since we weren't invited.

Across the room, Ashley was snoring like a freight train. ("I do not snore!" she snapped whenever anyone made a comment on her less than graceful habit.) Gabby had a summer cold and took Nyquil so she was out for the count as well. The two of them wore these satin sleep masks to block out the light, which made what we were doing even easier. We were in the cubby portion of the cabin, emptying all of Ashley's and Gabby's clothes into our backpacks. Em and I had already collected their shoes.

We were at war with our own cabin. And if we pulled this prank off, we were winning.

"Is that everything?" Grace asked as she zipped her backpack closed.

"Are you sure we shouldn't leave them at least one outfit?" Em asked. "What if something goes wrong and they lose everything?"

"Who cares?" Court shrugged. "They deserve it."

Court was beyond bitter this week. Even though 8B had made the talent show, thanks to Court's awesome cowgirl routine, we'd had to audition with one less team member — Court. Ashley's Capture the Flag prank cost Court full use of her ankle (the nurse said it wasn't sprained, but it was bruised, and Court needed to avoid physical activities for a few days). She would be off crutches in two days, but she was determined to pull off the stunt that night. It was Wednesday and that was the counselors' meeting/hangout time.

"What about their shampoo and stuff?" Grace wanted to know. "Should we take their toothbrushes?"

"I want them to have bad breath!" I said gleefully.

"You guys, that's pushing it." Em sounded motherly. "A prank is one thing, but if we take everything they own, they'll know it's us for sure."

"Em's right," Grace said. "Let's put back one ugly outfit each and their pj's."

Court sighed. "Fine." She pulled some of Gabby's stuff out of her backpack. "Now let's get out of here."

The four of us crept through the cabin, avoiding the wood plank under the shaggy pink rug that made a loud creak every time you stepped on it. Court secretly put a wedge in the screen door to keep it cracked open so we could get out without a peep.

We couldn't really make a run for it with Court on crutches, so we hobbled down to the lake. The rest of us were carrying flashlights to light the way, but it still wasn't that much illumination. In the distance, I heard a long, low howl.

"What was that?" I freaked.

"I'm sure it was a dog," Grace assured me, even though she sounded alarmed herself.

"We've got to keep moving," Em said. "Beaver is on night duty and if he catches us, he'll eat us for breakfast."

Beaver took night watch duty seriously. The week before, he had woken up our bunk at 3 AM when he barged in unexpectedly because he thought he heard a noise. It was probably Ashley snoring.

"These bags are really heavy," I complained as I hoisted my backpack higher on my shoulder.

"Hang in there. This will be worth it," Court said. "Since

we're putting a few of our own things in the canoe as well, Ashley and Gabby won't be able to blame the prank on us."

I had to admit Court's idea was brilliant. She made each of us put a few outfits of our own — ones we hated or had already stained — into the backpacks so that we looked like we were also pranked.

"Has anyone pulled this off before?" I asked.

"A few times in the years I've been here," said Grace. "Usually they only take one or two outfits — not their whole summer wardrobe — but one time it went really wrong. The night they pulled the prank there was a huge storm and the canoe they put the clothes in overturned. They lost everything. Hitch was so mad he sent the ringleader of the pranksters home from camp three weeks early."

Gulp. We walked in silence after that. I had gotten used to the dark campgrounds at that point and slapped my knee to ward off a mosquito attack (that was the worst part of the outdoors at night). The moon was high and bright and it seemed to be guiding us. I could see the lake in the distance and the water was as still as glass. A few canoes were tied to the nearby dock and I stared at them nervously.

I was starting to wonder if this prank was a good idea. I wanted to get Ashley back for being so awful, but I didn't want to get kicked out of camp for doing it. Ashley had been mean, but no meaner than some of the girls I went to school with. And did I play pranks on them? No. But I guess if I really thought about it, I would have liked to.

"There's the boat dock," Court whispered when we'd made it down the hill.

We stepped onto the dock and it creaked. The sound was louder at night when there weren't a million campers splashing about. I looked around. "I feel like I'm being watched."

"That's just because we're pulling a prank," Court said as she gingerly knelt down and began unloading the contents of her backpack into the closest canoe. I saw her place Ashley's favorite green American Eagle tee in the boat. "I always feel that way. But afterward, when the prank works, you're going to be exhilarated. Trust me."

It was eerie down at the boat launch at night. I'd never been down here this late. I knew Court had in summers past — it was where she had her first kiss — but it didn't seem romantic to me. It was spooky. I expected Jaws to pop out of the water at any moment.

We'd almost unloaded everything into the boat, including Gabby's rhinestone-studded Havianas, when I saw a light in the woods by the cabins.

"Someone's coming," Em croaked.

It was definitely a flashlight.

We were toast.

"Quick," Court instructed, hurrying to finish the contents of the bags and get them in the boat. She dumped the remaining few pairs of shoes inside. "Turn off your flashlights. We've got to untie the boat and push it into the lake or we're going to get expelled from camp for sure. If they catch us in the act, it's worse than just being caught out of bed after curfew."

Grace pulled Court to her feet. "You have to start walking now," she ordered Court. "You're the slowest. One of us will untie the boat and the other two will help you get away."

"WHO'S DOWN THERE?" It was Beaver. I felt a chill run down my spine.

"We're dead," Em freaked. She started to wheeze and quickly reached for her inhaler.

"You three go," I told them. "I'll untie the canoe and I'll be right behind you."

"No, I'm not leaving you!" Court said. "This was my idea. I should take the rap if we get caught."

"Go," I said forcefully and Grace started dragging Court and Em away. "I'll be there in a second."

"I CAN SEE YOU! STOP RIGHT THERE!" Beaver's voice was getting louder.

My heart was beating out of my chest. "Go so I can finish this!"

"We've got to go," Grace said. "Court, NOW."

"Untie the boat and push it as hard as you can," Court told me as they moved away. "Hurry, Sam!"

"Who are you?" I heard Beaver say as I fumbled for the knot that was tying the canoe to the dock. "Did you hear me?"

My hands were sweating and I was having trouble undoing the rope. "Come on, come on," I said to myself as my heart beat faster and faster.

"I'm radioing for Hitch! If you show yourself you'll get in less trouble."

Yeah, right.

The knot unraveled and I untied the boat. I gave it a hard push and it moved away from the dock. In an hour, it would be floating in the middle of the lake. YES! Good-bye Ashley's and Gabby's clothes! Have a good trip!

I looked up and I saw Beaver's flashlight was almost down the hill. I turned, started to run, and *boom!*

I'd tripped over my own two feet. When I stood up, I was missing one of my flip-flops. I could run without it and I started to, but then I remembered: Everything I owned at camp had my name on it. Stupid camp rules! If I didn't retrieve that flip-flop, I was as good as done for. I was afraid to turn my flashlight on and give away my face so I fumbled around the dock in the dark. I felt a splinter pinch my finger as I traced the worn wood planks. Finally I felt something rubbery. It was my flip-flop!

And it was stuck. It must have gotten wedged in the dock.

"Give me your name and maybe I'll go easy on you," Beaver yelled. "There is nowhere for you to run!"

I pulled as hard as I could. My hands were slipping because I was sweating a lot. I looked around. I couldn't see Court, Grace, or Em. If they were still somewhere on the beach, there was no way I could find them now. I gave one final tug and my flip-flop came free. I slid it on my foot and broke out into a full run, just as Beaver made it to the bottom of the hill.

"Get back here!" Beaver bellowed.

He was too close. There was no way I was going to get away from him. Any second he was going to shine his flashlight on me and I'd be recognized. I had to get off this beach.

"Did you hear me? Stop!"

I darted left into the dreaded woods. I could hear Beaver running after me, but I kept going even though I had no clue where I was headed in the dark. My arms brushed against tree branches and leaves and I forced myself not to freak out.

I was doomed.

And that was when it happened. All of a sudden something grabbed me and I screamed.

"Are you okay?" I heard Beaver say.

A hand slapped over my mouth and the next thing I knew I was hoisted into the air and over someone's shoulder. Instinctively I started to pound on their back.

"Calm down," I heard a familiar voice say. "It's okay. I'm getting you out of here."

It was Cole! I would have recognized that voice anywhere. I was so shocked I didn't say anything. Cole was moving quickly and Beaver's voice sounded farther and farther away. Before I knew it, we were back on a camp path. Cole put me down and looked at me. He was in a tee and sweats.

"You just saved my life!" I told him, and without caring what he thought, I wrapped my arms around him and hugged him. Neither of us let go for a while, and we just stood there quietly. I could feel my heart pounding out of my chest and I wondered if he could too. Finally, I reluctantly unwrapped myself. "What are you doing here?"

"I was looking for you," he said as if it was obvious.

Me? Cole was looking for me?

"Walk and I'll explain," he said. "We should get you back to your bunk before Beaver starts inspecting them to see who's missing."

We walked back in silence, but I kept stealing glances at him out of the corner of my eye. "I'm sorry I tried to hit you," I apologized.

"I'm sorry if I scared you. You've got a strong arm!" He laughed. "I came looking for you at your cabin and saw you guys heading down to the lake so I followed you. I guess it's a good thing I did, huh?"

"You saw the prank we pulled?" I asked in alarm.

Cole stopped and looked at me. "What prank?" he said innocently. "I didn't see you do anything down at the lake involving clothes and a boat."

I should have known Cole wouldn't say anything. "Thanks," I said, relieved. But I still had an unanswered question for him. "But, um, why were you coming to see me?"

My heart was pounding again. This time it was a different kind of fear. I was anxious to hear what Cole had to say.

"You were keeping me awake tonight," Cole admitted.

If I wasn't trying to avoid Beaver's capture, I think I would have fainted on the spot. "I was? But I was far away in bunk 8B." I was trying to be flirty, but I was nervous.

"I couldn't stop thinking about you before bed," Cole said. "There was something I wanted to ask you."

He turned toward me. Even though I felt dizzy, I stopped and turned too.

"I was wondering," Cole started to say. "I mean, I was hoping . . ."

"SAM!" someone whisper-shouted.

It was Court. I whipped my head around and saw Grace sprinting toward me. Court and Em were moving slowly behind her.

As glad as I was to see they got away, I kind of wished they weren't there at that moment.

"Cole, what are you doing here?" Grace asked as she reached me. "We were so worried! I thought you were going to get caught, Sam."

"I got away just in time," I said as Court slowly made her way over with Em. "Cole rescued me."

"What were you doing down at the lake?" Court asked. She looked at me curiously.

"Don't ask and I won't ask what you guys were doing there yourselves," Cole teased. Court laughed nervously.

"We better get back to the bunk," Court said. "I'm sure Beaver has alerted the counselors and they're going to be doing bunk checks any minute."

"You should go," Cole told me, but his face told a different story.

"You too," I said awkwardly. "But . . . ?" I left the sentence hanging there, hoping Cole would finish it.

"We'll talk some other time," he said and looked at my friends. "Goodnight, ladies." Then he turned and headed back to his cabin.

Grace grabbed my arm and the four of us hurried back to our bunk. I couldn't stop thinking about Cole. I had a feeling I would be the one tossing and turning now.

🌿 🌿 🌿

I was awakened the next morning by an ear-piercing scream.

"Where are my clothes?" Ashley was shrieking. She was in the cubby area and she was examining all the clothing places and running back and forth to her empty trunk. "Where the hell are my shoes?"

Ashley was always the first one out of bed in the morning. She liked to be the first one in the shower if she was showering before breakfast. She was a pro at using up all the hot water.

"Ash, calm down, maybe you just — OMG! Where is my stuff?" Gabby freaked out as she walked in behind her and saw all the empty cubbies. She ran to her trunk. That was almost empty too, except for the ratty things we had left behind.

I was sitting up. I looked over at the next bunk, where Grace was sitting up also. We didn't say anything, but we knew what to do. We jumped out of bed and acted alarmed. Em and Court were right behind us.

"Has anyone seen my gray sweatpants?" I asked as I reached my cubby.

"My Nikes are missing!" Em said, sounding shocked.

"Who cares about your stupid sneakers!" Ashley screamed. "Practically every piece of clothing I have is missing."

"Do you think it was those marshmallows, Ash?" Gabby

whispered. "You know, the girls you made cart the sleepover snacks? The ones you told to leave? They've been jealous of us all summer."

"They wouldn't be this stupid," Ashley said.

"Where is my navy sweater?" Court interrupted. "It's missing!" Her acting was perfect. I would never have known that she was the mastermind behind this whole prank.

"You mean the one I spilled ice cream on last week?" Gabby snapped. "Who cares about your ugly sweater? I'm missing my outfit for the dance!"

"Me too!" Ashley moaned. "I just knew it was a bad idea to tell everyone I was wearing Bebe!"

I glanced at Court out of the corner of my eye. She was smirking and she turned away. I will not laugh, I willed myself. I will not laugh.

Meg came running from her room, still in her pj's. "What's wrong?" she asked just as there was a knock at the cabin door. "Come in!"

It was Hitch and he was carrying a huge black bag that smelled like swamp water. I had a strong hunch I knew what was in there.

"I believe this belongs to this bunk," he said seriously. "At daybreak, when I was taking my morning jog, I saw a canoe floating in the middle of the lake. Donovan swam out and retrieved it and we found all these clothes inside that had this bunk's names on them. Someone obviously played a prank on you guys."

"That's it?" Ashley shrieked. "That's all you have to say? Daddy, I want whoever did this expelled."

Hitch chuckled. "Ashley, that's a little harsh. Thankfully, no harm was done — this is very different than what happened last time — but you may want to do some laundry since it rained this morning and everything is wet." Ashley continued to stare at him and Hitch cleared his throat. "I will be issuing a warning during announcements this morning. I do not want campers out of bed after curfew. It's dangerous."

Gabby grabbed the bag from Hitch and opened it, pulling out Ashley's green American Eagle shirt. She jumped back in disgust. "Eww! Everything smells like pond water."

"One of you did this," Ashley whirled around and turned to the rest of us. "I know it. You're jealous because I didn't want any of you at my sleepover."

"Ashley Suzanne Hitchens!" Hitch said sternly. "We agreed not to talk about the party in front of people who weren't coming, remember?"

"Ash, that makes no sense," said Meg as she began sorting through the smelly clothes. "Some of their stuff is in here too."

"But *all* of my stuff is in here!" Ashley yelled, hopping up and down in frustration. "I have nothing to wear today but a pair of skuzzy sweatpants or farty pj's that I hate!"

"Borrow some of your bunkmates' clothes," Meg suggested.

Ashley rolled her eyes. "I'm too thin to wear their stuff. It would fall off."

"Pul-eeze," Court couldn't help blurting out. "She wishes."

Meg handed Ashley the bag and smiled sweetly. "Well, if that's the case, then I guess you'll have to do laundry before breakfast. It will be quicker if you all do it together, since you all have stuff in the bag."

Ashley and Gabby dragged the bag past us and we followed. I was trying hard not to look at Grace, Em, or Court, so that I didn't give us away.

Victory was ours.

A few feet from the cabin, Ashley stopped suddenly and faced the four of us. "I'm going to find out who did this," she said in a low voice. "I know it was one of you. And when I figure out who it was, you're going to be supremely sorry."

▲ 15 ▲
The Hunt

I wanted to throw up.

Either that or I was going to jump off the stage and run screaming from the auditorium at any moment. Brooke, our drama instructor, was definitely wrong about me: I didn't have a bright future in the theater. I was standing on the Pines stage in full costume alongside the other CITs and counselors as Hitch explained the rules to the Guess the Counselor game hunt and all I could think about was the fact that I was less than an hour away from confessing to Cole that I seriously liked him.

"For those of you who are new to the Guess the Counselor game, let me explain how this works," Hitch instructed the entire camp from the front of the stage using his trusty megaphone. I secretly prayed he'd run out of batteries for it before the end of camp. It had started to squeak when he talked and sometimes you had to hold your ears the noise was so bad.

The auditorium was nothing like the one we had at school. Basically it was a big room with a basketball court for a floor.

There were folding chairs for seating and large rotating fans to keep everyone cool. (Or should I say they were *attempting* to keep everyone cool. With another heat wave hitting the area, the most you could hope for was a quick breeze passing through one of the large windows. Thankfully the sun would be going down soon and offer more relief. The auditorium smelled musty from the heat, and everywhere I looked kids were fanning themselves with the counselor hunt rules memo that Hitch had passed out earlier.) Lining the auditorium walls were camp posters and banners, similar to the ones in the mess hall. One heralding our upcoming talent show, written in sparkly purple lettering, was front and center. I had to admit, Court's routine was so fun that I was secretly looking forward to performing now. The other big banner was a replica of ones that were littering the camp: COLOR WAR IS FOUR DAYS AWAY! The countdown had begun and it was all anyone could talk about.

"Counselors and CITs are going to be hiding around camp in costume. The remaining staff, like Mrs. Morberry, Cara, Beaver and a few counselors," Hitch continued, "including myself, will be patrolling the grounds to help campers. After the counselors have had twenty minutes to hide, you may all head out with your bunks to search for them. Bunks should stay together for this game. When you come across a counselor, you will have three guesses as to who is behind the mask. Get the answer right, and your team wins a point. Once a counselor has been identified, they are out of the game and must go to our makeshift jail at the mess hall. The team with the most points at nine PM will be the winner and will get a free snack at the canteen every day for the rest of the week." A loud cheer rose from the heat-exhausted crowd.

"Less than an hour till you tell Cole you like him," Court reminded me. As if I needed reminding. She was dressed as Kermit the Frog. We had painted her with washable green paint and she was wearing green clothing. I thought she kind of looked like the Jolly Green Giant, but Court got mad when I said that. I was dressed as a rag doll. (Alexis came up with the idea.) I had white pancake makeup, big, red rouge circles on my cheeks, oversized glasses, fake red eyebrows, a clown nose, striped stockings, a baby doll dress, and red hair made of yarn. Court thought my costume was cheesy. Well, it wasn't as cheesy as Gabby being Catwoman. (She must have been sweating in those black leather pants.) Not one to be topped, Ashley went with the superhero theme as well. She was Wonder Woman, so she was wearing a black wig, a small gold eye mask, and a skintight leotard with stars on it that matched her gold go-go boots.

Ashley must have had ESP because at that moment, she turned her head and gave me a nasty look.

I knew she thought — rightly so — I was one of the culprits behind last week's prank. None of Ashley's and Gabby's clothes got ruined, but Ashley was still angry, mostly because she hadn't been able to prove it was us that did it. The good news was that Ashley wasn't talking to any of us (except Gabby, of course), so camp life had been attitude-free for a few days.

Still, I was convinced the truce would be short-lived. There was no way Ashley was not going to get us back for humiliating her. It was just a matter of time before I woke up covered in honey and feathers or found my bras swinging from the top of the flagpole.

"I've been thinking and I'm not sure telling Cole I like him during the game is such a good idea," I whispered to Court as Hitch continued talking. "I'm dressed as a rag doll! It's kind of hard to confess you like someone when you're wearing a yarn wig. Maybe I should just tell him the normal way, you know? Plus, how do I know I'm even going to find Cole? I have no clue what his costume is."

"Trust me, this is a good idea. And how hard could it be to figure out who he is?" she said as she glanced around the stage.

Very hard if you asked me. Most of the male counselors were smart enough to wear masks or papier-mâché heads. They were dressed in giant costumes like the Hulk, Barney, and a panda bear. Cole could be any of them, including the knight in armor, Darth Vader, Batman, or even that henchman from the movie *Scream*. I knew he wasn't Tarzan — that chiseled torso belonged to Court's beloved Donovan.

"Okay, this is going to be more difficult than I thought," Court admitted, reading my thoughts. "Usually the costumes are as lame as Gabby's and you can tell who someone is right away, but I guess this year the guys went all out."

"I have to find someone who knows who Cole is," I decided. "Then I have to get to him before a group of campers do *and* find my own hiding space before Hitch realizes I'm not actually playing the game."

"You can do it," Court said encouragingly. "When you find Cole, I think you should run up to him and kiss him."

I had to cover my mouth to keep from laughing. Kissing was all Court thought about. "I'm not sure that's the best approach," I said delicately.

I did have an overwhelming urge to kiss Cole. I'd had it for a while, but ever since he'd rescued me from Beaver the other night, I couldn't get the thought out of my head. I should have just done it then, when I had the chance. Cole must have had to ask me something important if he snuck out of his bunk to do it. What could it have been? I wanted to ask, but every time I saw Cole, someone interrupted us. Grace thought he wanted to ask me to go to the camp dance with him, which was during the last week of camp. If that was true, then that meant Cole definitely liked me. Just the thought of Cole liking me as much as I liked him made me melt faster than the Firecracker ice pop I'd gotten at the canteen that afternoon.

"So are there any questions?" I heard Hitch ask the revved-up crowd. For the first time tonight, the room was actually quiet. "Well, then, before I dismiss the counselors and CITS, I have more big news to announce — the names of this year's Color War captains."

The crowd got very excited. I glanced sideways at Grace, who was standing stoically. She had wanted that title since she was six.

"This year's Color War captains — who won't be able to celebrate at this exact moment for fear of their costumes being exposed — are Grace Weidinger, Tim Conway, Grady James, and Amy Josephs!" The crowd cheered. Court and I were louder than anyone onstage. Grace had to be ready to burst. "Details about

Color War will come soon, after I've met with the captains, but in the meantime, let's start tonight's game. It's time for the counselors and CITs to go into hiding. Good luck!"

We moved off the stage as quickly as we could. It was kind of hard when some of us were wearing such clunky costumes. Barney couldn't fit between the stair railings and had to be helped off the stage.

"Have you had any luck figuring out who they are yet?" Em appeared at my side. She was dressed as Minnie Mouse and she looked adorable with her big black ears, black foam nose, and red polka dot dress that she had borrowed from the camp secretary, Mrs. Morberry.

I shook my head. "They could be anyone," I complained. "The only way to find out is to get someone to tell us. Maybe if we can track down one of the other male CITs we can get him to spill the beans."

Em nodded. "Good idea. First we have to find another CIT. I'll head toward the lake and you head toward the upper campus. If either of us finds out who someone is, we'll meet on the path up to the bunks, right next to the water fountain — that is, if we're not captured first."

"Good luck," we both said. Em and I shook on it and headed in opposite directions.

It wasn't long before I came across Grace, who was posing regally in the middle of the tennis courts. She was dressed as the Statue of Liberty and her face was a funny shade of green. She saw me and frowned. "Sam, you're going to give me away! No one can see you talking to me."

I laughed. "Grace, you're standing in the middle of the tennis courts," I pointed out. "It's not going to be hard to find you."

Grace itched her left calf. All that green paint must have been miserable in the heat. "Yeah, well, I thought I'd help the peeps and hide somewhere easy. They still have to figure out who I am though and my crown is so big, I doubt they'll be able to do that."

"Congrats on the Color War pick, captain," I said.

Grace attempted a smile, her makeup cracking. "Can you believe it? I've always wanted to be captain and now I finally get my chance! I think it's so cool that Tim got picked too. We're both going to be such strong leaders." She sighed. "So, any sign of Cole?"

"This was a stupid idea," I said miserably. "There is no way I'm going to find him when he's in disguise."

Grace looked thoughtful. "You need to think about the type of costume Cole would pick. Has he ever talked to you about his favorite movies or anything? If he likes *Star Wars* then he's probably the one dressed as Darth Vader."

I gave her a skeptical look. "Are you saying there is a chance that one of the CITs or counselors actually watches Barney?"

She seemed to be having trouble moving her lips. "I see your point," she said. Her face brightened. "I do know someone you could hunt down and ask about Cole. Tim is dressed as Kung Fu Panda — but you didn't hear that from me."

My excitement at having a lead was momentarily forgotten with the news about Tim's costume choice. He was a jock, just like Grace, and I'd pictured him being something more active, like a lion tamer. There was one of those running around in a big, long-haired wig. "King Fu Panda?" I couldn't help asking. I tried not to smirk.

"I think it's cute," Grace said stiffly. "You know just because —" She paused. "Campers! They're coming this way."

The two of us turned around. Heading right toward us were definitely peeps, and they were being trailed by Mrs. Morberry. As they got closer, I spotted Mackenzie's pigtails. I had put her hair in them just before dinner when she complained it was hot out. "They're mine," I said breathlessly. "If they figure out who I am, I'll never get to tell Cole anything."

"Just stay calm," Grace said. "They're peeps, remember? Be happy they aren't marshmallows."

"We see you!" I heard Serena yell. She started running up the path ahead of the rest of the girls. She stopped when she saw Grace and me and I inhaled sharply. "You're Ashley!" she said, pointing at Grace. Grace shook her head. "Then you're Ashley," she said to me. I shook my head.

"Don't say a name till everyone gets here," reminded Mrs. Morberry gently.

"Hitch said we only get three picks," Callie told the girls. She whispered to the other excited little girls and they nodded in agreement. "Are one of you Meg?"

Whoo hoo! Two picks down. Grace and I shook our heads.

"I know who the rag doll is," Mackenzie shrieked suddenly. She ran up to me and I tried not to look her in the eye. My heart was racing. Mackenzie squinted intently. "Alexis!" I exhaled and shook my head. She looked at Grace, disappointed. "Are you Alexis?"

"No," Grace said in a deep voice. "That's three guesses. Sorry! Good luck."

The girls trudged off, looking dejected, and I almost felt bad for them. This was a pretty tough game for six-year-olds. I was surprised we didn't give them clues.

"That was close," I said to Grace. "I'm going to get out of here before anyone else comes looking." I didn't get much farther before my path was blocked by a group of pez arguing over which cabin to explore. I ducked into the trees to avoid being seen. When I came out the other side, I took a shortcut behind the arts and crafts cabin and almost ran right into Alexis, who was dressed as a fairy. I dove in front of the porch before she could turn her heavy wings around and see me.

My best bet was to get back to the path down to the lake and find Em. Maybe she had better luck than I did. The first area of the path was deserted, but as soon as I reached the hill leading to the lake I stopped and rested by a moss-covered rock. It was getting dark and that was only going to make it harder to find Cole. I bitterly swatted a mosquito away. That was when I saw Court whiz by me.

"HEY!" She spotted me and backtracked. She sat down on the rock next to me. Her dark hair, also sprayed green, was covered in pine needles. She must have been cutting through the woods. "A group of pez almost spotted me so I bolted," Court said, sounding out of breath.

I laughed. "Court! You're not supposed to move once you've gone into hiding. The campers are supposed to find you."

Court folded her arms defiantly. "You're one to talk. You haven't even gone into hiding yet!"

"That's true," I admitted sheepishly. "I'm still looking for Cole." I relayed what Grace said. "She thinks I should find Tim and he may tell me what Cole is."

"What's he dressed up as?" Court asked me.

"Kung Fu Panda." I giggled.

Court grabbed my arm, getting green paint on my white shirt. "Sam, I just saw a panda hanging out by the counselor lounge! That must be Tim!" The two of us looked at each other. "I'll go with you," Court said. "We'll take the woods. No one will see us."

It was hard to move quickly with all the trees and branches. First, my wig got pulled off by an unruly bush. Then Court snagged her green stockings on a tree trunk. Even though the sun hadn't gone down completely yet it was dark in the woods; the only thing I could see was Court's flashlight leading the way. Finally we made it to a clearing. Court held me back as a group of pez marched by with a disgusted-looking Gabby. Elmo, whoever he was, was right behind her with some marshmallows. When the coast was clear, we ran for it. After a detour around the inground pool, we made it to the counselor lounge where Tim was sitting on the steps. Even without Grace's tip, I would have known it was Tim. He was sitting with his panda head in his hands and his hair and face were drenched with sweat.

"What are you guys doing up here?" he demanded when

he saw us. He fumbled to put the panda head back on, but it tumbled down the steps.

"It's okay, Tim," I told him. "It's Sam and Court." I reached down to pick the mask up. I handed it back to him. "We're not spying. We were looking for you."

"Is Grace okay?" Tim asked, looking concerned. "I told her the tennis courts were a dead giveaway."

Court elbowed me. "I think Grace is fine. Congrats on the Color War news."

Tim beamed proudly. "Thanks. I'm really stoked."

"Tim, we were hoping you could help us find someone," Court said. "Cole. Do you know what he's dressed as?"

"We're not supposed to give away costumes, remember?" Tim pointed out. "It ruins the fun of the game."

No wonder Grace liked Tim. He was just as anal about camp tradition as she was. "I know," I said. "I won't tell anyone who Cole is. I just need to know myself. There's something really important I have to tell him."

Tim looked at me curiously and smirked. "OH," he said in a way that made me think he knew what I was talking about. "Okay. Cole is a knight," he said. "He's been eyeing that costume for weeks."

YES! Now I just had to get to him before a group of pez did. "Thanks, Tim! I owe you one. Court, wish me luck!" I yelled as I took off running down the dirt path.

"Don't be a chicken!" Court yelled back.

Before I even reached the cabins, I found my path blocked by Barney. Since I didn't know who was inside the purple dinosaur costume, I quickly ducked behind a tree. I wasn't fast enough though because Barney saw me. I looked into the spooky, darkened woods and heard an owl hoot in the distance. Or was it a wolf? The woods were my only chance of losing Barney. I'd done it once already, I could do it again. I turned on my flashlight, pushed a few branches out of the way, inhaled sharply and walked in.

"Sam!" I heard a muffled voice yell. "SAM!"

I turned around and flashed my light in the trees around me. Barney was wedged between two trees. I couldn't just leave him there so I rushed over and pushed his purple tail till he wiggled free.

"Thanks," Barney said and pulled off his mask. It was Dylan! His face was dripping with sweat. It must have been so hot in that thing. "Grace told me you were a rag doll. That's why I followed you. Have you seen Em?"

I shook my head. "No, but she might be down by the lake, and that's where I'm headed," I said. "She's dressed as Minnie Mouse."

"I'll walk with you," he offered. "Just in case I get stuck again."

I wasn't about to protest. Walking with someone in the woods was much better than going alone. It took us fifteen minutes to get to the lake — Dylan got stuck about four times, I tripped over a few rocks, and then we had to search for my wig again (it was stuck on a tree branch) — and when we finally made it, the place was deserted. Either the campers had given up on the area, or whoever had been hiding down there was already captured.

"Don't look so disappointed. Em could still be down here," Dylan said, not knowing who I was really looking for. "We'll head in different directions."

"AH HA!" A group of pez popped out from behind a nearby tree. "We have you!"

Dylan and I froze. I tried not to panic. I couldn't be this close and get caught now. The pez were older than the peeps, usually nine to eleven, and much more savvy. They circled us like we were their supper. Every once in a while they would whisper something to one another. Dylan and I stood back-to-back, waiting.

"You first," one of the pez said to me. "Our first guess is Gabby!"

"She's already been captured," I said in a high-pitched voice. "I saw it happen."

The group huddled together again, whispering. "Our next guess is Colleen!"

I shook my head. Just one more guess . . .

"Then you have to be . . ." A girl approached me and gave me the evil eye. "You have to be . . ." I held my breath. "You have to be Grace!"

"Wrong again," I squeaked. The pez looked disappointed, but I wanted to jump up and down and celebrate. They turned to Dylan. He had to get off too.

"We captured Tim, and Gavin is the lion tamer," the pez recounted out loud. "We've narrowed down who we think Cole and Hunter are so you must be . . . DYLAN!"

I couldn't believe it. They guessed right! Now Em would never get to tell him.

Dylan removed his head. "You've got me," he said with a smile. He looked at me and shrugged. "Good luck finding who you're looking for. Let them know I was looking for them too," he added cryptically.

One of the pez grabbed his arm. "Let's take him to jail," he said.

"Shouldn't we look for Cole first? Someone on the path said they saw a knight heading this way a few minutes ago. He's got to be down here somewhere."

"I don't see anyone," one of the others protested. "Let's just take Dylan and score a point and worry about Cole later. He's probably in the boathouse thinking no one would look there because it's usually locked. That's where my brother hid last year when he was a counselor. Apparently they unlock the boathouse for the hunt. We'll come back for him if we have time."

I wanted to reach over and kiss that pez right on the cheek! I couldn't believe they weren't rushing over to check right now. But their loss was my gain. If Cole was spotted coming this way and the boathouse was unlocked, then he could be in there. It was the only hiding place at the lake I could think of other than lying in one of the canoes. But they always had lake water hanging out in the bottom and were all moldy. Eww.

"Guys, we only have a half hour left," said one of the pez. "Let's get Dylan to the jail before it's too late."

They headed off, leaving me alone again and my eyes

narrowed in on the small, wooden boathouse. Instead of running, however, my feet felt like they were glued to the sand. I was possibly thisclose to finding Cole and part of me suddenly didn't want to. My hands felt sweaty, my mouth was dry, and I was beginning to hyperventilate. Maybe I wasn't ready to do this after all.

"I thought I saw a counselor go this way!" I heard a camper yell.

Maybe I didn't have a choice. The boat shack was a few feet away. I could make it inside before I was spotted. I fumbled for the door and miraculously it really was unlocked. I shut it quietly behind me and looked around hopefully in the dark. There didn't seem to be anyone in here. Disappointed, I waited till I heard the campers run by to continue my search.

The shack was kind of spooky at night. The only way I could see was the illumination of the moon shining in the windows. I tried not to think about spiders and counted the seconds till the coast was clear. That's when I heard a noise. I spun around and there in the moonlight was a knight. Cole! I gasped.

My heart started beating madly and I thought I would pass out. This was really happening. I was alone with Cole and I was about to tell him the truth. Cole moved to take off his mask. "No! Wait. Don't do that!" I blurted out. I could barely breath I was so nervous. I had to do this and I had to do it quickly. "I know it sounds silly, but I have something to say and it might be easier if I wasn't looking into your eyes."

I closed my eyes and tried to think of the words I'd practiced over and over in my head a hundred times before: I like you and here is why. I could hear them, but I couldn't get myself to say them out loud. I was too nervous to do it. "I . . ." I couldn't do this. Telling someone you liked them was harder than I imagined. How did boys do it? "I . . ." Think of Cole, I told myself.

I pictured Cole laughing at the mess hall, his curls bouncing as he held his stomach. I thought of that moment when he tackled me to the ground during Capture the Flag and took a few seconds longer than he should have rolling off me. I could see his bluer-than-Court's-bright-blue-nail-polish eyes looking at me at a campfire when he gave me his last roasted marshmallow. How he helped me through the woods to avoid being seen by Beaver the night of the prank. Cole wasn't afraid of being caught even if I was.

And that's when I realized: What exactly was I afraid of now? I'd liked Cole almost the entire summer and this was the first time I'd been afraid to be myself around him. That was silly, wasn't it? I'd never pretended to be someone else around him before and I wasn't about to do it now. I pulled off my wig and stared at his suit of armor.

"There is something I've wanted to say to you for weeks," I said slowly. "It's something I've never said to a guy before, but I know if I don't say it to you, I'll always regret it." I took a deep breath, letting the air fill my lungs before I finally spoke. "I like you," I blurted out. "I really like you and I hope what you were trying to tell me the other night was that you like me too."

There. I said it. I stood there in the dark, breathing in the smell of wet wood and I waited for Cole to say something. The seconds felt like hours. An owl hooted and I was still waiting.

And then Cole removed his mask and I heard myself scream, as if I was standing outside my body.

"I think you're looking for Cole," Hunter said, shaking his sweaty hair. I could faintly make out a smile on his lips. "But I like your forwardness, champ." Then he walked toward me, his armor creaking, while I stood cemented to the ground. Before I knew what was happening, Hunter grabbed my face, tilted my chin, pulled me toward him, and kissed me.

The seconds felt like hours. Before I could even react, I heard the doorknob to the boathouse jingle. "I bet someone is hiding in here," I heard someone say as Hunter kissed me. Terrified of getting caught with the wrong guy, I stayed frozen like a statue, knowing that a single sound from us and we'd be caught for sure. Please don't open the door. Please, please, please don't open the door. . . .

When camp started that summer, I used to wonder what a kiss from Hunter would be like. I would lie in my bunk and imagine what his lips felt like, what he smelled like, how experienced he was in the kissing department. And yet, now that it was actually happening, I was . . . disappointed. Hunter's lips were rough and he kissed me hard, almost banging my lips with every semi-sloppy lock. He was a pro, but it wasn't what I was looking for.

"We checked there already!" someone else said and I heard them leave just as quickly.

I pulled away from Hunter and looked at him. Part of me wanted to hit him, but he was a senior counselor. That move was out of the question. "But I'm supposed to kiss Cole," I said stupidly.

Hunter touched my cheek. "Maybe. But I've wanted to see what it would be like to kiss you all summer." He leaned forward again and I stumbled backward. A shadow passed Hunter's face and I turned around. Someone was staring in the boathouse window. I quickly opened the door. Ashley was standing there in her Wonder Woman costume, smiling wickedly.

I heard a whistle. The game was over. I looked from Ashley to Hunter, who was now standing in the boathouse doorway, holding his helmet, and the only thing I could think of doing was run. I ran as fast as I could, past a group of campers, past the horse stables, and didn't stop till I reached the main part of campus. I didn't know how to feel at that moment. My body and mind were numb. I was angry at Hunter, even though part of me was sort of flattered — when had a guy ever said something like that to me before? — and I was freaked out and upset that Ashley saw us. But my biggest concern was Cole. He was going to find out.

If I could have kept running, all the way back to Carle Place, I might have, but my lungs were on fire and my feet finally gave out. I stopped in front of one of the large leafy trees and rested my head on the bark.

Someone grabbed my shoulder and I whirled around. If it was Ashley, I was going to yell. Instead, there was a Scream mask inches from my face. Before I could react, the mask came off. It was Cole. I felt woozy.

"You were supposed to be a knight," I said weakly.

"Sorry to disappoint you," Cole said with one of his trademark adorable grins. "I wanted to be the knight, but Hunter pulled rank and I got stuck with this at the last minute." He pointed to his black robe and mask. "Pretty lame, huh?" He laughed.

But I didn't feel like laughing. My hands were cold and it wasn't because it was nine at night and we were in the mountains. The guilt was overwhelming me and my mouth was so dry I could barely speak. Hunter kissed me, my brain wanted to scream, but my mouth thankfully kept quiet.

Hunter kissed me and I didn't stop him. And Ashley saw me. Ashley saw me! She was going to tell Cole. He wouldn't know that it was all an honest mistake on my part. And then any chance I had at being with Cole would be over.

"Don't say anything," Cole said. "I want to ask you this before we're interrupted again." He moved closer and grabbed my hand. His felt warm and sweaty. "What I was trying to tell you the other night was that I wanted you to go to the dance with me. I know that probably sounds strange since everyone at camp has to go to the dance, but I want to feel like I'm there with you and only you."

Cole was saying exactly what I hoped he'd say and I couldn't even look at him. I was staring at the ground. He put a finger under my chin and made me look at him and I thought I might cry. My perfect moment with Cole was ruined because of Hunter, and I knew that when Cole found out he would be crushed.

"Sam, I like you," he said. "I've liked you for a while and I wanted you to know."

"Cole," I said hoarsely. I should tell him right now what happened. Before he heard it from someone else. It wasn't fair to keep it from him. I had to be honest. It was an honest mistake. An accident. He *had* to understand. Right? "Cole, listen," I started to say.

Somewhere far away I heard Hitch's whistle again. Cole tugged on my hand.

"We should get to the mess hall, but you have to give me an answer first," he teased.

A group of screaming campers ran by us and my heart sank. I couldn't tell Cole in front of other people. We needed to be alone. Here. Now. And we had to go. "Cole, I . . ."

Even in a black robe, Cole couldn't help but look good. His curly hair was kind of matted thanks to the *Scream* mask, but his eyes looked amazing in the moonlight. His face was so open and hopeful.

"Cole, we've got to go!" one of his bunkmates yelled as he hurried past.

Cole pulled on my hand again and I looked down at our fingers. They were intertwined. I was afraid to let go. "Of course I'll go with you to the dance," I said.

That made Cole smile wider, which only made me feel worse. "I was hoping you'd say that," he said. "Ready to go?"

I wanted to hold Cole's hand and walk back to the mess hall more than anything, but I couldn't. I felt too guilty. I shook my head. "I have to wait for Em," I said. "You go ahead."

Thankfully, Cole didn't question me. "Don't take too long."

"I promise," I said weakly.

When Cole was gone, I sank onto the grass and let the tree support my limp body. Maybe they could plant me there and I'd never have to move.

"Sam! Sam!" I heard Em's voice. "Guys, she's over here." Em ran over. "We just saw Cole *and he was smiling!*" Em said gleefully. "Did you tell him, Sam? Because I was all set to tell Dylan when I got captured. Then Dylan turned up in the holding cell and he said it to me first. We're going to the dance together!"

My face must have said it all because suddenly Em's face was dark and it wasn't because the moon had just hidden behind a few clouds. "Sam?" she said nervously.

"She doesn't look good," Grace said, leaning down to my level and taking my pulse. "Sam? Talk to us."

"She's fine!" Court said. "She's probably just in shock. Did you kiss Cole? What happened? Was he a bad kisser?"

I never got to answer that question. Ashley was standing right in front of us.

"Hi girls," she said, a little too cheerfully. "Did you have fun?" She smirked at me. "I know you did, Sam, but we can talk later. Kiss kiss!"

Court looked at me. "What is she talking about? Did Ashley see you kiss Cole? Who cares! I'm so proud of you! You did it, Sam! How was it?"

I felt faint. "No," I said weakly. "*Hunter* kissed me. And Ashley saw it happen."

⚴ 16 ⚴

Confession Is Good for the Soul

Saying the truth out loud didn't make it any easier to swallow. Nor did it make it easier for my friends to understand.

"How could this have happened?" Grace asked for what felt like the millionth time as Court kept my palmcorder on me to record my misery.

"I was in shock," I said miserably, going over the moment yet again. "I'd said everything in my heart to the wrong guy. By the time I realized what was happening, Hunter had started kissing me. He just heard me say all these things he knew were meant for Cole and yet he kissed me anyway! How could he do that to Cole, his CIT? Or to me?" I buried my head in my lap. "I can't believe I kissed Hunter."

"Would you stop blaming yourself as always?" Court reprimanded me. "Hunter kissed *you*. He's the bad guy here."

It was almost three hours after the infamous Hunter incident and I was supposed to be tucked into my bunk bed dreaming about kissing Cole. Except it wasn't Cole who had kissed me, it was Hunter. My perfect daydream had turned into a nightmare.

That was why we had snuck out to the canteen shack. Even though it was risky to sneak out right now with Ashley and Gabby watching our every move, everyone agreed that my crisis deserved an emergency sleepaway girls meeting.

The canteen was the first place we thought of, since Hunter had already found us in the mess hall kitchen. The canteen was dark, but we had our flashlights and I could see bags of potato chips and mounds of candy bars lining the shelves. The freezer, full of ice cream and frozen yogurt pops, purred in protest of our arrival. I could have eaten everything in the room and it still wouldn't have calmed my nerves.

No one wanted to risk turning on the lights and getting caught so we took a seat on the floor and placed our flashlights in a circle. The light illuminated our faces, making us look pale and nervous, which was exactly how I felt.

"Are you sure no one saw us leave?" Em took a puff of her inhaler. "I could have sworn I saw Ashley's head pop up when we left the bunk."

"You're just imagining things," Court said dismissively. "They were both asleep. Gabby was snoring louder than Ashley."

"Were they real snores?" Grace asked, worriedly. "Maybe they were trying to trick us. If Ashley saw Hunter and Sam kissing, she's not going to wait long to take Sam down." Grace looked panicked. "And us with her! If she saw us sneak out tonight, I could lose my Color War captain status!"

Grace looked like she was going to bolt, but Court grabbed her arm. "You won't lose your Color War title, okay? They were asleep. I swear. Ashley would not miss her beauty sleep to tell Cole what she saw." Court looked at me. "She'll do it in the morning."

I moaned. "There is no fixing this, is there? What I did is beyond forgivable."

"Stop it!" Grace yelled. "Hunter is the one who should be apologizing. He knew you were giving this big speech about Cole and then he came on to you anyway. He's such a pig." Grace rolled her eyes. "I'm going to tell him that when I see him!"

"Ooh, this is good," Court said and turned the camera on her. "I like Grace angry."

"I'm not sure this is a memory I want to keep," I complained. I held my hands to my stomach and curled into a ball. No one said anything for a minute.

"Did you kiss him back?" Court asked suddenly. I hit her. So did Em. "What? It's an honest question! You're all wondering the same thing and you know it."

"I don't think I did," I said tentatively. "My lips were frozen. I know Hunter is gorgeous, and it was obvious he knew what he was doing in the lip-lock department. I was in shock. I didn't feel any fireworks. I was actually disappointed."

Em nodded appreciatively. "You wanted a first kiss and Hunter gave you sloppy seconds. It happens all the time in my books. A kiss doesn't feel right if it's not from the right guy."

"A kiss is a kiss," Court scoffed.

"You're just saying that because you probably haven't had a great one yet," Em said defensively. "Kisses are different depending on who they're from."

"You kissed Dylan, didn't you?" Court freaked.

"SHHHHH!" We hushed her. Em covered her face with her hands.

"Em, I'm so proud of you!" Court said, jumping up and down. Court's camera work was going to be all over the place. I was sure when I watched it, I would throw up. Not that I didn't feel like doing that already.

"I didn't want to say anything because Sam was so upset," Em said awkwardly, "but Dylan kissed me after he asked me to the dance and it was . . . perfect." She had a dreamy expression on her face.

I grabbed her hand. "Em, I would have been happy for you. I *am* happy for you! Just because I screwed up doesn't mean your big moment doesn't matter."

Em smiled shyly. "Thanks. I keep replaying it in my head. I actually banged my head on his chin when he leaned in to kiss me, but then we laughed, got our positions just right, and he kissed me."

Grace sighed. "That does sound perfect."

"It really does," I agreed, feeling sorry for myself all over again, which was terrible, I know, because we were supposed to be enjoying Em's moment.

"Oh, Sam, don't worry," Em said, putting an arm around me. "It'll work out."

I buried my head in her shoulder. "I don't know about that.

I screwed up big time. I think what makes this whole disaster worse was that it happened with Hunter. Cole knows I used to like Hunter. Now he's going to think I liked Hunter this entire time."

"He won't because the truth is you don't actually *like* Hunter," Court reminded me. "Yes, you thought he was hot. It's okay to think someone is hot other than the guy you like. Like, I love Joe Jonas, but that doesn't mean I like Donovan any less. I have zero chance with Joe Jonas. At least there's some possibility with Donovan."

"I think what Court is trying to say is that Cole has to appreciate the fact that Hunter does want you — that's obvious now — but you don't want him," said Em. "You want Cole."

"Em's right. You just have to get to Cole before Ashley does," Grace said darkly. "If she tells him first, she's going to spin the story differently, like she did to the peeps with your commercial. You won't be able to explain how you told Hunter your speech was for Cole, and he kissed you, not the other way around. That's the most important thing to stress. Your lips were meant for Cole that night, not Hunter. You have to make him understand that it's him you want, not his senior counselor."

I groaned some more. Why did love have to be so complicated? At the start of the summer, all I was looking for was some independence. I didn't even think I'd grab one guy's attention, let alone two.

"Cole is a good guy," Em said to me. "When you tell him you like him, he's going to realize that you don't like Hunter and that the kiss was completely accidental."

"And what if he can't forgive that it was Hunter?" I asked quietly.

"Then he wasn't worth your time anyway," Em said simply.

I didn't think that was true, but I knew Em was just trying to make me feel better. I covered my face with my hands and took a few deep breaths. They were right. It was an accident. An honest mistake. Hunter kissed me! But I should have pulled away quicker. Why didn't I do that? It didn't matter now. I had to stop beating myself up over it. "I'll tell Cole the truth tomorrow morning," I said, determined to make things right. "I'll grab him when we take the peeps for their allergy shots."

Em hugged me. "We'll be here if you need us," she said. "You don't have to be worried about doing this alone."

"Thanks," I said to all of them. "I don't know what I would do without you guys."

Grace smiled. "Now that Sam has a game plan, let's get to bed." She started to gather her things.

"You mean you don't want to talk about Tim?" Court teased.

Grace shook her head. "Not tonight. I just want to get out of here and back to our bunk. I feel like we're being watched."

Court laughed. "You've seen one too many horror movies, but fine, let's g —"

Before Court even got out the word "go" the canteen door swung open. Ashley and Gabby blocked the exit.

"How long have you two been out there?" Court demanded.

"Long enough," Ashley said smugly and looked directly at me with such a chilly expression I actually felt cold. How much did she hear?

She didn't get a chance to say because Hitch came running up behind them, sounding out of breath. He had under-eye circles and bed head, and I got the impression he had been woken from a sound sleep. He was still in his pajamas — green sweats and a Navy Seals tee. "I came as fast as I could," he said frantically. "Is everyone okay? No one's hurt?" He looked around in confusion. "Did you put the fire out?"

Court, Em, Grace, and I looked at each other. "What fire?" Grace asked, alarmed.

"Ashley said the canteen was on fire," Hitch said, looking at his daughter for answers.

Meg was the next to arrive, sprinting up to the doorstep and pushing her way inside. When she saw us, she burst into tears. "Thank God you guys are okay." She threw her arms around us.

"What are you guys talking about?" I couldn't help asking. "There was no fire."

"If there was no fire, then why did you tell me there was one, sweetie?" Hitch asked Ashley.

She looked up at him with big, round eyes. "I'm sorry," she quivered. "I woke up and didn't see any of my bunkmates."

"So she woke me," Gabby interrupted.

"And we ran to the window and we saw the girls heading toward the canteen, so we followed them," Ashley said worriedly. "We didn't want them to get hurt."

"And that's when we saw the lights in the canteen," Gabby added. "We thought the place was on fire."

"Those lights were our flashlights," Grace growled.

"We didn't know that," Ashley snapped, and then quickly

composed herself. "We were worried so we called you, Daddy. And we woke up Meg."

Meg looked away. I got the feeling Meg wasn't in bed either.

"I also ran and told Alexis, but she said she couldn't leave her bunk unattended," Ashley added, looking directly at me.

Of course she told Alexis. Ashley was still determined to make Alexis hate me.

"Well, I'm glad there wasn't a fire, but I don't understand what you were all doing at the canteen at midnight." Hitch frowned.

"We were just talking," Court tried to explain.

"You couldn't have this conversation tomorrow morning at breakfast?" Ashley wanted to know. "Why do you guys leave us out all the time?" She started sniffling and tearing up.

I glanced at Em nervously. Ashley was out for blood and she was going to use every trick in the book to make sure she got it. I looked at Hitch. His expression was pained. He put an arm awkwardly around his daughter.

"Hitch, I can handle this," Meg interrupted. "This is obviously a bunk issue and I'll be sure that the girls are spoken to and reprimanded properly."

"Since I'm here, I think I should handle this, Meg." Hitch looked at the four of us. "Is there anything you want to say?"

"Ask them if they were stealing more clothes," Ashley said.

"That's enough, Ashley," Hitch's voice sounded stern. He turned back to us. "I didn't expect this sort of behavior from you four."

I glanced at Grace. She looked like she might cry as she waited to hear what Hitch was going to say. If he took away

Grace's Color War status I would die. This was yet another thing that was my fault.

Normally if a camper was caught sneaking out, they'd be punished by their counselor. Hitch didn't get involved unless there was a vicious prank occuring or the person was a repeat offender. But Ashley had gotten him involved and now he wasn't going to walk away.

"We're sorry," Grace pleaded. "We weren't doing anything wrong. We swear. We didn't take anything. We just wanted someplace private to talk."

"Since this is a first offense, I'm going to go easy on you," Hitch said despite Ashley's obvious gasping. "Even so, your senior counselors will be told of this infraction. Your punishment is that you'll be excused from all activities tomorrow and will have to help Beaver in the kitchen all day. You'll eat all your meals in there and will have no contact with anyone. In the evening, we'll meet again and talk."

"You're not going to take away our Color War privileges?" Grace asked tearfully.

Hitch shook his head. I thought I saw a small smile on his lips. "You worked hard for that position, Grace. It was meant to be yours."

Ashley had a coughing fit. "But they broke into the canteen! And they were out after curfew! They could have set the place on fire. You're not taking away anything but a stupid day of activities? What about the talent show? Don't you think they should be banned from it?"

"Ashley, I said I would handle this," Hitch told her. "I suggest you get back to bed before I decide to make you go home to your actual bed this evening."

Ashley shut her mouth and glared at her father. "Fine," she huffed. "Come on, Gabby."

Hitch sighed and turned to Meg. "You'll see to it that they get back to bed?"

"Yes, sir," Meg said, blushing slightly. Meg was a model counselor. I knew getting caught with her whole bunk out after curfew couldn't be easy on her. I had really made a mess of things.

"Well, then, I'm going back to bed," Hitch said. "And I'll see you four bright and early in the morning. Make it seven."

It was just us and Meg. She sighed heavily. "Girls, I know counselors and campers sneak out sometimes, but after what happened with that prank last week, I thought you guys would have been more careful. Ashley still thinks it was one of you who took her stuff. She's watching your every move."

"This is my fault, Meg," I started to say. "I begged the girls to come out tonight because I was having a problem and I needed their advice. Don't blame this on them."

Meg shook her head. I noticed her eyes catch something and she stopped. She grabbed Grace's flashlight and shined it at Court's feet. The video camera! Court looked like a deer caught in headlights. "What's that?" Meg asked and grabbed it before Court could. "Whose is this? Is this the camp's?"

"It's mine," I said quickly. "I brought it from home."

"Sam, you know you're not allowed portable electronic devices at camp, and especially not something this expensive!"

Meg scolded. "I'm going to have to hold on to that till the end of camp."

I looked at the girls. Our sleepaway girls conversations were sacred. I knew if they were safe with anyone, it was Meg, but I hated the idea of being banned from making more. We had already filled up three ninety-minute tapes with our other conversations. The last few weeks of camp weren't going to be as fun if we couldn't have sleepaway girls confessionals.

Court reluctantly handed over the backpack containing my tapes, and Meg tucked my camera inside.

"Let's talk more in the morning," Meg suggested and slung the backpack over her arm. "Right now, I just want to get to sleep."

Meg led the way back to the bunk with the four of us walking slowly behind her.

"I can't believe Ashley did that to us," Court seethed. "It's bad enough she's going to try to destroy your chances with Cole. She has to get us put on probation too?"

"It's not that bad of a punishment," Grace said. "It's just one day without camp activities. At least he didn't take away Color War."

"Or the talent show," Em added.

"Meg did take away our camera," Court grumbled.

"We'll have to talk to her about how important that camera is to us," Em said.

I stopped walking. "Guys, I just realized something. If we're on kitchen duty all day tomorrow that means I won't see Cole. What if Ashley gets to him first?"

Em looked as if someone just called and said her cat died. "It will be fine. It's only for one day, right?" Em said uncertainly.

It was just one day. But one day was an awfully long time when you were at camp and people spent every waking moment together.

One day could be all it took to ruin my life.

▲ 17 ▲

Food for Thought

Desperate times called for desperate measures. It was time to reach out to the big guy upstairs.

   God, if you're listening, it's me, Samantha Montgomery — you know, the girl who is always praying you'll permanently de-frizz my crazy hair, and for six months last year asked that you let one guy at Carle Place High be more interested in me than in my best friend? It's okay that you haven't answered my prayers yet. I know you're really busy and all, with the polar ice caps melting, and having to deal with Amy Winehouse's meltdowns on an almost daily basis. But my last shout-outs were nothing compared to the urgency of this one. If you could PLEASE see to it that no one tells Cole that Hunter kissed me before I have a chance to explain myself, I promise to do anything you want. I'll be more green and stop using so many paper towels. I'll be a better granddaughter and not groan when Grandma visits and wants to eat every meal at Olive Garden. I'll even come clean to my mom about being the one who put her favorite wood Crate and Barrel bowl in the dishwasher even though I claimed it was that housekeeper, Stella, who only lasted a week. And . . . oh! Wait! That's Meg's alarm clock. I have to get in the shower before Ashley stops snoring and someone hears the alarm. But don't forget — I'm counting on you with this one. Amen.

When I was finished, I tiptoed around the bunk, trying not to disturb Courtney, who flipped and flailed all over the place when she was sleeping. I moved stealthily to the bathroom, grabbed my best camp shirt (the tie-dyed one we had made the week before in arts and crafts — everyone said it wasn't a camp session if you didn't at least tie-dye something) and my khaki shorts that made my thighs look killer, and then I dove into the shower. I used as much hot water as I wanted since I was the first one in. To make up for being less green, after having just promised God I would be more so, I rescued a spider on the shower door by dropping him into my shave gel container top. I needed as much good karma on my side as I could get. By the time I'd tied my sneakers, Gabby was just starting to stir, which meant her snores were about to turn into snorts, and would wake up the entire room. Thankfully, I slipped out the door before her first grunt.

The sun hadn't even poked its lazy head above the mountains yet and the air outside the cabin was cool. I put my shower gel container on the ground and let the spider rush to safer surroundings. I was shivering in just shorts and a t-shirt, but I wasn't going back for a sweatshirt. I hadn't had a face-to-face with Ashley in almost eight hours and I wasn't about to now.

I knew she saw Hunter kiss me. All I could hope was that she hadn't gotten to Cole yet. Grace had tried to get some information for me. She'd stolen a few minutes with Tim during the dinner rush the night before when she told Beaver a table requested an extra helping of his sloppy joes (as if that would ever happen). She asked Tim if he saw Ashley with Cole at all —

when the rest of us were on mandatory kitchen duty — and he said no. He told her Cole was fine. But what did fine mean? Did he not know about Hunter and me yet? Or was he fine hating me? I had to get to Cole and find out. I knocked on my peeps cabin door and Alexis answered.

"Hey," she said. She was still in her pajamas. "Mackenzie is all ready for you." Mackenzie skipped to the doorway, clutching her bear.

I'd never been so thankful to be the one who took her for her allergy shots before. Hitch wouldn't let me take her yesterday because of my probation so Alexis had to take the whole bunk with her and go. I wondered what Cole thought when he saw Alexis there instead of me. Cole and I took our campers at the same time every morning, which meant I was guaranteed some alone time with him before breakfast and I needed that today of all days.

"We'll see you at the mess hall in a half an hour," Alexis said to me with a smile. I knew she knew about my punishment for sneaking out after-hours, but she wasn't saying anything about it in front of the peeps. I was sure I'd hear it later.

Mackenzie and I trudged up the hill to the nurse's station and my heart was pounding the whole way there. I was seconds away from seeing Cole, and as much as I wanted to be the first one to tell him what happened with Hunter, I was scared too. Mackenzie burst through the door first, and a rush of cool air greeted me. My eyes immediately went to the waiting room bench. Caleb was there, but Cole wasn't. Caleb was actually alone.

"Where's Cole?" Mackenzie asked before I could.

Caleb yawned. "He went for an early jog. He dropped me off here first. He said I was a big boy and I could come by myself today," Caleb said proudly.

"I want to come by myself too!" Mackenzie tugged on my sleeve, but I couldn't concentrate enough to actually answer her.

Cole went jogging this late? He usually got up an hour earlier and went. I could never understand why he did it. They gave us so much mandatory exercise around this place I couldn't imagine anyone wanting to do more on their own. Even my waistband was loose, although that could be on account of the fact I was eating less since I couldn't stand looking at another burger or nacho salad surprise.

When Mackenzie's shot was over, I practically carried her to the mess hall. I didn't want to have my conversation with Cole there, but I didn't have a choice. At the front doors, I was greeted by Court.

"What's wrong?" I panicked.

"Nothing," Court said soothingly. "What about you? Did you talk to him?"

"Mackenzie, why don't you go inside?" I said. "I'll be over to the table in a minute." Without hesitation, she opened one of the doors and I could hear the noise level increase. Then I told Court what happened. "I don't know if he wasn't there because he was avoiding me or if he really just slept late before his jog."

Court was deep in thought. "I'm not sure either," she admitted. "If Ashley got to him first, she isn't acting any differently. The gruesome twosome have been in the bunk all morning acting completely normal. And by normal, I mean complaining that someone used all the hot water, telling Em her shirt was ugly, and forcing Grace to abandon her K.T. Tunstall CD for Chris Brown." Even though we weren't allowed electronics, every bunk at the Pines had a CD player for communal use.

"That is pretty normal," I admitted. Maybe Ashley was holding on to the Hunter kiss as a way to blackmail me. I wouldn't put it past her. That meant I still had time to get to Cole first.

Thank you, God, for hearing me! Seriously, I don't know if you have Verizon FiOS up there or what, but you worked your magic in record time.

"Thanks for making me feel better," I told Court.

"I told you everything would be fine," she said. "You want to know how I knew? I was at the flag-raising and Donovan came up to me, and in front of Gabby said, 'Court, I hear you're taking over the talent show with that cool routine of yours.' Me. Cool! Can you imagine? Then he said he'd see me at lunch. That's a major improvement over last week's 'see ya!'" Court stared at the nearby meadow and I half expected to hear the flowers singing.

"That is an improvement," I told her. All of the sleepaway girls had made progress in the guy area since we'd started our camp confessionals. Em and Dylan had kissed, and Grace and Tim were Color War captains. In sports speak, that was true love.

Court patted me on the back. "Now go in there and get your man! We'll be waiting at the table for you." She opened the door and pushed me through.

I took a deep breath. The walk to Cole's table felt like the longest walk I'd ever taken, and that's not just because Hitch stopped me on the way to tell me how much he appreciated my "grown-up" attitude during yesterday's kitchen confinement. When I broke free, I strode over to Cole's usual table. Dylan saw me and pointed to the peeps. My heart sunk. Cole was sitting with his charges today? That meant Hunter would be at the same table. But when I looked over, I saw Hunter wasn't there yet. It was just Cole and a few of the kids. They were drawing on a piece of paper and Cole was scribbling furiously while a few kids laughed. That had to be a good sign, right? If Cole was making people laugh, he couldn't be upset about anything as major as me kissing a guy he didn't respect.

When I reached the table, my hands were shaking. Cole was inches from me, but he didn't look up. "Hey," I said casually, hoping he couldn't hear the nervousness in my voice.

"Hey," he said. Just hey. No smile, no jokes. No flirting.

"Mackenzie and I missed you this morning at the nurse's office," I said. "They had the Today show on in there and I actually got to hear the weather forecast for someplace other than here."

"I got going on my jog late," Cole said, still not looking at me. "And Caleb wanted to go on his own for once."

I was starting to sense that Cole was anything but okay, and my heart beat out of my chest, kind of like the way it did when I'd drank too much hot chocolate before bed, or when I was watching The Eye with Jessica Alba. Still, I couldn't help babbling.

"Mackenzie is really jealous. I'm sorry I wasn't around all day yesterday," I blurted out. "I was on mandatory kitchen duty with Beaver, and let me tell you, you do not want to see what goes on in that kitchen when you're there all day. You'd never eat again."

Caleb laughed at my joke, but Cole still didn't say anything. I finally glanced at his paper. He was playing a game of hangman.

"Cole?" I said it almost like a question and he looked up at me.

I instantly wished he hadn't. His blue eyes were sort of partly cloudy, just like his expression. And that's when I knew for sure: Cole knew. Even though Court told me to act calm and unaffected, I was anything but.

"Guys, could you excuse me for a minute?" Cole asked the peeps. Cole walked out to the mess hall porch and I followed. Kids were still streaming in around us. I was surrounded by kids eager for sugary pancake syrup, zipping by us on their way to their tables, yet I couldn't hear them. I could have heard a pin drop as I stood next to Cole waiting to hear what he was going to say. I had to beat him to the punch.

"Please let me explain," I said hurriedly. If I could just get it out before he interrupted me, I might be able to salvage things.

"You don't have to," Cole said. "I get it."

"You do?" I asked incredulously and Cole didn't say anything. "I swear, I didn't mean for it to happen. You have no idea how sorry I am. I haven't been able to eat, or sleep or do anything but think about talking to you. I was under arrest all day yesterday," I added. "I hated not being able to tell you myself."

"It's fine." Cole shrugged. "You like Hunter. I knew you did. I kept telling you that. I just wish" — his face was pensive — "you would have been honest with me."

"I don't like Hunter! The kiss was an accident. He kissed me.

I swear! I was looking for you. I was coming to tell you that I liked you. That's why I came down to the lake. Someone told me you were there, but then Hunter was there instead and he kissed me," I said, feeling queasy.

"Did you kiss Hunter back?" Cole asked quietly.

I felt the wind whip up behind me and a shiver ran down my spine. How could I answer that honestly? I didn't pull away immediately, that was true, but I was in shock. And yet, I still felt guilty. It was my nature. "I, well, you see, not really." Cole's face darkened.

"That answer says it all," Cole said. "Ashley told me the rest. At first, I thought she was lying, considering it was Ashley and knowing how much we don't like each other. But then I confronted Hunter and he confessed. He told me he kissed you and you didn't stop him."

I felt like the bottom of the porch dropped out from under me. Suddenly I could hear again. The noise was deafening, but somehow my voice was louder than any of the kids. "Did he tell you that I gave him a huge speech about liking *you*?" I practically cried. "Did he tell you that I thought *you* were dressed as a knight and that's why I said all those things to him?"

"No," Cole said. "I hit him before he could say anything else."

My jaw dropped for the second time. Cole hit his senior counselor?

"The fact is, Sam, you didn't stop Hunter," Cole said softly. "You didn't pull away. If you were looking for me to kiss, you would have turned Hunter away, but you didn't."

"Cole," I tried again and reached for his hand. He slipped his away.

"I can't look at you right now, Sam," he said. "I'm sorry." Then he walked down the porch steps, away from the mess hall. That's when I snapped. ASHLEY. She had gone too far.

I pulled open the mess hall doors and thundered through the room to my own CIT table. Meg wasn't there yet, but my bunkmates looked up at me. All but two of them.

"Sam." Em said it so gravely that I wanted to cry. I wanted to cry anyway, but not there. Not then. Not until I had said everything I needed to first.

"You and I need to talk," I told Ashley and made sure I sounded like I meant it.

She looked up at me with those doe eyes of her and said, "What?"

I didn't know if it was her sarcastic "what?" or her face, but the whole interaction just made me madder. I was aware that the room around me was quiet, except for the quiet scraping of silverware. I had an audience. Ashley seemed to realize the same thing, and she didn't like it.

"Keep your voice down," she hissed. "We're not putting on a show."

I wasn't thrilled either. Somewhere nearby, my peeps were hearing this, and I was embarrassed. But I couldn't back down now. "You couldn't keep your mouth shut," I said shakily. "You just had to tell Cole what you saw."

Ashley flashed me a vindictive smile. "Why wouldn't I? Cole is a good guy. He deserved to know the truth."

"BFD," Gab defended her best friend with an equally ghoulish grin and I knew she meant *big freaking deal*. "Cole had a right to know the girl he likes is a two-timer."

"He had a right to know the *real* story!" I couldn't help but shrill. "He deserved to hear it from me, not some bystander out for my blood."

Ashley shrugged. "I saw what I saw. There's no denying the truth."

"He kissed me," I said hoarsely, "even though he knew I was looking for Cole, and that my whole confession about liking Cole was not for him. Not that you deserve to know any of this, but it's the truth. Now Cole won't even listen to me."

Ashley sighed. "It's just as well," she said. "Cole's too good for you anyway."

"You insensitive, pampered brat," Court seethed and slid out of her chair to come to my aid. Ashley, sensing danger, ducked behind Gabby, who reached for a fork and held it menacingly at Court's chest.

"Stay out of this," I told Court and gently pushed her aside. "This is between Ashley and me." I continued to glare at Ashley and she actually stood up. She folded her arms over her chest defiantly and I could see she was wearing her tie-dyed t-shirt. She'd been bragging about how perfect hers was all week. Hers had her name painted on the front with little hearts all around it. You had to watch out for a girl who put hearts around her name or dotted her i's with little valentines. Erin Marble, who sat behind me in third grade, always did that and she was the one who told the whole class I was a baby because I still believed in Santa Claus.

"You're right, Sam, this is between us," Ashley said, knowing all eyes were on her. "And we should finish it right here. So let's go. You've been jealous of me from the moment you arrived. You hated how popular I was. You were embarrassed that I didn't invite you to my sleepover. And that's why you pulled that prank with all my clothes."

I hated that my peeps could be hearing this. I was nervous that Alexis was too, but it was too late to turn back now. "Fine, I'll admit that I was part of that prank with your clothes, but if you think I did it because I was jealous of you, you're wrong. I was tired of you pushing me around. I hated how you embarrassed me in front of my peeps and how you always had it out for me. I can't help it if I settled in to camp just fine, without any help from you. I can't help it if I happened to be part of my mom's commercial and you felt threatened. It's also not my fault that I got your sister as my senior counselor. I tried not to rock the boat, but that was never good enough. You telling Cole was cruel." My voice was starting to crack. "That's one thing I've never been to you."

Ashley's eyes darkened. "You think you're so hot," she seethed, "but you want the truth? My dad made a huge mistake by hiring you. Everyone knows it. You aren't cut out to be a CIT. My sister can't stand you. She says you're the worst excuse for a CIT she's ever had. I doubt you'll be asked back next year."

"Give it a rest, Ashley," Grace warned.

If I was angry before, my body felt like it was on fire now. Ashley was lying. I knew it, but my mouth was too dry to contradict her. I was too tired to yell anymore. I didn't have the words in me to fight. My hands, however, were fine. I spied the plastic pitcher of bug juice on the table. Not thinking, I picked it up and hurled the whole pitcher at her with full force. The pitcher splashed over her shirt, over Gabby, and dripped down her hair. Ashley started to scream and I couldn't help but grin. Good. She deserved that.

I was so proud of myself, and the reaction of everyone at the table, which was total shock, that I wasn't quick enough to see Ashley retaliate. She grabbed the orange juice and heaved it in my direction. The ice cold drink drenched my shirt and my arms.

The rest of the scene seemed to play out in slow motion. I couldn't stop. I grabbed the cheap, no-name brand pancake syrup and squirted it at Ashley's head, causing her to jump out of the way, and making me hit Gabby. A furious Gabby grabbed the eggs and flung them across the table, hitting me and Court in the process. Court stood up and spilled the pitcher of water in Ashley's lap. It wasn't long before Em was throwing pancakes. Even Grace was flicking jelly out of the jelly jar. Everyone was grabbing for food now, pulling at the table for everything and anything left. Ashley took the butter and smashed it into my already frizzy hair. I grabbed a handful of cream cheese and stuffed it in her chest. We both stopped when we saw a platter of waffles, which weren't even on our table since Gabby claimed waffles gave her heartburn, fly past our heads. We both ducked.

When we turned around, Ashley gasped.

My stomach churned. It wasn't a good sight.

We weren't the only table having a food fight. The entire mess hall had joined in and the place was in chaos. Counselors were trying to stop it, but it was no use. We'd caused a war. Beaver had come out of the kitchen, wielding wooden spoons, but he didn't make it far before he slipped on a pancake and crashed into a table. Meg was across the room and trying to reach us, but she got hit with a flying orange juice pitcher. Hunter had finally made it here. Thankfully, he was too caught up in separating two peeps fighting over a plate of sausage to see me. Ashley's CIT counselor, Morgan, was two tables away from us when she got sideswiped by a carton of milk.

Suddenly there was a loud whistle. And another. And another. I felt myself getting dragged by the back of my shirt. Ashley was being pulled right next to me.

"Let go of me! I didn't do anything! She started it," Ashley screamed, punching the air with her fists.

It was Beaver. He'd survived his brush with pancakes and had gotten to our table. He pulled us through the stunned mess hall all the way up to Hitch.

"THAT IS ENOUGH!" I heard Hitch yelling into his megaphone. I wiped peanut butter off my eyelid and took a good look at his face. OH. Um . . .

Hitch's hair was covered in jelly, and an orange and bug juice concoction was dripping down his army-navy game shirt. He looked at Ashley and me and pointed his finger shakily in our direction. "YOU TWO. IN MY OFFICE. NOW."

18

Crime and Punishment

"In all my years as a camp director, I have never seen two CITs behave this irresponsibly," Hitch ranted at Ashley and me as orange juice continued to drip off his shorts. "We've never had a camp-wide food fight before! What do you two think this is? A Disney Channel movie?"

"She started it," Ashley mumbled.

Alexis, Meg, Morgan, and Hitch were standing in front of us. They all looked furious and I felt like I was in front of a firing squad. Meg had egg in her hair, Alexis had pancake syrup down her shirt, and Morgan was covered in jelly.

"I am so disappointed," Meg seconded as yolk dripped from her hair onto her shirt. "I never expected your rivalry to go this far."

"Rivalry?" Ashley snorted. "She isn't even worth rivaling."

Sadly, even covered in chocolate Quik and jelly, Ashley still managed to look beautiful. She could have done a commercial for the cleaning power of Tide right then and it still would have been an instant YouTube hit. I was sure I didn't look anywhere near as cute with peanut butter up my nose.

"Ash, that's enough," Alexis said wearily. And then to me Alexis added: "I'm used to Ashley getting into mischief, but Sam, I'm stunned — and not because it's going to take three showers to get this sticky syrup out of my hair. I never expected this sort of behavior from you."

I hung my head sadly. I hated to let Alexis down, but I didn't regret what I'd done to Ashley. I wanted her to look as dirty as she really was for spilling the beans to Cole. I would have poured ten more gallons of OJ on Ashley if I had been given the chance.

Hitch sighed. "I knew you two weren't getting along, but I didn't know it was this bad. Camp is about gelling with people you normally wouldn't and learning how to live together despite your obvious differences. No one said you had to be best friends. We just wanted you to coexist. Instead, you two have caused camp-wide chaos and destruction in the mess hall."

"And wasted all that food," Morgan added sternly.

"What kind of example is that for CITs to be setting?" Alexis pointed out.

Ashley rolled her eyes. "Sam humiliated me on several occasions and all you care about is how our food fight affected the camp atmosphere?"

"Do either of you want to apologize for what happened?" Hitch asked, incredulous.

"I'm sorry," I said, and I meant it. I wasn't sorry for hitting Ashley with a plate of pancakes, but I was sorry that I had disappointed all the counselors and Hitch and had disrupted the camp schedule. I overheard Beaver tell Hitch they needed to move lunchtime to try to get the place clean in time. There was even talk of having a barbeque outside if they couldn't.

"I'm sorry Sam started it," Ashley sniffed.

Hitch crossed his arms, making his biceps bulge. "I think the best punishment would be to make the two of you clean up the mess hall all by yourselves."

"Eww," Ashley said under her breath.

"Okay," I agreed, afraid to even look at Alexis or Meg.

"That's it?" Morgan asked, stunned. "All they have to do is clean up their mess? These two set a bad example for the entire camp."

"And their loathing of each other has been a sore point all summer," Meg added.

"Counselors, calm down. That was just the first part of their punishment," Hitch said. He waved them over into a group huddle. "This is what I also had in mind, as long as it was okay with you."

I heard the words "lesson," "compromise," "fit the crime," and "team," but it was hard to hear more over Ashley's moaning.

"If I have to sit the talent show out because of you, you're dead," Ashley threatened me as she continued to pull stray pieces of egg whites from her hair. How it still looked perfectly straight, I had no idea. Between the humidity and the syrup, mine probably looked like a clown wig.

I rolled my eyes. What more could Ashley do to me? She'd already ruined my chances with Cole. And she couldn't steal my friends. "Bring it on," I told her, my voice dripping like the syrup all over me.

"Girls," Hitch interrupted. "We've decided on an appropriate punishment for your actions."

Ashley cried out. "You're not taking away the talent show from me, are you?" Her lip quivered and for a moment I thought she might actually cry. Over the talent show. I knew the performance was a big deal to all the CITs, since this was their last year performing as campers. After that, they'd get to do the group counselor number, but it wasn't the same thing.

"You'll still get to be in the talent show," Hitch said and Ashley breathed a sigh of relief, "but you're not doing the routine you've rehearsed. Your bunk will do that without you."

"Good," Ashley said happily, "because Court's routine was so beyond boring. If we go back to my original suggestion, I'm sure —"

"You won't be doing that either," Hitch cut her off. "Instead you'll be doing a new routine." He paused. "One that you come up with *together*."

"What?" Ashley and I said at the same time.

"Her and me?" I clarified. "Together? Alone?"

"Your punishment is that you're going to spend the next several days together and only together." Hitch sounded proud of himself. "You'll spend all your time as a team, figuring out a performance that the two of you will give."

If our punishment started right away, that meant we'd be . . . "We're missing Color War?" I asked. I felt a tinge of disappointment. I still didn't understand what all the fuss was about, but the nine million daily reminders — via posters or campers talking, plus Grace's daily Color War talks — had gotten me excited.

"Yes," Hitch said firmly. "We all feel that your behavior today merits being excluded from this activity. Color War is about teamwork and togetherness, two qualities you both need to learn before you can participate."

I side-eyed Ashley. She didn't look crushed, not that I was surprised. I'd overheard her say on more than one occasion, "I don't run because I hate to sweat."

"I'll miss Color War," Ashley said, as if she was devastated, "but I'm not performing with her. I won't commit social suicide in front of the whole camp."

If I had to spend every minute in Ashley-confinement, how was I going to hunt down Cole and explain myself? Just the thought of having to live with the unfinished conversation in my head for several days was making me nauseous. "Shockingly, I agree with Ashley," I piped up. "Given our history, I don't see how we can team up together."

"You don't have a choice," Hitch said calmly. "Ashley, it's either this or Boca Raton and your grandmother's condo. And I mean it."

"Noo, not there!" Ashley looked horrified.

For once, I could relate.

Hitch looked at me. "Same goes for you, Sam. If you don't do the show, then I will send you home early, which, of course, means I have to tell your mom what happened."

Gulp. Mom wouldn't be too thrilled to hear I'd disrupted the entire camp's meal with a food fight and everything was wasted. She got aggravated when I pushed my peas around on my plate and didn't finish my organic burrito because it tasted like paste. "There are children out there who would kill for a cup of rice," she always said. Even brown, whole-grain rice? I found that hard to believe.

"And while I know missing Color War is a huge blow," Hitch said sadly, "it's just the first of many things you'll miss if you don't accept your punishment like adults. If you're leaving early, you'll also miss the luau dance and the sleepover on the lawn."

The sleepover on the lawn was supposedly the best thing ever. I didn't want to miss that. Or the luau, even if Cole was avoiding me. I sighed. "I'll do it."

"Ashley?" Hitch asked.

"I guess," she said with a loud sigh.

"Good." Hitch looked satisfied. "I know you'll both work together and come up with a brilliant routine. You'll have to. You're closing the show."

Double groan. Court said the final number was usually reserved for the best group. Camp gossip traveled faster than wildfire so it wouldn't take long for everyone to hear that Ashley and I were the ones doing it. How was I going to face Cole?

"Your counselors will take you back to your bunks to collect some things and then you'll report to the mess hall to start cleaning," Hitch told us. "We'll be putting you two in the isolation cabin near the horse stables for the next few days. This is the first time it's been used the whole summer." He shook his head sadly. "I'll check in on you later." Then Hitch left, presumably to go shower, something I wished I could have done.

"Can we at least change out of these gross clothes?" Ashley complained.

Meg, Morgan, and Alexis looked at each other. "Okay," Meg said. "Alexis will take Ashley back first, and I'll head down with Sam in a few minutes. That way you both have some alone time before your confinement."

I smiled gratefully at Meg. When it was my turn to go, I quickly washed up, grabbed my things, and stuffed them in my duffel bag. Meg escorted me back to the mess hall. Ashley wasn't there yet, but I was so keyed up, I wanted to start cleaning anyway, just to blow off some steam. But I stopped short when I walked into the mess hall and saw the aftermath.

The floor was littered with syrup, assorted jellies and cream cheese. Orange juice was still oozing off the tables, and pancakes hung to the walls like plaques. The floor was so filthy with food and broken dishes that you couldn't even see it. The whole place smelled awful too. The combination of all that food, sitting in a hot room for two hours, made an unbearable stench. I quickly ran to the windows to open them higher.

"I guess you should start cleaning," said Meg, looking around in horror. "I'll leave you to it."

Ashley still wasn't here yet — of course, she was probably delaying her arrival as long as she could — but I knew this job was huge and I should probably dig in. I grabbed a mop and bucket, filled it with soap and water and began scrubbing, but there was so much food in the way that I had to get down on my hands and knees and start throwing stuff away before I could even begin to clean the floors. Thankfully I had gloves. I wanted to throw up several times as I grabbed squashed pancakes, toast and jelly from the floor. When I had finally cleared the area around two tables, I started to mop and the stains came right up. That was the nice thing about housework. No matter how dirty something got, you could fix it. I wished the same could be said for what had happened between me and Cole.

When the mess hall door finally opened, Ashley strode inside looking like she was ready for a date. Her hair was pulled softly into a low bun. Her foundation was flawless, her eyes had been freshly painted, and she was wearing lip gloss. I, on the other hand, had scrubbed my face and walked back out the cabin door. No one would be seeing me for three days, so eyeliner wasn't a necessity. I felt like the two of us were acting out a scene from *Beauty and the Beast*. I couldn't help but smile at the irony.

"What?" Ashley growled.

"Nothing," I said. "You just look good. As usual."

Ashley snorted. "You can drop the act. There's no one here but me to hear it."

"I'm serious," I said, exasperated. "You always look perfect, even after we've done the high-ropes course. That's why I don't get it."

"Get what?" Ashley asked, as she picked up a pair of gloves and stared at the room in disgust. Rather than sounding aggravated, for once she sounded intrigued. She slid them on and then remarkably got right to work, grabbing a black garbage bag and depositing food from the tables into it.

Maybe I'd said too much already, but it was too late to stop now. I wanted to ask a question that had been on my mind since the beginning of the summer. "I'm not a supermodel," I pointed out. "I'm not an actress. My commercial was a one-time-only thing. I haven't stolen any of your friends. Yet you go out of your way to make my life miserable. I don't see how hating me is even worth your time."

Ashley didn't say anything at first. I figured she was going to give me the silent treatment. Either that or she was going to direct her answer to the antler chandelier hanging above her head. Then she said three words I never expected to hear: "I was jealous."

"What?" I wiggled my ear, wondering if it was clogged with orange juice. "I don't think I heard you right."

Ashley glared at me again. "You don't have to be sarcastic. I was jealous of you, okay? I saw how excited everyone was when they'd heard you'd been in the Dial and Dash Phone commercial. Everyone, including my bunkmates, was hanging on your every word! You were an instant camp star and suddenly my little camp videos looked stupid. It didn't help that my dad thought you were going to be a CIT Wonder Woman even before he met you," she added, rolling her eyes. "He kept droning on about how you were untapped, raw talent, and how he and Alexis were going to mold you to be the perfect counselor. Alexis couldn't wait to meet you. I couldn't stand hearing your name and you hadn't even arrived yet!"

All I could do was stand there, holding my mop, which was dripping water all over the floor, and listen. Ashley looked away guiltily. "I know I said at the mess hall my dad and Alexis regretted hiring you, but it's not true. Alexis is always going on and on about how great you are. My dad too. But somehow, I never do anything they find worthy."

No wonder Ashley hated me. I would have hated me too if my family talked about my arrival as if I were Super Girl.

"I knew they liked you, but I really had no idea you were going to wind up as Alexis's CIT," Ashley added. "Everyone wants Alexis and everyone thought my CIT year it would be me. We're always competing with each other, but when it came to camp stuff I thought we were on the same team. Then she goes and passes me up for you. That was my slot. It's like you set out to take everything that was mine and once again I was nothing more than Alexis's younger, less competent sister."

I was going to need cosmetic surgery for sure because my jaw must have permanently fallen off my face. I accidentally dropped my mop and I scrambled to pick it up.

"Stop looking at me like that," Ashley snapped.

I was still trying to digest what just happened. Ashley Hitchens, the most popular girl at camp, was jealous of me? That didn't make sense. "I'm just surprised," I said. "Everyone at the Pines worships you, especially the guys. I wouldn't think you'd be threatened by anyone."

"I will never be the perfect counselor Alexis is, and she's already made it clear to me that you might be," Ashley pointed out. "Being pretty doesn't make it any easier to live in your sister's shadow. I've spent my whole life trying to keep up with her. If she wanted me to do something, I did it, trying to make her happy. But when is my happiness just as important as hers?" She looked away again. "I don't expect you to understand."

Whoa. That feeling sounded sort of familiar. Wasn't that the way I sometimes felt when I was with Mal? I adored her, but sometimes I felt like her less important stepsister. I couldn't believe it was possible, but Ashley and I actually had something in common. It was time both of us broke the chain.

I looked at Ashley. Suddenly I saw how hard it probably was to be her and live in Alexis's shadow. "I understand more than you know," I said. "I have a best friend named Mal and we've always done everything together. Or should I say, I've done everything Mal wanted to do, which was pretty ridiculous. I think sometimes you love a person so much that you get lost in what they want and forget what you want."

Ashley looked at me curiously. "Yeah," she said. "That's exactly it."

Neither of us said anything else. We went back to cleaning and I was glad for the silence. I was feeling pretty overwhelmed, realizing what my relationship with Mal had always been, how similar Ashley's situation was, and just how much had changed in a matter of minutes.

Suddenly Ashley spoke up. "Just because we have the same problem doesn't mean we're friends or anything," she said. "If you tell anyone what I said about Alexis, I'll deny it."

But despite her words, I saw her smile a little, and not maliciously either. We had bonded, just slightly, and maybe that was a start.

⋀ 19 ⋀
Common Ground

While our first day of confinement had led to a partial break-through, the next two days were much less pleasant. It was as if Ashley had all but forgotten our conversation in the mess hall and had decided to go back to loathing me. So we spent our days in the isolation cabin, just glaring at each other. The bunk looked just like 8A, but it was smaller, with just two bunk beds, and it was anything but homey. The walls were bare, the sheets on our beds plain white, there were zero snacks, and the whole place was sort of depressing. The only thing we had to do to pass the time was stare at each other. If glaring were an Olympic sport, I was sure I could win a gold medal.

We were sitting on opposite sides of the room avoiding each other like one of us had the plague. I was sitting on the window seat and Ashley was on her bunk, flipping through a magazine. She looked up and glared back at me almost as convincingly as she used to. She could probably win the silver in this competition. Outside the cabin, you could hear two things: Horses neighing in the nearby stables, which meant their stench could waft over this way too, and campers screaming excitedly about some Color War activity going on. My hope was that everyone was so wrapped up in the game that they had forgotten all about the food fight. I already felt miserable about the fact that I would have to apologize to my peeps about my behavior. They may have been young, but even they wouldn't have thrown orange juice at someone if they were mad.

"Don't you think we should talk about the talent show?" I asked the wood-planked wall in front of me that had "I heart Nick!" carved on it. I was talking to Ashley, but Ashley and I didn't actually look at each other when we talked. "We're supposed to have our routine ready to show Hitch by the end of the day today," I reminded her. "Today is our last day in this cabin."

My question was met by silence again and I felt like I was having déjà vu. I'd been saying the same thing over and over every few hours and every time I got the same response. I was tired of the silent treatment by six o'clock yesterday. Today I was growing agitated and worried. Hitch expected a routine and if we didn't give him one, he'd probably send us both away early. Then I'd never get to patch things up with Cole. I glared at Ashley again. Every time she ignored me, my sympathy about her and her sister shrunk a little more.

"I'm going to the bathroom," Ashley told the ugly lamp next to her.

This was hopeless. We were never going to come up with a talent show routine this way. I was going to have to save myself like the time I got stuck with Bobby Dwyer for my English project partner and he was so busy reading some manga book that I had to work on our *Animal Farm* presentation all by myself. (I still got an A. But so did Bobby.) I'd have to do the same damage control here and come up with a solo routine.

The word solo flashed in my brain and I stopped myself. Who was I kidding? There was no way I could get up onstage all by myself. I'd rather perform with Bobby Dwyer than do that.

DINK!

The sound startled me, not because it was big, but because I hadn't heard it before in the days I'd been confined here. I knew every sound in the cabin by heart since Ashley and I were pretending to be monks sworn to a vow of silence. I'd already deciphered the leaky faucet in the bathroom, the hissing of the overhead light, and the buzzing of the fly trapped in this nightmare with us.

DINK!

There it was again. I looked around, wondering where it came from.

DINK! This time I saw a small pebble hit the window next to me. DINK! And another.

I looked for Ashley. She was still in the bathroom. I knew from her previous trips that she could be in there for an hour. I leaned over to the window and pried it open. I looked down and saw Court, Grace, and Em staring up at me. Court and Em were wearing matching purple T-shirts and Grace was all in yellow, down to her ponytail holder.

"What are you guys doing here?" I whispered, excited to see some friendly faces.

"We brought you a survival kit," Em said. She handed me up a Twix, a bag of Baked Lays, a Diet Coke, and an old US *Weekly* that had Mrs. Morberry's name and the camp address on the return label.

"Thanks," I said and hid my loot behind my bed pillow. "Ashley's in the bathroom doing God-knows-what, so your timing couldn't be more perfect."

"We had a quick break between events," said Grace. "Not that I can stay long, being captain and all." I tried not to smirk. "How are you holding up?" she added.

"Great! We're telling secrets and doing each other's nails." I rolled my eyes. "Another hour of silence and I think I'm going to go insane."

"Just a few more hours," Em said. "You can make it."

"I don't know about that." I frowned. "We still haven't come up with a routine and Hitch is not going to let us out of here until we do. I just don't get her. When we were cleaning the mess hall the other day, we had this major breakthrough, and since then she's said nothing." I quickly filled the girls in on Ashley's and my conversation. They listened carefully, glancing at each other every once in a while as I spoke.

"Finally!" Court said to the blue sky.

"What?" I asked, confused.

"Sam, you've had a major revelation," Em said excitedly. "I finished this book last month called *The New You Inside and Out* — totally not my usual reading material, I know, but it was on Oprah, and anyway, the book said that some people spend their whole lives being people pleasers. They do everything for someone else and don't worry at all about what they really want. Don't get mad at me for saying this, but you, Sam, are a people pleaser."

"Definitely," Grace agreed. "I'm just glad you finally realized that."

"It's not as bad as Ashley and her sister, right?" I asked.

Grace gave me a look. "You've spent every morning getting up early to take a camper for allergy shots when you could be sleeping in. You always let someone else have the shower first. You volunteered to help Alexis on visitors' day even though you could have the day off. You're more than willing to let Court have the last pancake at breakfast. I could go on."

"It's true," Court agreed. "I mean, I'm happy to let you be my lackey if you want the job, but you're too good for the position, Sam, and you know it."

"Okay, okay, I see your point. I am a people pleaser." I sighed. "I've always been one, especially when it came to Mal. The Pines is the first thing I've ever done without her."

"That means you're growing," said Em brightly. "And you've stopped spending your free time making videos for your friends too. I think you've made huge strides, Sam. You just have to keep making them even when you're not here."

"And you have to practice using the word no," Court pointed out. "Say it to yourself over and over until it sticks."

"I will." I smiled and glanced over my shoulder. "So quickly. Tell me what's going on in the outside world. Have people stopped talking about the food fight?"

"We had to put Gabby in her place," Court said darkly. "She

was walking around telling everybody how you approached our table with a steak knife and tried to kill Ashley, but Gabby stopped you," Court said. "We have that rumor under control now."

"And most people are so into Color War they don't even remember you guys are in here," Grace added.

"And Cole?" I asked tentatively.

"I think he's avoiding us," Em said awkwardly. "I talked to Dylan about it and he said we shouldn't take it personally. Dylan said he's kind of been keeping to himself when we're not at war."

"The anger seems to have done wonders for his sportsmanship," Grace said brightly. "We're on the same Color War team and Cole is beating the hell out of everyone. Not that I should be talking about a teammate or anything when we're not playing. I don't want to give away any yellow team secrets."

"Would you give it a rest?" Court groaned. "I tell you this every year: It's only a game! You're allowed to talk to your best friends even if we're not wearing the same color pinnie."

"Color War is important to me, Court," Grace looked hurt. "Why can't you respect that?"

The two of them started to bicker and I couldn't help but laugh. I needed this. "I miss you guys," I said.

They stopped fighting and smiled. "We miss you too," the three of them said.

I heard the handle to the bathroom jiggle and I knew I had to bolt. "Ashley's coming," I whispered quickly. "You guys should go."

"We'll try to sneak by later and bring you more food," Em said before the three of them hurried away.

Ashley walked out of the bathroom and went straight back to her magazine on her bunk. She didn't even notice I'd broken confinement rules.

"Are we going to talk about the talent show or not?" I tried again.

Ashley shrugged. "I've been thinking about it, and I think you should come up with a routine and then I'll *consider* doing it with you. If you want out of here so badly, that's what you'll do because I'm not about to sit here and come up with one with you."

The old me might have agreed to that arrangement. But the new me, the one that desperately needed to be broken in, knew I couldn't agree to that.

"That's not going to work for me," I said. Ashley looked startled. "If we're doing this, we're doing it together or we're not doing it at all."

Ashley sighed. "How are we supposed to do that when we can barely look at each other?"

"We did fine talking the other day, didn't we?" I reminded her. "Don't you think we could put our differences aside and try to do that again?"

Ashley shot me a disdainful look. "I told you not to bring that up again," she snapped. "And as for the talent show, you may think I'm a snob, but I'm not fake. I can't get up there and pretend I like you for a three-minute song. I just don't see how the two of us are ever going to be able to perform together."

But if we weren't going to perform together, what else was

there to do? Our routine had to be about us and camp and we were supposed to close out the show so our number had to be good. How could we merge those two things without acting like we were best buds?

Suddenly I had an idea. "Maybe we don't have to actually act, sing, or dance together," I said slowly. "Maybe we can just work together."

Ashley looked at me like I was crazy. "What do you mean? All the acts are acting, singing, or dancing. What else could we do?"

"What if we did a camp newscast?" I asked her. "We'd be working together, but we don't have to act like we're best friends. We can interview campers and the staff about the summer."

"Eh," she said, sounding bored. "We already have a camp video that Daddy sends out at the end of every season."

"Yeah, but isn't that just clips of everything you've done during the year?" I wanted to know. "Maybe ours could be like a camp yearbook — camp heartthrob, camp flirt, camp crush. We could make it really funny and have interviews and everything. Nothing mean," I stressed.

"I don't like it," Ashley said, flipping through her magazine. "If we're on camera, then no one gets to see me actually perform. That's my favorite part."

I could see I was losing her and I knew I couldn't. It was my last chance to fulfill Hitch's punishment, and get out of confinement. So that's when I said the words that I knew would click: "I'll videotape and you can be the show's star. You'll be the host.

Like Tyra Banks on *America's Next Top Model*. You *are* the one with the acting experience."

I was finally speaking Ashley's language, and her eyes popped wide open in recognition. "That could work, if we did it my way," she said thoughtfully. "Maybe we could do a camp reality show like *My Super Sweet 16* or *The Real Housewives of Orange County!*" Her eyes were darting around the sad-looking room. "Ooh, mine would be so much better. MTV would pick it up in a hot second because I'll look amazing on camera!"

"Anyway," I interrupted, "if we get out of confinement today and Hitch likes our idea, then we still have two days before the talent show to go around camp filming things. We just need to get permission from your dad first." I grabbed a pad from a nearby table and started writing notes furiously.

This video could actually be — dare I say it — fun. Ashley seemed excited too.

"I have to figure out what I'm going to wear on camera," she said. "I need something that will really bring out my eyes." She stood up and started pacing the room. "I might have to borrow something from Gabby so that no one has seen my outfit before. I'll definitely need to wear more makeup. Oh! And I want to do good interviews, you know? I'm not interviewing just anybody," she insisted. "If this is going to work, I need a big story. I'm not interviewing Mrs. Morberry about her years of Pines service. I want a story with juice."

A story with juice. That was it! Ashley was a genius. I couldn't believe what I was about to say.

Ashley frowned, her bottom lip curling into an Angelina-worthy pout. "Are you writing any of my suggestions down? Just because I'm the star of this project, doesn't mean I don't get any say on the production, you know."

I cut her off. "I completely understand. You can have a ton of creative control. But there is one story I have in mind that you have to do. Everyone will be talking about it. It's juicy," I added, knowing that would do the trick.

"What is it?" Ashley asked, her smile getting bigger by the second. She folded her skinny legs under her. "Spill it."

I took a deep breath. This had to work. If it didn't, I was out of options. And time. The talent show was just a few days before camp ended. "I'll tell you everything you need to know for the interview," I said, "but you have to listen and for once, you have to promise not to interrupt till I'm done."

🐝 🐝 🐝

When Hitch stopped by the isolation bunk later on and heard our pitch, he thought it was brilliant. He stressed we needed to keep the story PG so that the peeps could watch, but beyond that, we could interview anyone we wanted. And after that, we were free. Walking out of the cabin and into the open mountain air never felt so good. Starving, I headed right up to the mess hall to see if I could beg Beaver for an early dinner. I was steps from the porch when I saw Mrs. Morberry trying to flag me down.

"Samantha! You have a phone call on the main line," the older woman said frantically. "It's your mother. She said it's urgent. I said I'd find you. I'm glad I didn't have to go far to look because this leg is killing me."

I hadn't had a call all summer. I'd called Mom when we'd been allowed to phone home, but she'd never called here looking for me. Did Hitch tell my mom about the food fight after all? If so, it was not going to be a pleasant conversation.

I followed Mrs. Morberry a few yards away to the main office and stepped inside the air-conditioned cabin. She pointed to her desk phone. "I'll give you some privacy," she said, and headed into the other room to heat up her dinner. The smell of her lasagna leftovers made my stomach growl.

"Hello?" I said, holding the phone as far away from my ear as I could so that Mom's yelling didn't shatter my eardrum.

"Sam? It's me!"

Wait a minute. That didn't sound like Mom. "Mal?" I whispered.

"Yes, it's me, silly," she said. "This is the only number I could find for camp. I wasn't sure they'd get you if I said I was a friend, so I said I was your mom."

Just hearing Mal's voice was comforting, like my favorite fleece blanket that I always wrapped myself in at home while I was watching *American Idol*. Any thoughts of being mad at her for betraying our video secrecy to Mark went flying out the window. This was my best friend on the line, and I needed her. "More than okay," I whispered as Mrs. Morberry walked back into the room.

"I'm going to eat outside on the porch," she told me. "Just hang up when you're done."

I nodded and waited till she'd let the door slam behind her to continue. "Thank God you called, Mal; I've made a huge mess of things up here."

"I knew something was wrong!" Mal said, her voice jumping the way it did whenever she got excited. Usually it was over a picture of Johnny Depp or a viewing of The Notebook. "I haven't gotten a video from you in weeks. That's why I hunted you down. I thought something had happened to you."

That made me feel guilty, and even though I knew my time was limited, I had to speak my mind. "About that," I said slowly. "There is a reason I haven't sent you another video."

"What do you mean?" Mal asked, sounding surprised.

"At first, it was because I was mad about your last video," I explained. "It was so short, which mine never were, and on top of that you showed it to Mark. I thought our messages were sacred."

"I'm sorry about the tape," Mal apologized. "I felt guilty as I was taping it. I knew it was short, but Mark was always around and I didn't want him to hear everything I had to say. How could I talk about him suffocating me when he was there? It's so annoying, Sam!" She groaned. "He wants to spend every single second together, even if he's just playing Rock Band and I'm watching. I told him I needed time to do something alone, but when he didn't get the hint, I let him be part of it. But when I mailed it to you, I instantly regretted it. I knew I was breaking our friendship code. Anyway, after a few more weeks of Mark being all over me, I'd had enough. We're kind of on a break," she told me.

Cole would never be that kind of boyfriend. He was too self-reliant. But I didn't tell Mal that. It would just bum her out if I told her how cool the guy I met was compared to her suck-the-life-out-of-you boyfriend. But in a weird way, maybe it was good that Mal had that experience. Her and Mark being attached at the hip was kind of the way she and I were pre-Malomark. Too much togetherness is never good. You have to stand on your own two feet.

"I'm sorry about Mark," I said. "And I shouldn't put this whole tape thing on you. It's my fault for promising to send you so many. I was killing myself trying to get the tapes done and I really didn't have the time. I missed you, but I was enjoying camp and things were so busy that I got tired of sneaking off during my rare free time to send you a video."

"You should have said something," Mal pointed out. "I had no idea you were so busy."

"I know," I admitted. "I guess I realized there's nothing wrong with having fun separately."

"Yeah, but I like doing stuff together too," Mal said, sounding slightly hurt. "I thought you did too."

"I do," I said quickly, "but sometimes, well, I have a confession to make." I had to tell her the truth. "Sometimes I do things because you want to do them. Like kickline. I don't want to be a Rockette. I like cheerleading. So maybe I do cheerleading and you do kickline and that's okay."

The other end of the line was silent. "You're right," Mal said finally, her voice quieter than it was before. "I had no idea I was being so demanding. It didn't even occur to me that maybe you'd want to do something else. You never say anything."

"That's going to change," I promised. "I'm going to tell you if I don't want to do something. I'm not going to be afraid to try new things alone. I think I learned something about myself this summer — figuring things out on my own can be kind of scary, but it's also kind of fun." I filled Mal in a little bit on the sleepaway girls and about Cole and Hunter and the drama of the last week and Ashley and my talent show plan.

"I cannot believe you started a food fight!" Mal giggled. "Neither of us can stand Patty Prince and her snide comments on the lunch line, but you've never thrown orange juice at her. Why haven't we thought of that before?"

I couldn't help but laugh. Quietly, of course. If Mrs. Morberry didn't hear me, maybe she wouldn't realize how long I'd been on the phone. "I've definitely become braver on this trip," I added.

"I can tell," Mal agreed. "I think camp suits you — even if I do miss you like mad. Having Mark as my sidekick this summer just wasn't the same thing as having you here. There is no way I'm going to let you go back to that place next year!"

We both laughed again. Mal because she was being funny, and me because deep down I knew I couldn't imagine spending my summer anywhere but at the Pines. I was starting to understand why Grace marked the days till the first day of camp on her school year calendar. And why Court traveled two thousand miles from home to sleep on a lumpy mattress. But I didn't need to say that to Mal. Not now anyway. I was coming back to camp next year, no matter what. But instead of saying that, I asked Mal something I knew she could answer. "So what do you think about my plan for Cole?"

"I'm so proud of you, Sam," she said. "You sound so sure of yourself for a change. I think if Cole hears what *really* happened, he'll forgive you. If he doesn't, he's an idiot."

"Sam?" Mrs. Morberry interrupted us. "I'm sorry, but I have a newsletter to get out before dinner."

"Mom, I'm sorry, but I have to go," I said regretfully. "I miss you and I can't wait to see you in a week."

"Hang in there, Sam," Mal told me. "If anyone can clean up this mess, you can. I'll see you soon. Good luck!"

I hung up, thanked Mrs. Morberry for patching "Mom" through, and headed to the mess hall for some grub. For once, I felt ready to take on the world.

▲20▲
The Talent Show

I could smell Ashley's perfume before I saw her. "Hey," she addressed me stiffly as we waited backstage at the Pines Theater for the talent show to begin. Even though our show entry was a video and not live, Ashley was dressed as if she was presenting at the Oscars. She was wearing a black mini dress, her blond hair was swept up into a chignon, and she even had on a camp first — heels. I guessed it was easy to look good when your actual bedroom and full wardrobe were only minutes from camp property, not two hours away. I, on the other hand, was "dressed up" in jeans and my nicest shirt — a pink fitted American Eagle polo and matching flip-flops that had rhinestones on them.

"Did you go over the sound check with my dad?" Ashley asked me impatiently.

We were never going to be friends, but over those last few days, we somehow managed to make our tape without killing each other. Everyone we wanted to interview said yes, and agreed to stay mum till the video aired, so we'd been pretty busy. Busy enough to keep my mind off Cole.

I'd managed to avoid him — and Hunter — till that night. But that didn't make me any less nervous about what was going to happen. I knew they were both on the other side of the curtain, sitting with the peeps, waiting for the show to start, and just the thought of that made me want to throw up. Once they saw our video, things between the three of us were going to change, and I only prayed it was for the better.

"I took care of everything," I told Ashley soothingly. "Your dad knows we're going to introduce the clip and then they'll start it. He said we show the relationships in a PG way and it's okay for the peeps to watch."

Ashley gave me the once-over and her lip curled into a frown again. "You're going to change before we go out there, right?"

"Nope," I said simply. "Not all of us had our spring fling dress with us."

She gave me a disapproving look. "You're going to *so* clash with my outfit, but I guess the production person isn't supposed to look as good as the star." Ashley was taking her newest star turn quite seriously. She thought she was Diane Sawyer and I was just a lowly P.A. sent to do her drudge work. She gave her chignon a quick pat and walked away. "Gabs!" she yelled. "Gabs! Where are you? I need a quick touch-up on my makeup!"

Gabby came clomping over in cowboy boots, short-shorts, and a white tailored guy's shirt tied at her toned waist. All that was missing was a cowboy hat. "CIW?" she said, which after weeks of

Gabby-speak, I knew meant *can it wait?* "We're on in six," Gabby added. She tossed Ashley a jumbo-size makeup bag, which looked like it was ready to burst open, and left Ashley standing there.

I turned away so she couldn't see me laugh, and that's when I saw him. Cole.

He was backstage talking to three of his peeps, who were performing in the show. I could feel my breath begin to shorten at just the sight of him in a collared shirt and khaki Docker shorts, his hairy extra wavy. When he looked up and caught me staring, my breathing stopped completely. I managed to somehow give a casual wave, knowing I wouldn't get one back.

But Cole did wave back and even went so far as to mouth the word *hey*. For some reason that made me feel guilty all over again and I quickly turned away.

"You'd think someone no longer being held hostage would look happier," Grace said as she, Court, and Em approached me. The three of them were dressed just like Gabby, except they were already wearing their cowboy hats. They looked like they were competing on *Dancing with the Stars*. From the looks of it, they could actually win. Grace looked over my shoulder and saw Cole. "Don't stress," she said.

"When the show is over, you'll have a ton of chances to talk to him," Court added, glancing in the same direction as Grace.

Em took a puff of her inhaler. "Can we worry about this *after* the show?" she asked. "No offense, Sam, but at the moment, I can barely walk and talk, I'm so nervous."

"Why?" I asked. "You've done the talent show before."

"Yeah, but never in something like this," Em said, and fiddled uncomfortably with her tied shirt.

Court grabbed Em's firm belly and shook her. "Who knew Em had abs like that hidden under her J.Crew tees?" Court asked. "When Dylan gets a load of her onstage, he's going to flip."

Em shooed her away. Her face was bright red. "I could kill Gabby for picking out this outfit." Even though Em lived and breathed romance novels full of twisted love triangles, betrayals, and torrid love affairs, actually talking about her own love life obviously freaked her out. "What about you, Sam?" she said, changing the subject. "Are you ready to prove the haters wrong?"

"There are no haters," Grace said firmly. "Especially not now, after my team won Color War and during my speech I told everyone that the Pines was lucky to have someone like Sam Montgomery on staff."

"Thanks," I told Grace, "but the truth is, I am a source of hot gossip at the moment. Ashley's and my 'friendship' has become a sensation worthy of *YouTube* worship."

Grace smirked. "Well, I guess some people *are* talking about you. Everyone wants to know what's on your video."

"So do I," said Court. "Can't you tell us what's on it? We're your friends!"

I laughed. "I promised Ashley I'd stay sworn to secrecy till the big reveal." Our reel was so hush-hush that even Hitch agreed to not play it during our dress rehearsal. Ashley wanted it that way so that she could get people talking. I wanted it that way so our final interview would air for the first time in front of the whole camp. I just hoped I had made the right decision.

"I can't believe you and Ashley have a secret together," Em marveled.

"As Gab would ask, 'Are you BFFs?'" Grace joked.

"I don't think we'll be doing any future productions together," I said as the group of us watched Ashley berate a marshmallow assigned to lighting. "But this one came out pretty well. I think. I hope." I sighed. "There's a lot riding on it."

"That's why you should tell us what it's about!" Court complained. "If you're going to use the video camera, you could at least explain what's on the tape. She's not going to join the sleepaway girls, is she?"

"No way!" I said indignantly. "That's just ours. Speaking of which, if we can get Meg to give us back the camera permanently, we should tape a final installment before we go home. She still says I can only have the camera for the talent show."

"Go home," Grace repeated, her voice shaky. "I can't even think about it."

"Well you should," Court pointed out. "It's just a few days away."

"GOOD EVENING, CAMPERS!" I heard Hitch yell into his megaphone. He had just taken the stage. "I'd like to welcome all of you to our annual talent show!" Cheers rocked the room. "Our first act is the boys from 6D doing a Frank Sinatra medley!"

"We better get in position," Court told the girls. "We're on next."

"Good luck," I told them as a camper next to us burst into

tears because she kept messing up the steps to her Bazooka Gum dance. The whole backstage area had gotten more chaotic since Hitch's announcement. I strained to see Cole, but I didn't know where he'd gone. Hopefully he was back in the audience, where he belonged.

The auditorium had been semi-transformed since the day of the counselor hunt. Most of the acts had a background, made out of cardboard or plywood, that could be slid onstage before their performance. The scenery wasn't as professional-looking as the ones we used for Carle Place High shows, but that was mainly because so many different people had worked on the backdrops. Everyone was able to audition for the show — from peeps to CITs (counselors performed too, but they didn't have to audition) — so the level of art skills varied depending on the age of the camper. Some of the peeps had done nothing more than paint large, sloppy flowers on a big piece of paper that was pinned to a curtain.

Once the boys of 6D took the stage, the show moved along quickly and I barely had time to freak out. Our bunk's number was a huge hit, getting the most applause by far, and I wasn't sure if it was due to Court's tricky choreography or Gabby's wardrobe choices, but either way, I could tell Ashley was less than thrilled they did so well without her direction. Cole's peeps did an adorable magic act, bringing Mrs. Morberry onstage to saw her in half, which got a lot of laughs. The girls of 8A did some kind of hula dance, I guess as an ode to the upcoming dance with the same theme. Some of the marshmallows put together a rock band and played instruments that were surprisingly in tune. The biggest hit of the night though was when some of the guy counselors and CITs got onstage to do a karaoke version of the Jonas Brothers song they were sick of all the girls singing that summer. I thought Court was going to pass out when Donovan sang Joe's parts. After the girl counselors — minus the CITs, who were all in the show already anyway — finished their skit on "what counselors do when they have time off," it was finally time for Ashley and me.

"For our final act, we have a number from Ashley Hitchens and Samantha Montgomery," Hitch told the crowd enthusiastically. He was the only one who had seen our tape — which was kind of mortifying for me, having to sit in front of him as he watched it — but he wouldn't let us air it without making sure it was safe for the peeps. I just prayed he didn't tell my mother about it. Ashley and I caught him on the phone with her when we dropped by the office to show him our reel and I think both of us wanted to gag when we overheard him say how much he was looking forward to seeing her again. It was just two weekends earlier that Hitch had driven down to New York on his day off to meet Mom in the city to see Mamma Mia on Broadway. Mom had gushed to me what a great time they'd had.

"Let's give them a warm welcome!" Hitch said to the crowd as Ashley and I took the stage and people cheered. The auditorium was buzzing. I looked around for Cole and spotted him sitting with his peeps. Hunter was sitting on the opposite end of the row. It was the first time I'd seen him since our infamous kiss and his black eye was faded, but still purple.

"Ashley, you're hot!" someone yelled.

"Go, Sam!" My friends screamed in unison, drowning out the whistles. They were in the back of the auditorium, still in costume, standing by Meg.

Hitch handed us each a microphone and smiled. Ashley and I thought it was a good idea to introduce the video before it aired. I took my mic. I was afraid it was going to fall out of my hands they were sweating so badly. Ashley was the first to speak.

"Hi. I'm Ashley," she said confidently. "I guess there's not a person here who doesn't know what happened to me and Sam last week." She looked at me expectantly. A few people laughed.

I took a deep breath and tried not to think about how badly I was shaking. "And so it's no surprise to any of you that Ashley and I don't like each other." I heard a few more chuckles. When Ashley and I had to come up with an opening, we thought it was best if we played to our strengths. After all, I'd learned the hard way that honesty is the best policy.

"We can barely tolerate being in the same room," Ashley agreed on cue, eliciting more laughter. "Let alone have to perform in the talent show together."

I looked out at the audience and saw a lot of smiles. It was working. "That's why we came up with this idea instead," I said as the video projector screen lowered behind me. "A video we like to call: The Real Lives of Pines Campers." More laughter. "This, of course, includes the real deal on my mess-hall meltdown." Now they were roaring.

"Sit back and enjoy," Ashley said giddily. "Sam and I — or should I say just I since I'm the star, will be available for autographs after the show, before MTV swoops us up and you can't get near our entourage again."

The two of us exited the stage and stood on the side as the ten-minute video began to play. I felt really jumpy and kept shifting my feet uneasily. There was no turning back and I was only eight minutes away from hearing my video self reveal one of the hardest things I'd ever had to say in public.

The first few seconds were of Ashley, dressed in a suit, reporting from the lakefront where she introduced the segment and announced that she'd be doing an exposé on camp life at the Pines. Ashley wanted to make sure she interviewed her crush, Patrick, on the day-to-day life of being a counselor. She also managed to interview every hot male on campus and did a segment on Donovan and Gavin talking about the safety of knowing how to swim. She drew laughs when she interviewed Mrs. Morberry about who on campus got the most mail (apparently it was Dylan, Em's crush, whose large family inundated him with twice-weekly care packages plus cards), and had the audience cracking up at her interview with Beaver, who showed the camp the ingredients to his famous mac and cheese (it turned out it was just Kraft with some breadcrumbs and parmesan cheese sprinkled on top).

"The audience is eating it up." Ashley elbowed me as the segment on the camp love triangles began. It was a who's who of all the known crushes on campus (those that no one minded if we revealed). The funniest part was when Ashley showed Hunter's picture, and said, "And this guy is crushed on by everyone in this room — including Mrs. Morberry!" I glanced at Hunter. Even he laughed.

It was at that moment in the video that I zoomed in on Ashley's almost angelic face. "And now the moment you've all been waiting for. The answers to the Ashley/Sam saga that unfolded in the mess hall. To get to the bottom of what happened, I thought it was best to have a sit-down with Sam herself."

I glanced nervously at Cole. He was watching the screen with interest. My heart was pounding harder than it did when I was near him. If Mal were here, and she knew what I was about to say, she would have been floored at my brief burst of courage.

The crowd grew quiet as an image of me, taking a seat on Ashley's bed, came on screen. It was the first time I'd actually been seen in the ten-minute video. For this part, we put the video camera on a stack of books. Ashley's back was to the camera and she was the one asking all the questions.

"So, Sam," the video Ashley said, reading from her notes, "tell us what led you to going postal in the mess hall." The crowd laughed.

I let Ashley get away with posing the question that way because I knew it would be funnier. I also knew it was going to be one of the few things Ashley would get to say in the next two minutes. This was my time now. "I was mad at you," I said, "because you told the guy I liked that you saw me kissing someone else." Somewhere in the audience, you could hear someone whistle.

"Why did that bother you if it was true?" Ashley prodded.

Deep breaths. Deep breaths. Here it came. "Because it wasn't the truth," I explained. "Yes, you saw me kissing another guy, but *he* actually kissed me."

I looked over at Cole, whose head was down, and I couldn't see his face. Hunter had dropped lower in his seat and I couldn't see him either.

"I had gone to the boathouse to find the guy I liked and tell him I liked him, but it was during the Guess the Counselor game and I got his costume confused. I wound up spilling my guts to someone else — the guy who kissed me. Afterward I felt so guilty. I should have pushed the guy away, but I was in shock. I didn't see it coming and didn't know how to react."

One or two guys were still whistling immaturely, but the rest of the room had grown quiet. Either that or I couldn't hear anyone over the loud whooshing sound in my ears. I looked over at Hunter nervously. He was watching the screen again, but his face was sort of blank.

"If you could tell the guy you liked one thing, what would it be?" Ashley asked, trying to sound like a serious journalist.

Video me sighed. "I would tell the guy I liked how sorry I was for what happened and how I never meant to hurt him. I was hoping to kiss him that night. Not the other guy."

My face was reddening by the second. I wanted to look over at Cole and see his expression, but now I was afraid of his reaction.

"I was going to tell the guy I like the truth the next day, but then I got in trouble for something and had to wait a whole other day. By that time, you had already told him and he wouldn't listen to my side of the story," I added.

"And that's when you went psycho," Ashley filled in the gaps.

"And that's when I got mad," I clarified. "You were mad at me, for reasons we won't disclose here, and to get me back, you told the guy I like your version of what happened. I was so mad, I confronted you."

"You threw bug juice at me and ruined my new shirt," Ashley accused.

"I did," I agreed. "I was so mad that I grabbed the first thing I could and threw it at you. And it snowballed from there."

"And you ruined breakfast," Ashley added.

"I want to apologize for the damage I caused," video me said directly to the camera. "I shouldn't have acted so immaturely. That's not how a CIT should behave and I really hate the fact that I let my senior counselor and peeps down. The Pines has been one of the best summers of my life and I've made some great friends here. I also fell for a really great guy," I added, and even on camera you could see me blush, "and I feel awful that he got hurt because of what happened."

Ashley turned and faced the camera, flashing it a bright smile. "Well, there you have it. A story of love, betrayal, and downright stupidity. All in a day's work for Sam Montgomery," she said brightly. "For The Real Lives of Pines Campers, I'm Ashley Hitchens. You can check out more of my work at my MySpace page."

The clip ended, the screen went blank, and the house lights went up. We didn't have to wait long for a reaction. Campers were applauding wildly. I looked over at Ashley, who was beaming. She hurried off the stage to greet her well-wishers.

Seconds later, I was tackled by Court. "I can't believe you told the whole camp you liked Cole," she screamed in my ear. "Well, you didn't say his name, but *everyone* knows that's who you meant. I'm so proud of you. How do you feel? Are you okay?"

"I'm freaked out," I admitted, "but I'm glad I did it."

Em, Grace, and Meg were the next to congratulate me. Alexis hugged me for a job well done, telling me she was proud that I was her CIT. Even a girl from 8A complimented me on being one of the few people true to my soul at camp, whatever that meant. So many people stopped to talk to me about the tape, my head was spinning. When the crowd started to die down, I headed backstage to get the tape back from Hitch. The area was all but deserted.

"Sam?"

I turned around. Cole was standing just a few feet away.

"Hi," I said awkwardly.

Saying you liked a boy on video was a lot easier than facing him in the flesh.

He moved a few inches closer. "Hi," Cole said back, and I noticed he was smiling. Smiling at me. "I wanted to compliment you on your video genius. I think you might be the next Scorsese."

"Thanks," I managed to squeak out. Cole was looking at me intently and I was finding it hard to focus on actual words. I didn't remember feeling this nervous in front of him. But then again, this was the first time I'd talked to him since . . . well, since everything happened.

Cole moved a step closer. If I reached with my hand, I could touch him. But I didn't. I kept my eyes on his to steady myself. But it didn't work. I was shaking like a leaf on a tree on a windy day. Cole's eyes were so clear; I could dive in and stay there. "That took guts to do what you did," he said.

"I needed to prove to you that I was telling the truth," I explained, "and I had to wait till you were a captive audience." I sighed. "I'm telling the truth when I say it was you I wanted to kiss."

"I wish it was me too," he said with a grin. "That's why I hit Hunter. I immediately felt bad afterward, but Hunter was cool. He said he had it coming. He and I have smoothed things over, but I don't think he'll be coming anywhere near you again this summer." Cole smiled. "He did bring your name up to me once since then — he told me that you liked me, not him, and that if I was a smart guy, I'd realize that and forgive you. I was actually planning to talk to you after tonight's show."

"So are you telling me I confessed my true feelings for you to the entire camp and I didn't have to?" I freaked.

"Pretty much," Cole said with a grin so cute I could have reached out right then and kissed him. I wanted to. I really wanted to, but I couldn't move my feet. They were welded to the scuffed-up, sticky floor.

Cole moved even closer. This time we were so close that I could feel his breath on me. "So you're sorry, and I'm sorry for not giving you the chance to explain. And I've admitted I like you and you've admitted you like me. I guess there's only one thing left to fix."

I held my breath. "What's that?" I asked hoarsely.

"I think it's time you kissed the right guy," he said and he reached out and took my chin in his hands.

When Cole's lips hit mine, I felt the difference immediately. His mouth was soft and fit mine like my favorite pair of Dolce & Gabbana leather gloves that I scored at TJ Maxx. The sensation in my mouth was the same way I felt when I ate too many Sour Patch Kids at the same time — tingly, fired up, and left wanting more. Thankfully the wanting more part wasn't a problem.

When we finally came up for air, Cole said, "Well, what do you think?"

"I think I could get used to this," I admitted.

"Good." Cole grinned. And then he got back to granting my wish.

🌲 21 🌲

So Long . . . for Now

"Guys, stop laughing or we'll never finish this!" I said, even though I couldn't stop laughing myself.

Court, Grace, Em, and I were huddled at the lakefront filming our last sleepaway girls testament of the camp season (Meg had kindly given us back the recorder this afternoon along with my backpack full of our tapes). The final campfire had just ended and we were supposed to be gathering our sleeping bags and heading to the great lawn for the sleepover party. Ashley and Gabby ran ahead to ensure they got a prime location near Patrick and Gavin. But for the rest of my bunk, there was something more important than boys that we had to take care of first.

I placed the palmcorder gently on the window ledge of the boathouse and made sure you could see everyone in the viewfinder. Then I ran back to the girls to begin taping. The four of us linked arms. I pressed record on my remote.

"This is our final sleepaway girls entry for the summer," Court narrated. "I'm pretty sad. But even though I live farther away than any of you, I know this won't be our last tape of the year."

"You said you're going to ask your parents to come to New York for Christmas," Em reminded her. "Or the Thanksgiving Day parade."

"And we're going to beg our parents to let us visit over spring break," I added.

"I'm definitely not missing the chance to climb Squaw Peak." Grace was obsessed with this mountain in Phoenix loads of people liked to hike. I didn't want to burst her bubble by telling her hiking and physical activity weren't going to be on my vacation agenda.

"I'm going to really miss you guys," Court added, and for a second she sounded choked up, which was pretty rare for Court. She never showed emotion about anything other than describing Donovan's abs.

Em sniffled. "We'll call and e-mail all the time." Her eyes were misty too.

"I know," Court squeaked. "And who knows? Maybe my parents will let me use their video camera and we can tape each other messages."

Em and Grace squealed while I, on the other hand, moaned. "I thought I was done with the lengthy video monologues," I jokingly complained. "Remember? I have a life now. I'm trying not to be a people pleaser anymore. This school year is all about the new, assertive, in-control me." Court nudged me. "But I guess I could do a few, time permitting, if you all sent tapes as well."

"Do you think we should say something important?" Em asked. "Like sum up our summer?"

"Grace could be here all night doing that," Court kidded. Grace gave her a stern look that reminded me of my mother.

"Why don't we just tell the truth?" Grace asked. "This summer was ten times better than summers past because Sam was here."

I blushed. "You guys are just saying that."

"I'm serious!" Grace said, and coming from her, I know she must have meant it. "We've always gotten along, but we've never been as close as we are this year, and that's because of you and this video madness."

"Next year we're going to rule this place," Court said gleefully. "I can't wait to be an official counselor. Well, a junior counselor at least. If Donovan comes back, then we can actually date!" Donovan had told Court at the dance last night that he thought she was really cute, and that next year he might be able to say more than that if she was a junior counselor. Court practically did backflips around the hamburger line.

"You're definitely coming back, right, Sam?" Grace asked worriedly.

"You're stuck with me." I grinned. "And so is Ashley."

Em was teary. "I don't want to go home!" she complained. "I-I-I don't want to face the school year without you guys."

Grace shushed her. Court actually hiccupped. I thought I might cry too.

That first day, I didn't even think I'd last a week. Now I didn't want to leave the girls or Cole. The last few days with him had been amazing. We'd gone on early morning jogs (me jogging!), taken walks around the lake at dusk, and spent every possible moment we had together. Just when we were finally getting to really hang out, I had to go home and, unlike Grace and Em, who only lived about an hour from me in New Jersey, Cole lived up here, only a half hour from the Pines; a whole two and a half hours from me. I was trying not to think about what that meant for our chances.

"Grace and I are going to see you next Saturday to go school clothes shopping in Manhattan," I reminded Em. That seemed to calm her down a little bit.

"Why don't we forget about our goodbyes and go get our sleeping bags?" Court suggested. "There'll be time for crying tomorrow. Right now I want to score a sleeping location with a view of Donovan." The three of us glared at her. "As long as it's near you guys, of course."

We all burst out laughing. Again. I almost forgot the camera was running, but I looked over and saw the little green light blinking. "Guys, we're still taping! Any last words?"

"I'm thankful that I have friends who could pull me away from my books," Em said.

"I'm thankful for friends who put up with my type-A personality and competitive sportsmanship," Grace said.

"I'm thankful for people who put up with my boy craziness!" Court laughed.

They all looked at me. "I'm thankful for the sleepaway girls."

And on that note, it was time to stop recording.

Ten minutes later, we'd made it to the cabin and we were grabbing our stuff for the sleepover — our sleeping bags (which hadn't been used once all summer since we didn't go on the optional overnight camping trip in the mountains. I refused for fear of wolf sightings), warm sweatshirts, extra socks, snacks that Em's mom sent us, extra pillowcases and a Sharpie, so that we could all sign each others' pillowcases. It was a camp tradition, kind of like a school yearbook. We were down the steps when I realized I forgot my disposable camera. Court groaned.

"We're already late," she complained. "Do you really need it?"

"Yes, I need it," I told her. "I want to take pictures of the four of us."

"She means she wants to take pictures of her and Cole," Grace said dryly.

I didn't deny it. "You guys go on ahead and I'll meet you there. Get me a good spot!" I headed back up the steps and walked inside the now bare bunk. It had been stripped down. The walls were empty, the cubbies were clean, and Meg's tattered pink rug was rolled up in the corner along with the rest of her stuff. Before I got too depressed, I located my camera, rushed back out of the bunk and — OOOF!

"Sorry about that," I laughed as I banged smack into someone walking by. I looked up.

It was Hunter. I hadn't seen him since the talent show. He

looked as cute as ever in a backward Dodgers ball cap, jeans, and a red American Eagle sweatshirt. His black eye was gone and his cherubic face was annoyingly, once more, perfect.

"Hey," I said, feeling awkward.

"Hi, champ." He grinned, and his smile practically lit up the path. "How have you been? I haven't wanted to get too close for fear Cole might deck me again."

I blushed. "Yeah, about that . . ."

He cut me off. "You don't have to say anything. I get it. My man Cole won. I can handle defeat."

Defeat? What was Hunter talking about? I stared at his face, so smug. How did I not see what a flirt he was on that first day? "Funny," I deadpanned. I clutched my sleeping bag to my chest, hoping it would somehow put more space between us. "I've got to go." I started walking away and then I turned back around. Hunter was still standing there, watching me. I had the overwhelming urge to say something, and if I didn't do it now, the words would haunt me all winter.

"You kissed me, you know," I told him.

Hunter kind of chuckled, and looked down at the ground. "I know that," he said, and adjusted his cap. "You made that painfully clear in your video." Then he looked up at me and his stare moved right through me. "But as I told you that night, I wouldn't have kissed you if I didn't want to."

Freaked, I gripped my sleeping bag tightly to keep from passing out. I knew if I answered him, I'd say the wrong thing. So I said nothing and just turned around again, feeling Hunter's eyes on me as I walked away and tried to keep his words out of my head.

"Hey!" Alexis said, spotting me as I made my way onto the great lawn a few minutes later. She was talking to our peeps, who were lined up in a row, snuggled close together. A few of them were crying as they signed each other's pillowcases.

The lawn was packed. There were so many red, blue, yellow, and purple designer sleeping bags; I had no clue where my friends had put theirs. A huge projector had been set up at the edge of the lawn and was playing *Iron Man*. Beaver was in one corner serving hot chocolate and cookies. Everywhere you looked, people were hugging, or laughing, or crying. It felt like a high school graduation.

"We were wondering when you'd get here," Alexis said to me. "The girls have been asking. They have something for you."

Mackenzie reached into her sleeping bag and pulled out an oversized card made of poster paper. I could see it had hearts all over it and notes scribbled in crooked handwriting. She handed it to me. On the front it said, "TO THE BEST CIT EVER!"

I thought I might cry. I began hugging each and every one of them, sitting down for a few minutes to sign their pillowcases and to have them sign mine. Serena actually cried when I hugged her. I was going to really miss all of them.

"They loved having you as a CIT," Alexis told me a few minutes later. "And I have too."

"Really?" I asked softly. "Even after everything that's happened?"

Alexis laughed. "You certainly haven't kept in line as well as some of the other CITs I've had over the years," she admitted. "But you have spunk, and you've got a great way with kids." Her face turned serious. "I couldn't be happier with my CIT choice for this summer and I think my father will be lucky to have you as a junior counselor next summer, that is, if you'll come back."

"UGH, Alexis, do you have to fawn all over her?" Ashley appeared, hovering over us, her cranky expression the only thing darkening her beauty.

It may have been close to 10 PM, but Ashley looked like she was ready for a party. Her hair was down and sort of curly and she was wearing a Juicy tank and low-slung jeans, even though it had to be 75 degrees. Ashley would suffer through anything for beauty. "You're not coming back, are you?" she asked hopefully.

She already knew my answer, but I guess she wanted to hear me say it. "Sorry to disappoint you, Ash," I said sweetly, "but I am *definitely* coming back next year and the year after that one."

Ashley rolled her eyes. "At least I have ten whole months to forget about you before we do this all over again."

"My thoughts exactly," I agreed. If there was one reason to look forward to the camp off-season, it was not having to see Ashley.

Alexis tried to stifle a laugh, but she couldn't help it. She was looking at us both, and she covered her mouth, but the laughter was uncontrollable. "I'm sorry," she practically panted, "but if you could see your faces. I just, you guys, I hate to break this to you, but I have a feeling you're going to be seeing each other this winter and I have to say the thought of that makes me smile. You may not like each other, but by next summer, I predict this rivalry will be long over."

"Why?" we both asked at the same time, our arms crossed defiantly.

Alexis didn't say anything. Instead she just pointed in the direction of the Pines offices, a few feet away from the end of the great lawn. The lights were on in the windows and you could see the outline of two people standing with their arms around each other in a tight embrace. I already knew who the mystery couple was.

"Our dad's and your mom's little flirtation appears to be sort of serious," Alexis told us, trying not to laugh too hard. "I overheard them talking a few minutes ago, and they were definitely planning on some more get-togethers that just might include the two of you. I'll be at college so I'm spared."

"SHUT UP!" Ashley looked like she might pass out. "You're joking, right?"

"I'm not joking. Sam's mom came up early to go on a date with Dad," Alexis explained cheerfully. "She's so sweet, Sam. This is the first time I've met her, but she seems great for Dad. I'm rooting for them to make a go of things. And, of course, I can't wait to watch you two squirm during family dinners when I'm home on break."

"You're lying," Ashley said over and over again. Alexis kept shaking her head. I felt a little dizzy. I knew there was a chance this could happen, but I had been pushing it out of my head. On the one hand, I did not want to spend weekends with Ashley.

On the other, if Mom was driving up here, we were only half an hour away from Cole.

"I'm going up there," Ashley declared and stomped off. I quickly followed. The two of us had to sidestep dozens of sleeping bags to get to the office. Several people said hi to Ashley along the way, but she ignored them. Her face was determined and her jaw was locked in concentration.

"Hi, sweetie," Hitch said, when he looked down and saw Ashley standing by the deck with her arms crossed. "Hi, Sam." He nudged my mom, who lifted her head and looked at me guiltily.

"Hi, Ashley. It's nice to meet you. Hi, honey!" she said to me cheerfully. Her hair was a little longer than I remembered it, and she was wearing makeup and perfume. She hadn't done that in a while. "Just pretend I'm not here. I don't want to ruin your sleepover party. I wasn't going to bother you till tomorrow. I came up early to see, um, well, Alan."

"You don't say," Ashley muttered under her breath, but thankfully Mom didn't hear. Daughter or no daughter, Mom would have had something to say about Ashley's attitude, even if Hitch did put up with it.

"We were going to tell you both tomorrow," Hitch said worriedly. "We're both so new to this dating thing we're not sure how it will work with the distance, but we're hoping to take some weekend trips — you guys coming up to us, us coming down — to see how things go."

Cheering erupted behind us and I saw on the big screen that Robert Downey Jr. had slipped into his Iron Man costume.

"You both should get back to your friends," Mom insisted as Hitch put his arm around her waist again. "We have plenty of time to catch up — and get to know each other — tomorrow."

"Your house better have a guest room and more than basic cable," was the only thing Ashley said to me as we walked back across the lawn.

"Ditto," I told her and was thankful when Ashley veered right to sit down next to Gabby, Gavin, Patrick, and a bunch of girls from 8A.

"What took you so long?" Court wanted to know when I finally, FINALLY dragged my sleeping bag over to the girls and collapsed on top of it. I mumbled my response to my pillow. I was afraid to turn around and see Hitch and my mom kissing.

"We thought you got eaten by wolves," Grace told me. This made me sit up.

"You guys saw wolves?" I freaked. "And you let me walk down here alone?"

The three of them laughed. "I can't believe you still fall for that one," Grace marveled. She was in her sleeping bag and all I could see was her head. She had the bag rolled up to her neck. Em and Court were on either side of her.

"There you are," Cole said, as he, Dylan, Tim, and some of their bunkmates made their way over to our little patch of grass. They placed their sleeping bags in a row behind us — Hitch kind of made it clear that guys should not be sleeping directly next to girls — and took a seat. Em scrambled out of her bed and shyly sat next to Dylan. I noticed that for the first time she didn't have a book with her to read before bed. Tim crouched down next to Grace and the two of them started whispering. I looked over at Court and she rolled her eyes.

"I guess I'll go get some final flirting in," she said, and slid out of her sleeping bag. She walked over to Donovan, who was sitting with a few other counselors.

"Hey," Cole said as he leaned down and kissed me. It was just as good the hundredth time as it was the first — I felt like the Fourth of July fireworks were exploding over our heads. And even though my Mom could technically be watching from a distance, I couldn't help but enjoy the moment. It was hard not to when you were with Cole. After more than a week of not talking, we'd spent the last few days talking till our jaws locked.

When we came up for air, I said: "My mom is here. She's on a date with Hitch, and — are you ready for this? — they're going to try to do the long distance thing."

Cole looked surprised. "Are you serious?"

I shook my head and laughed. "Ashley and I were just with them and they were talking about mom and me coming up to visit some weekends."

Cole's eyebrows shot up. "You mean up here? A half-hour from my house?"

"Mmm-hmm."

He broke into a wide grin. "That's not such a bad thing."

"No?" I questioned. I mean, we were inseparable here, in the Pines bubble, but back in the real world, would Cole like me just as much? As much fun as I'd been having, the nagging thought had entered my mind a million times over the last few days.

He shook his head. "I know you can't stand Ashley, but if your mom dating Hitch means you get to come upstate more, which means I can see you, then I think it's a win-win situation."

"So you're not sick of me?" I joked.

"Samantha Montgomery, I don't think I could ever get sick of you," Cole said seriously.

And you know what? When he said it like that, all brooding and sexy like he was Nate on *Gossip Girl*, I believed him.

"I don't think I could ever get sick of you either," I said shyly.

"Good," Cole said with a grin and put his arm around me, right where I knew it belonged.

Acknowledgments

Sleepaway Girls couldn't have been written without my fabulous editors, Cindy Eagan and Kate Sullivan. This story changed so much—for the better!—from the initial proposal to the final edit and became something I grew to love more and more with every edit. Thanks so much for all your suggestions and camp knowledge ("Is it sleepaway or sleepover camp?") and for your pep talks along the way.

The same goes for my wonderful agent, Laura Dail, who patiently reminded me there was a whole book to write, and not just the first nine chapters, which I crazily rewrote four (yes, four) times and then later wound up rewriting a fifth. Thank you for always helping me keep my head on straight.

To the amazing team at Little, Brown Books for Young Readers—Ames O'Neill, Melanie Chang, Andrew Smith, Lisa Laginestra, Melanie Sanders, and Tracy Shaw (who amazes me time and again with her great cover designs)—I'm so lucky to work with all of you.

To the always knowledgeable Mara Reinstein—this time the questions were more of a camp than a Hollywood variety, but still! You always had the answer I needed. The same goes for my camp- and non-camp-going friends who put up with my teen romance questions, camp q's and everything in between—

Lisa, AnnMarie, Joyce, Joanie, Elena, Miana, and Erin. A special thanks to Christi, my high school best friend and fellow camp counselor—who was nothing like the Mal in this book!

To my mom, Lynn Calonita, who helps out more than a grandmother ever should just so I make all my book deadlines. It's because of you that I always get everything in on time! Love also to my dad, Nick Calonita; my grandfather, Nick Calonita; Nicole and John Neary; and Gail and Brian Smith for their endless support.

Finally, to my wonderful family—my husband, Mike; my sons Tyler and Dylan; and our super-pampered Chihuahua, Jack—thank you for all your love, laughter, and large supply of kisses.

Friends don't let friends do reality shows.

When Charlie signs herself and her friends up for their own reality television show, she discovers that having cameras following them everywhere and interfering producers surreptitiously scripting their lives start to affect the four best friends' relationship. As soon as Charlie realizes what's going on, she figures out the perfect way to give the studio and her home audience a much-needed reality check.

Turn the page for a sneak peek at
RealityCheck,
Jen Calonita's newest look
at what really happens behind the cameras.

Coming June 2010

Lights, Camera, Action!

"Okay, girls, just act natural," Addison tells us with a big smile. "Forget about the cameras. Just pretend we're not here." Everyone keeps saying that, but it sounds impossible. How am I supposed to pretend that there are not *three* cameras surrounding our table right now, all of them focused on us?

We're sitting at the Crab Shack, Hallie's parents' restaurant/ boat dock, for our first-ever taping of *The Cliffs*, and at the moment, I'm so nervous I want to dive off the dock, swim to nearby Shelter Island, and live there permanently. I have my cell phone and my toothbrush in my bag. What more do I need to survive?

"Should we look at the camera?" Keiran asks Addison nervously.

Addison shakes her head and the pencil behind her right ear falls onto the dock. She leans down to pick it up, rests it on her clipboard, and fixes her Bluetooth again. It's been glued to her ear the whole time we've been here and she's had several calls, which she's disappeared to answer. This is the first time I've gotten to see Addison at work, but she seems to be really on top of things. The crew hangs on her every word, and she's been pretty efficient about our time, knowing we can't tape all day.

Unlike the rest of us, who agonized over our outfits for days, Addison is not worried about her work wardrobe. She's wearing a long-sleeved blue shirt, jeans, and sneakers. She doesn't have on anywhere near as much makeup as the makeup artist (yay!) put on us. "I know this first taping is overwhelming for you girls, but I promise, it will get easier," Addison assures us. "Just think of us as the fourth wall to a room. We're not here. Don't look in this direction unless there is something over here other than us that you need to see. In a few days you won't even realize we're around. You're going to become pros fast. You'll see."

Taping started faster than we could have imagined. Addison actually called the day after the signing to see if would mind getting a day or two in *that week*. I almost fell off my chair I was so surprised, but I guess jumping in headfirst is a good thing. I didn't think we had anything exciting planned for that week, but Addison thought everything I mentioned sounded "super" or "perf." She stressed that Susan wanted us to be as natural as possible, so whatever we normally do together should be fine. We decided our first taping should be at the Crab Shack. Hallie's parents were more than happy to let us shoot. The crew got here early to set up and passed out waivers to everyone (they have to make sure people sign one if they're going to be on camera). By the time we arrived, everyone was ready for us.

"Promise you guys won't mention where I live, okay?" Brooke whispers to me while Addison is still on her call.

"Brooke, we swear, but you know they're going to find out eventually," I tell her. "It's nothing to be ashamed of."

Brooke's house is a stately old colonial, and the barn on her property is fully functional and has a bunch of horses that we all take riding. She has a bigger room than any of us, which seems to be redecorated in Pottery Barn Outlet stuff every two years. What's not to like about Brooke's home sweet home?

"Charlotte," she says stiffly, sounding like my mother. "I'm not a farm girl and I don't want certain people to think I am one."

I know who she's talking about. Brooke's never gotten over Marleyna Garrison's ribbing in ballet class about how Brooke smelled of horse manure.

"Okay," I assure her. "Just relax." I have to admit, I'm alternating between nausea and fits of giddiness. We are about to start taping our very own TV show.

"You're right," Brooke says and breathes a little easier. "This is our starring moment. What am I worrying about?"

"So, Addison, how do we start?" Hallie asks. "Should we tell a funny story? Or talk about boys?"

"Or gripe about homework? Family?" Keiran asks. "Should we avoid sounding negative? I don't want to come off as cranky."

Addison laughs. "Just do what you'd normally do. Chat. Talk about school, especially since we can't tape you guys there."

The four of us nod. Talk about school. Talk about school.

What about school? Do I mention my possible date with Zac? No, no, that wouldn't be good because then it would be on tape. I'd be talking about him to the world and I have no clue if he'll be around long enough to hear it on TV. Okay, school. Classes? That's boring. Homework? Nah. How much I hate Mr. Sparks? That would just get me an F in social studies. School...

"Ready?" Addison chirps. "We'll go slow and we can always stop when you want."

The girls and I look at each other. Brooke puts her hand out and we all give it a squeeze. "Let's get this party started!"

We've already ordered our usual: mozzarella sticks, clam strips, and a round of Cokes. The order covers the checkered tablecloth. The furnishings at the Crab Shack are pretty cheap—white plastic chairs and patio tables with tacky tablecloths. A large canopy hangs over the fifteen or so tables, giving us some relief from the sun. Food is ordered at the shack window and then your number is called over a staticky intercom so you can pick it up. Definitely not fine dining, but the place is always packed. Not many restaurants around can beat the spectacular scenery. The dock is right on the water and overlooks Shelter Island, a quiet residential town a short ferry ride away. Sailboats and small yachts slip by or dock right here, some with local license plates, others from as far away as Florida.

"Girls, I've got the perfect opener for us," Hallie says. "I figured we could start out talking about the spring fling. At least that sounds exciting, right?" Hallie fingers her green V-neck sweater that brings out her eyes. It's her favorite shirt and she's wearing it with a denim skirt, tights, and her brown knee-high boots that we covet.

We all nod. "What do you think, guys?" I ask the crew, but their faces are blank. Fourth wall. Fourth wall. I have to remember that. They're not going to answer us.

"Perfect!" Addison says enthusiastically. "Let's try it on for size." She turns to the crew, who jumps into action, yells out a few commands, and then someone says "Rolling," faster than I can even catch my breath.

"Can you guys believe the spring fling is next month?" Hallie asks, trying to sound natural even though I know her voice is an octave higher than it should be.

"Um, yeah, that's pretty close," Keiran seconds, her eyes moving toward the cameras and back again. I notice she's shredding the napkin in front of her.

"Has anyone started thinking about dates?" Brooke asks, a mischievous smile on her face. "It's never too early to start." She turns to me. "I know Charlie has her eye on someone."

My face burns—and it's not that hot out. Thanks, Brooke! "Maybe," I say cryptically. "Don't you?"

"I always keep my options open." Brooke winks.

"What are you thinking of wearing?" Hallie asks. "It's never too early to think of a dress."

"Oooh! I saw something in *Seventeen* that was sweet," Keiran gushes and then she's off and running describing it. This somehow turns into a conversation about the lack of great places to shop out here on NOFO. And then before I know it, I'm weighing in on where to find cute clothes, and Brooke is boasting about her amazing sales collection, and Addison is calling cut.

"Girls, that was amazing!" Addison says and sounds like she means it. "You guys totally forgot the camera was there."

"We did, didn't we?" I say to the others excitedly, my confidence growing. "That was fun."

"And surprisingly easy," Brooke admits.

"A total rush," Hallie agrees.

"Take a breather, get a drink, and we'll start up again in a few minutes," Addison says as she walks away to take yet another call.

"Brooke, I loved that line you gave about Tanger being the new Target—everyone who is anyone goes there." Tanger is the outlet mall where we shop.

Brooke grins. "That was good, wasn't it? And Kiki, you were so cute describing that dress."

"Do you think we were trying too hard?" Hallie asks with a frown. "I had to work it to be that witty."

"Nah," I dismiss her. "It's good for us to be funny on camera. They'll like us more, won't they? It's not like we were lying." I did notice our conversation was hipper than normal, but who cares? It was still us. I'm sure it will tone down the more comfortable we get.

The four of us are so busy rehashing our lines, we barely hear Keiran's phone ringing, "It's my mom," she says. "Hello? What?" She freaks out, making me jump. "Now? I can't. I'm *working*. Remember, *working?* But, Mom? Mom? FINE." She runs her fingers through her hair and looks at us worriedly. "I have to go. My mom needs me to watch my brother while she runs to a parent-teacher conference."

"Kiki, you can't go now!" Brooke complains. "We're in the middle of taping."

"I have no choice," Keiran says, coming down off her high.

She throws tip money down on the table and grabs her bag. "I'm sorry," she says, looking at Addison.

"It's okay," Addison tells her and motions to some of the guys. "We'll send a small crew with you on your babysitting gig and the rest of us will hang here. Keiran, tell your mom we're coming and we just need a few minutes to set up, okay?"

"Really? You don't mind?" Keiran asks, her shoulders relaxing.

"Of course not," Addison says. "We knew your babysitting skills were very much in demand. We love shooting this sort of stuff."

"You guys are awesome," says a camera guy named Hank. "The way the sun hits Charlie's hair is perfect."

"Perfect," seconds Phil. "She looks like an angel."

"Me? An angel?" I joke. "That's a new one."

"The rest of you look great too," Addison adds and I hear her phone ring. Again. Her face darkens. "I have to take this. Excuse me."

I lean back in my chair as Keiran gets whisked home with a small camera crew of three people. "This is pretty cool," I say to the others. "I thought it might be a little weird taping our conversations, but I don't mind it."

"Me either. But I hope we all get to shoot some individual scenes, don't you?" Brooke asks.

"I'm sure we will," says Hallie and nudges me.

"Hal! Hal! Someone here for you," a voice crackles over the intercom. We turn toward the Crab Shack window and see a cute guy wearing shorts (in April no less) and a hoodie, with curly blond hair, waving at Hallie.

"Whoa, who is he?" I have to ask.

Hallie's whole face flushes. "Patrick Waters. He goes to Greenport. He works here at the restaurant and—guys, do I look okay?"

"You look great," Brooke tells her. "I dressed you so I should know. Go talk to him. Why do you look so nervous? You never have trouble talking to guys, Hallie."

"This one is different," Hallie says shyly.

Addison appears again. "Oooh...who's that?" she asks Hallie.

"Hallie's crush," Brooke teases.

"Do you think he'd appear on camera?" Addison asks. "If so we just need to ask him to sign a release."

"Let me run and ask him," says Hallie. Hallie talks animatedly for a few minutes and then we watch as Phil hurries over with a camera while Patrick signs the form. Hallie backs up and they tape her walking over as if it's for the first time.

Brooke sighs. "She's getting good airtime." I hit her. "I know, we're all going to get it. I just wish mine was now. I really like being in front of the camera."

"You?" I tease. "Never." She swats me back.

"All this talking is making me thirsty," Brooke says, holding up her empty Coke.

"Me too," I realize. "I'll get us refills," I grab our cups and head to the counter. Hallie's mom is always telling me to just walk into the kitchen, but I feel funny doing that when there are paying customers around. Instead, I wait in line, making sure to stay out of the way of the cameras taping Hallie. I feel a tap on my shoulder and turn around quickly, almost knocking the cups of ice into the person's chest.

"Whoa. I wanted a cool drink, but not extra ice." It's Zac, and we're standing so close, with the cups between our chests, that I can smell his minty mouthwash. His curly hair is damp and he's wearing a plain navy long-sleeved shirt and khakis. But it's his eyes, those awesome blue eyes that seem to pick up every speck of light in this place and reflect my image back at me.

"Hey." I try to sound calm and natural even though I'm anything but.

"Hey yourself," he says. "I have a confession to make: I thought I might find you here."

"Really?" He came here looking for me?

Zac nods. "I didn't see you at the office at lunch, and someone mentioned you were heading here after school, so I decided to track you down."

He tracked me down? Wow. "Here I am." I try to smile. "Everything okay? They didn't kill my piece on the band's trip to Disney World, did they?"

"Nope, nothing like that," Zac says. "I just wanted to make sure we were still on for Friday night. I was hoping you weren't avoiding me."

"I wasn't avoiding you," I say quickly. God no. Never. It killed me not to go to the office today. "I had to get some homework done early since I'm..." I realize I've never told Zac about the show.

Zac looks over to where Hallie is talking to Patrick. "Is there a reason why a camera crew is following Hallie?"

"Um…" Okay, this is awkward. How do I explain this in less than five minutes? "You see…"

"Charlie?" Addison has now joined our little twosome. Her clipboard is in hand and she's smiling. "Who is your friend?"

"I'm Zac," he says, extending his hand and shaking Addison's.

"Addison," she says. "I'm Charlie's show producer."

"Show producer?" Zac says with a cock of his head and a curious grin. "As in theater?"

"As in TV," Addison corrects. "For *The Cliffs*, Charlie's new TV show."

"Charlie is getting her own TV show?" Zac looks really confused now.

"Um…yeah," I admit, feeling awkward.

Addison looks at me apologetically, but I smile. "Addison, could you give us two minutes so I can explain?"

Addison nods. "Sure, and make sure you explain this too." She hands me a release. She walks away, dialing her phone again.

I stand there holding the release in my hand. "So."

"So," Zac repeats. "Let me guess, you're secretly Hannah Montana and you've never told me?"

"Not exactly," I tell him sheepishly. "Remember how we were talking last week about paying for college? Well, the short story is that I was approached to do my own reality show on the Fire and Ice Network. If I do this for even one season, it will probably pay off all my college and then some."

"What kind of reality show?" Zac looks interested. We've moved off the line now and I'm still holding the empty cups, which are freezing my hands thanks to all the ice.

"One about me and Keiran, Brooke, and Hallie," I say, knowing how silly it sounds out loud. "This executive from the network was watching me at work and she approached me about the show. Today is our first day of taping." I glance over at the table where Brooke is talking to Hallie and Patrick. Addison motions for me to hurry up.

"Do you they follow you all the time?" Zac wants to know.

"No, they have to get our permission to tape things before-hand, which is why I'm holding this release," I explain, feeling embarrassed. "If I talk to you on camera, you have to sign this saying you're okay with being on the show."

"I think I'll leave the spotlight to you today," Zac says, and winks. "I want to hear more about your new career tomorrow though. See you at the office? Without the cameras, of course."

"Of course! I'll see you there," I tell him.

When I walk back over to the girls, Addison is eagerly waiting. "Charlie, he's adorable! Did he sign a release?" She watches Zac closely and 1 see him grab a brown bag from the pickup window and take it to go. He gives me a little wave and I wave back. "Where is he going?" Addison asks worriedly.

"He didn't want to be on camera today," I tell Addison.

"Oh, okay," Addison says, looking dejected. "He's just so cute. He'd look gorgeous on celluloid."

I giggle. "Back off, Addison, he's *my* crush." She laughs.

"Did you tell him Patrick signed a waver?" Hallie asks me. I shake my head.

"Maybe he'll change his mind," Addison suggests. "The more, the merrier! We want to feature you four and your larger circle. Patrick is a cute addition, and Brooke said she has some prospects that sound good. Zac would be perfect too. We want this show to cover your whole lives, not just pieces, so we're interested in seeing everyone who's a part of it if we can."

"Sure," I promise. I like how into showing the real us Addison seems to be.

"Okay then, let's get back to work." Addison puts her headset back on and I feel a rush of excitement. "Hallie? Make sure you talk about Patrick now that he's gone," Addison instructs us. "And Brooke, tell that story about the girl in gym class. I loved that. And Charlie?" She smiles. "You just be Charlie. Got it?"

"I think so," I tell her.

Addison grins. "Good. And we're rolling!"